Maurice Procter and The Murder Room

>>> This title is part of The Murder Room, our series dedicated to making available out-of-print or hard-to-find titles by classic crime writers.

Crime fiction has always held up a mirror to society. The Victorians were fascinated by sensational murder and the emerging science of detection; now we are obsessed with the forensic detail of violent death. And no other genre has so captivated and enthralled readers.

Vast troves of classic crime writing have for a long time been unavailable to all but the most dedicated frequenters of second-hand bookshops. The advent of digital publishing means that we are now able to bring you the backlists of a huge range of titles by classic and contemporary crime writers, some of which have been out of print for decades.

From the genteel amateur private eyes of the Golden Age and the femmes fatales of pulp fiction, to the morally ambiguous hard-boiled detectives of mid twentieth-century America and their descendants who walk our twenty-first century streets, The Murder Room has it all. >>>

The Murder Room
Where Criminal Minds Meet

themurderroom.com

T0351561

Maurice Procter 1906–1973

Born in Nelson, Lancashire, Maurice Procter attended the local grammar school and ran away to join the army at the age of fifteen. In 1927 he joined the police in Yorkshire and served in the force for nineteen years before his writing was published and he was able to write full-time. He was credited with an ability to write exciting stories while using his experience to create authentic detail. His procedural novels are set in Granchester, a fictional 1950s Manchester, and he is best known for his series characters, Detective Superintendent Philip Hunter and DCI Harry Martineau. Throughout his career, Procter's novels increased in popularity in both the UK and the US, and in 1960 *Hell is a City* was made into a film starring Stanley Baker and Billie Whitelaw. Procter was married to Winifred, and they had one child, Noel.

Philip Hunter

The Chief Inspector's Statement (1951)
   aka *The Pennycross Murders*
I Will Speak Daggers (1956)
   aka *The Ripper*

Chief Inspector Martineau

Hell is a City (1954)
   aka *Somewhere in This City*
The Midnight Plumber (1957)
Man in Ambush (1958)
Killer at Large (1959)

Devil's Due (1960)
The Devil Was Handsome (1961)
A Body to Spare (1962)
Moonlight Flitting (1963)
    aka *The Graveyard Rolls*
Two Men in Twenty (1964)
Homicide Blonde (1965)
    aka *Death has a Shadow*
His Weight in Gold (1966)
Rogue Running (1966)
Exercise Hoodwink (1967)
Hideaway (1968)

Standalone Novels
Each Man's Destiny (1947)
No Proud Chivalry (1947)
The End of the Street (1949)
Hurry the Darkness (1952)
Rich is the Treasure (1952)
    aka *Diamond Wizard*
The Pub Crawler (1956)
Three at the Angel (1958)
The Spearhead Death (1960)
Devil in Moonlight (1962)
The Dog Man (1969)

Hell is a City

Maurice Procter

An Orion book

Copyright © Maurice Procter 1954

The right of Maurice Procter to be identified as the author of this work
has been asserted in accordance with the Copyright, Designs and Patents
Act 1988.

This edition published by
The Orion Publishing Group Ltd
Orion House
5 Upper St Martin's Lane
London WC2H 9EA

An Hachette UK company
A CIP catalogue record for this book is available from the British Library

ISBN 978 1 4719 0263 5

All characters and events in this publication are fictitious and any
resemblance to real people, living or dead, is purely coincidental.

No part of this publication may be reproduced, stored in a retrieval system
or transmitted in any form or by any means without the prior permission
in writing of the publisher, nor be otherwise circulated in any form of
binding or cover other than that in which it is published without a similar
condition, including this condition, being imposed on the subsequent
purchaser.

www.orionbooks.co.uk

CONTENTS

PART ONE

MARTINEAU

I

THE black police Jaguar surged powerfully up a steep and narrow moorland road, nosed carefully round a walled corner, and emerged on top of the world. Or so it seemed. The way ahead ran comparatively straight along the edge of a high moor, and on one side the ground sloped away, down, down, down to the lower lands.

Detective Inspector Martineau was sitting beside the driver of the car. "Where are we now?" he asked, in a tone which suggested that he would be surprised if the other man could tell him.

Detective Constable Devery was the driver. "I don't know, sir," he replied, with astonishment in his voice, as if it were indeed strange that he of all people did not know exactly where he was.

Martineau gave the young man an amused sidelong glance, then he turned to look at the view. Though the day was dry and clear, there was not much to see: only rough fields stretching away downhill until they faded into the haze from several hundred square miles of smoking chimneys. Down there, ten miles away, was a city of a million people, but the city was only the hub of a wheeling spread of suburbs, satellites and close neighbours which made it, in reality, one of the very big cities of the world. It was the commercial capital of a closely packed area which supported, and was supported by, millions of hard-working and skilful people.

"I don't know about London," he said. "They should have called Granchester the Big Smoke."

"The Metropolis of the North," said Devery. "What Granchester says today, London forgot yesterday."

Martineau considered the gibe. Devery was a Liverpool man, and such remarks were to be expected from him. But they were not to go unanswered.

1

"I'd sooner be a church gargoyle in Granchester than the Lord Mayor of Liverpool," he said.

"Every tomcat likes his own back-alley," Devery retorted, and then he was worried by a sudden fear that he had said too much.

But Martineau's face wore the taut grin which was one of its characteristics. "You had to come there to make a living, anyway," he said. "Life too hard in Liverpool, was it?"

Without waiting for a reply, he reached forward and turned on the two-way radio. "Headquarters range is about ten miles, I believe." he said. "We might be able to hear something up here."

"I hope we hear that somebody has collared Don Starling."

"Same here," Martineau agreed. "It's been three days now, and we haven't had the faintest whiff of him. I don't like it at all."

It was business connected with Don Starling which had taken them into the hills. A County policeman in a remote hamlet had detained a tough-looking stranger who answered the description. But when the policeman had tried to lock his prisoner in a small room to await the arrival of prison officers, the man had fought him so successfully that he had escaped. To Granchester police, when they heard of it, that sounded just like Don Starling. Moreover, if Starling had been avoiding roads and keeping in the heather, the moorland village was a likely place for him to be seen. It was on a direct line of route between the prison which had failed to hold him and his home town of Granchester.

Because they knew Starling so well, Martineau and Devery had been sent from the City to help the County in the hunt. They had travelled eagerly to the out-station, only to be disappointed. The stranger had been rearrested, and he had not been Starling, but only a vagrant with claustrophobia. There had been nothing for the City men to do but get back into their car and go home. On the return journey along secondary roads, Devery had lost his way.

When the radio had warmed up, Martineau turned it on to full power. Immediately he caught the last words of a message: ". . . dark saloon car of American type, rather old and shabby. There are several men in the car with the girl."

"Something happening in town," he said, leaving the set at 'receive'.

"Hit and run, maybe," Devery guessed. Then he stopped the car. They were at the top of a steep declivity, and the way ahead was revealed. The narrow road curved and twisted away downhill, but not in the direction they wanted to go. It headed back into hill country. It was joined by a stony, rain-gullied track which did indeed descend towards Granchester, but it was much too rough for the precious Jaguar.

"I think I know where we are," said Martineau. "The good road takes us out of our way, but it brings us to the main Granchester-Halifax road."

Devery set the car in motion and started the long descent, taking the numerous bends only as fast as perfect control would allow. Like most young men, he looked his best when he was absorbed in the efficient handling of a vehicle. He held his broad, big-boned frame erect, and his long, rather handsome face was set calmly and firmly.

The voice of Headquarters spoke again: "GCPR to all cars. Message two-sixteen. Further to robbery-violence and abduction in Higgitt's Passage. American car believed to have gone eastward from scene of crime."

Martineau looked at the empty winding lane, the deserted moorland, and the high grey clouds, but in his mind's eye he saw Higgitt's Passage in the throbbing heart of the city. A narrow thoroughfare among crowded streets, surrounded by buildings thronged with people. Robbery with violence at the busiest time of a fine Saturday morning. A sudden shout, a scream maybe, a rush of feet, a slamming of doors followed by the snarl and squeal of harshly used brakes and tyres: momentary overtones in the city's roar. A slick, quick crime, obviously. A city crime committed by city denizens. Denizens of the underworld. Rats. Like rats they crept out of their holes to attack and steal, and scurry away.

Out there in the wide spaces of untainted air the city's fume-laden atmosphere, the city's crime, and the city's rats seemed to be distant in time and space. Something had happened in another world; another world ten miles away.

"So it's a job," said Martineau.

"And what a job. Kidnapping, no less. It's a long time since we had anything of that sort."

"So long I can't remember. It must be the girl who's been abducted. I wonder who she is."

"And I'm wondering what time it happened. The car is heading in this direction. . . . It might take the Halifax road. . . ."

"Yes. Go a bit faster if you can."

Devery began to show that with a Jaguar he could go quite a lot faster. Presently, a mile away, the main road came into view. It climbed straightly up to the higher moors. There was traffic on the road: tiny crawling beetles on a grey ribbon.

Martineau kept his glance on the distant moving vehicles. Was there a pre-war American car among them? A Chrysler or a Dodge or a Studebaker? Carrying some city rats away from their holes for a while? The man who had first used the term 'underworld' in connexion with criminals had known what he was talking about. Rat runs. Sewers. Well, there were cats to deal with the rats. Patient and painstaking cats. In that respect Martineau did not mind being referred to as a tomcat who liked his own back-alley.

There were a few houses and a pub at the road junction. When they reached it Devery drew in at the near side, close to a low stone wall. Looking over the wall they could see traffic approaching at speed from the Granchester direction, taking a run at the long hill and rightly ignoring the junction with the minor road.

Martineau glanced at the pub with a certain longing. At times, in suitable company, he liked to drink in pubs. After an uninteresting drive and an anticlimax, this could have been one of those times. He thought of a cool bar and a pint of foaming ale. He began to whistle softly as he watched the road.

"If the job happened half-an-hour ago, the Yankee car could be away, past us," he said. "Anyway, we'll give it fifteen minutes."

"We're out of our jurisdiction here," Devery reminded him.

The inspector nodded, and continued to watch the road. Devery considered him, wondering what action he would take under certain circumstances. He studied the blunt-featured, not unattractive face. The eyes were noticeably grey, and the blond hair was grey at the temples. An unobtrusive grey suit completed that colour scheme, and the suit covered the body of a heavyweight athlete. Devery comfortably reflected that if there were any trouble with 'several men' in an American car, the hardest hitter in the Granchester police would be on his side.

Martineau drew his attention to the leisurely approach of a County policeman in uniform. They watched the man saunter towards a blue-painted police pillar.

"Going to make his contact," Devery guessed.

When the P.C. was a few yards from the pillar, the red light on top of it began to flash in and out. The man did not quicken his pace. He strolled to the pillar, turned off the light, opened the door and took out the telephone.

"Here's where he gets further news about robbery-violence in Granchester," said Martineau.

But the constable's attitude changed too abruptly. His back was turned to the men in the Jaguar, but his interested, almost tense attitude was unmistakable. What he was hearing was more immediately and personally important than any crime in Granchester. As he listened he looked round at a red-and-white bus which was approaching at speed. It was a North-Western Lines single-decker, bound for Bradford via Halifax.

As the bus drew near the policeman's attitude became strained. He scarcely had time to hear all the message. He gabbled something into the phone, slammed it into its box, and ran out signalling to the driver of the bus. The bus rushed past him and stopped twenty yards beyond him. He sprinted after it and boarded it. The bus went on its way up the hill.

"What do you make of that?" Martineau asked.

"Accident up the road," Devery surmised. "Fatal accident, happen."

5

"When you were in uniform, did you run so hard to a fatal accident?"

"Well no, I don't suppose I did."

"There's lots of work, lots of responsibility, and little glory attached to a fatal accident," said Martineau. "I'm thinking he'd have listened longer and let the bus go, to give the motor patrol a chance to beat him to it. He'd reckon it was their job, anyway."

"Yes, sir. But it's certainly none of ours."

Martineau thought about that. "I think we'll go after that bus, Devery," he said.

They followed the bus up, up, up to the dark rolling moors. In a few minutes they were close behind it. The County policeman was still standing on the step of the bus, looking ahead.

"Overtake," said Martineau. "We might be wasting time."

In the long black car they fairly zoomed past the bus, but it was still in sight behind them when they saw a car standing beside a lonely farmhouse. Near the car there was the small figure of a man in the road, looking their way. This, then, was the source of the County policeman's message.

The man looked at them expectantly as they approached. He was a small, neatly dressed man, and they guessed that he was a commercial traveller. Devery drew up the car beside him.

"Police?" the man asked.

"Yes," said Martineau.

"It's about three hundred yards further up, in the dip there," the man began.

"Get in the car," said Martineau, reaching to open the rear door.

The man got in, and they went on in silence. He seemed to think that they knew all about the matter in hand.

Devery said quietly, from the side of his mouth: "The County people aren't going to like this, you know."

Martineau looked at him, and he said no more.

They were driving up to the skyline. There was a crest, then the gradient eased. There was a short, level stretch of road before the climb began again. This was the 'dip' which the traveller had mentioned. From it, all that could be seen was four hundred yards of grey road, a slope of dark moorland, and the limitless grey sky.

"Just here," the traveller said.

When the car stopped he was out before them, hurrying into the waste of dark grass and heather.

"Hold it!" Martineau called. "Don't go jumping about there." He knew what it was. He felt that he had known for some time, ever since he had seen the P.C. board the bus.

The traveller waited, and allowed the detectives to lead the way. They stepped carefully over the rough ground, looking about them as they walked. Ten yards from the road there was a small hillock. Behind the hillock, on bare black peat-hag, lay the body of a girl.

The girl had been young, smart, and pretty. She lay where she had been dropped, and she was graceful even without life in her. Her head was thrown back, and there were bruises on her tender throat. Her right wrist was linked to a ripped leather bag by a bright steel chain. Besides the marks on her neck, part of a great dark bruise was visible on her chest above the neckline of her dress. Her eyes were wide open, and Martineau reflected sadly that the last thing they had seen had been the face of her murderer. Her eyes had photographed him, and his image had been filed away in a remote cell of her brain. Now the brain could never recall that picture. It was unobtainable.

There was no sign that the girl had been 'interfered with'. Her skirt was around her legs, her stockings intact. The inspector thought bitterly: 'A nice, clean, bloody inhuman murder'.

"It's the girl from Gus Hawkins' office, and she's dead," he said over his shoulder to Devery. "See if you can reach Headquarters from here. If you can't, go down to the farmhouse and phone."

As Devery got into the police car the North-Western bus drew up, with passengers staring through the windows like goldfish in a tank. The County policeman dropped from the step and came bounding towards the hillock.

"Steady," said Martineau. "Watch where you're stepping."

The authority in his voice halted the constable, because he was used to authority. But: "Who're you?" he demanded.

"Inspector Martineau. C.I.D., Granchester City. Has anybody boarded that bus since you did?"

"No," said the P.C.

"Then send it on its way. Otherwise the passengers will be getting out and messing up the whole place."

The uniformed man did not like the order, but he could see the sense of it. He turned and waved to the bus driver. The driver nodded, put the bus in gear, and drove off.

"Now, what's all this?" the P.C. demanded.

"Let's get back to the road."

"I don't take orders from you," said the man, still obeying. "This is some sort of a fast move. I saw your car pass the bus. You're off your manor."

"I'm aware of it," said Martineau. "But I think it's a City job. Did you get a message about a robbery-violence in Granchester, and a girl being snatched?"

"Sure I did. And I guess this is the girl." The man's voice was angry. Probably this was the first time he had ever been closely associated with a murder, and but for the City men he would have been the first policeman on the spot. No doubt he would feel that he had been robbed of an opportunity to attract favourable notice.

Martineau seemed about to reply, then he lapsed into a thoughtful silence. Anyone who knew him could have told the frowning constable that he and his annoyance were not only ignored, they were completely forgotten. Martineau was thinking of the job; the murdered girl, and the murderers. How he was thinking of them! It was a City job, all right. Like grey vermin the men had emerged from the smoke. Soon, no doubt, they would be returning to it.

The girl was employed by Gus Hawkins, and the ripped cashbag with the steel chain told her story only too lucidly. Gus Hawkins was a bookmaker, and everybody knew that the bookies had had a good day yesterday. Not one favourite had won. Probably Gus had been shouting the odds at Doncaster, and he had come home loaded. This morning he had sent the girl to the bank with a bagful of money. She had been waylaid. The chain had been too strong, and the thieves had taken both girl and bag. Maybe she had recognized one of them. Anyway, one or more of them had been the death of her. Strangled, by the look of her. Strangled for a few hundred pounds of punters' money.

For a long time Martineau had been expecting something of the sort to happen. In England, the safe country, where policemen went unarmed and the criminal world had a climate less violent than in most other lands, employers and businessmen not only disregarded the possibility of robbery in the street, they asked for it. Near any bank, in any town, on any weekday morning, possible victims could be seen; from the elderly commissionaire and small shortsighted clerk transporting the payroll of a big factory, to the office boy or shopgirl going casually to and fro with a handful of fivers. They asked for it. And when they sent out a young girl with money chained to her wrist, they asked for murder.

Gus Hawkins had done that, and Gus Hawkins was a nice fellow. An extremely nice fellow. Gus Hawkins, who went to the races with a minder as big as a Carnera to protect his money, would be very sorry about the morning's happenings. Perhaps, in future, he would send his minder to the bank with the takings. A retired heavyweight wrestler wouldn't strangle quite so easily as this girl here.

Martineau's bitter thoughts were interrupted by the return of Devery, who was followed by a County police patrol car, with two uniformed officers. After a brief conference with their disgruntled colleague they glanced curiously at the City men, then sped away in the direction presumably taken by the fugitive American car.

The inspector turned to the commercial traveller. The man's name was Hartley, and he lived at Harrogate, and, after acting boldly in the public interest, he was beginning to be nervous and careful. He was involved in a murder. It was possible that the police would not believe what he told them. Persons who discovered bodies were often suspected of being the killers.

Martineau observed his uneasiness. "Don't worry," he said. "We already know what's behind this. Tell me what you saw."

"I was just coming over the brow up there, on my way to

9

Granchester," said Hartley with restored confidence. "As this bit of road came into sight I saw a car stopped here, facing towards me. A man was just walking away from the car, carrying something in both arms. It looked like a body. He dropped it there, where it is now, and ran back to the car. I put on speed, to try to get past the car before it got going again. I didn't quite succeed. It started to move, and the driver waved me down. It crossed my mind that the last thing he'd want was a smashed-up car, if he was on some crooked game. So I sounded my horn for him to keep out of my way, and kept going."

"You did well," said Martineau. "You're a quick thinker. So they let you go."

"Well, the driver made a half-hearted attempt to make me swerve off the road, but I held my course and he didn't risk a bump. I watched the car in my mirror when I was past. It went off the way it had been facing. I stopped at the farm down there and dialled nine-nine-nine."

"What sort of a car was it?"

"A Buick, I think. An old Buick. Pre-war. It was a sort of dusty black colour. The coachwork looked very shabby and neglected. I bet it hadn't been cleaned for ages."

"Did you get the registration number?"

"Sorry, no. I'm afraid I didn't."

"Did you notice any part of the number, or any of the letters?"

"No. I never looked at the number. I was more concerned with watching the driver, and the front wheels."

"Would you know him again?"

"I doubt if I would. When I got near, he put his hand across his face. I think they all did."

"All? How many men in the car?"

"I'm pretty sure there were four of them. The car seemed to be full."

"What about the man who carried the body?"

"He was back in the car before I got near enough to have a good look at him. He seemed to be a big, hefty man."

"Tall?"

"I wouldn't say he was as tall as you, but he struck me as being pretty big and burly."

"About what age?"

"Thirty, forty. Hard to say. He was wearing a dark suit and a soft hat. I couldn't say just what colour."

"Do you remember anything else about any of the others?"

"No. Just eyes; staring eyes over their hands. They'll all know *me* again."

"Don't worry about that, either. They'll be too busy to bother about you," said Martineau.

He spoke to Devery. "What did you find out?"

Devery looked at his watch. "It happened fifty-five minutes ago, at ten to eleven," he said. "The girl, Cicely Wainwright, was taking cash from Gus Hawkins' office to Lloyd's Bank. We don't know how much, yet. She was accompanied by a youth, Colin Lomax. They were attacked in Higgitt's Passage. There were three or four men involved. They sapped the boy; he's been taken to hospital. They shoved the girl into their car because she was chained to the handbag. They cleared off with her. They couldn't unlock either the chain or the bag because they hadn't time to look for the keys. The boy had them in his pocket."

Martineau nodded. It had been more or less as he had supposed.

Another car arrived, and plain-clothes men tumbled out of it. They were detectives of the County police, Granchester Division. Their leader, with a cold important frown, spoke to the constable in uniform. Then he saw the City men, and the frown deepened.

"Martineau," he said. "What are you doing here?"

Martineau was not disposed to be diplomatic about wnat he considered to be a triviality.

"I got here first, that's all," he said. "I was passing through when I picked up word about the job."

"Picked up word from where?"

"From Granchester—City."

"Oh." Some doubt crept into the County inspector's frown. "I suppose you would regard it as a City job. But the girl's body is here, and we don't know just where she was murdered."

The City man could have replied that the violent act

11

ending in murder had started in Granchester, but he refrained. He just nodded and waited. The County man was perplexed, not knowing how to handle him. He had heard things about Martineau.

"What have you done, so far?" he asked.

"Nothing, except stop people from trampling all over the place. By the way, there's a witness. This gentleman here. It occurs to me that one of your men could be taking his statement."

The County man nodded. His hostility had vanished. If the question of technical trespass had any importance, which he doubted, it could go in the report and be dealt with elsewhere. The job was the thing. Get on with it. He turned and gave an order, then he said: "Now then, let's have a look."

Martineau led the way to the body. The County man took a deep breath when he saw the bruised throat and chest. "That's nice, I must say," he muttered angrily.

Then Martineau noticed something. He squatted on his heels and lifted one of the limp hands. There were faint greenish stains on the fingers. He lifted the other hand, and the stains were there too.

The two inspectors looked at each other, and then Martineau did a strange thing. He spat on the end of his forefinger, and rubbed the spittle on one of the girl's fingers. The green stain showed up more clearly.

"By God!" said the County man. "Malachite green?"

"It looks like it, doesn't it?" the City inspector replied. "If it is. . . . What a break!"

II

The biggest city and county police forces of England—Lancashire, the West Riding, Birmingham, Liverpool and a few more—hardly ever call upon Scotland Yard to help them solve their major crimes. There was no question of Granchester calling in the Yard. Granchester City Police was a big force and a proud force. The Granchester men had their own forensic scientists and their own murder specialists —of whom Martineau was one—and they were of the opinion that on their own 'manor' they could do anything Scotland Yard could do.

Detective Superintendent Clay took charge of the Granchester end of the Cicely Wainwright case, with Martineau as his right hand man. Martineau had a comment about that. "All this and Don Starling, too," he said.

"You can stop thinking Starling is your own personal property," Clay answered briskly. "He's everybody's problem. We don't even know yet whether he's within a hundred miles of us."

Clay was big, stout, and very shrewd. Martineau respected his shrewdness. Still, he contradicted him. "Of course we know," he said. "He has no contacts anywhere but here."

"That we know of," Clay amended. "If you want to look for Starling you can do it in your spare time, and you'll have precious little of that. Just now, go and see what Gus Hawkins has to say."

So Martineau and Devery went to Gus Hawkins' office, but on the way they stopped to look at the scene of the crime. Higgitt's Passage was an alley which connected a quiet street of offices with a busy main street of shops, banks, airline offices, shipping offices, hotels, etc. It ran from Gaunt Street to Lacy Street. Gus Hawkins' office was in Gaunt Street, a mere three minutes' walk from Lloyd's Bank in Lacy Street.

The passage itself was like the shorter bar of a T, the longer bar being the back street between that part of Lacy Street and Gaunt Street. The attack on the boy and girl had occurred at the junction of the two bars of the T.

Martineau spoke to the detective-sergeant who was in charge of inquiries there. "Any developments?" he asked.

The sergeant pointed to a small plain van which was parked in the back street.

"That," he said. "We've just found out it's been stolen. It belongs to a greengrocer out at Highfield. He goes to market with it every morning, then he leaves it behind his shop till shutting-up time. He's busy serving in the shop. Didn't even know it had been pinched."

"You think it was used on this job?"

"We're guessing it was. One or two of 'em could have hid in it, and jumped out at the right moment."

13

"Where was the Buick?"

"Right here, as far as we can tell. A woman in one of these back rooms heard a scream. She thinks there was only one scream. She ran to the window and saw the car full of men dashing off along the back street. She said there seemed to be a bit of confusion in the back seat. But she didn't say anything at all till she was asked. Silly bitch. Lost us nearly twenty minutes."

Martineau gazed around. His glance settled on a small, old public house whose windows looked along the back street. It was a secluded place for a pub, and the pub itself was unobtrusive. It's faded sign bore the words 'The Prodigal Son. Free House', and above the door a small board announced that Hannah Savage was licensed to sell ale, porter, wine, spirituous liquor and tobacco. The attack on the boy and girl had taken place right outside the door of the Prodigal Son. But the people in there, though they must have become aware of unusual happenings, were apparently not curious. Nobody looked out from either door or window.

"Doug Savage's place," said Martineau reflectively.

The sergeant nodded significantly.

"Of course, it wouldn't be open at eleven o'clock," the inspector went on. "Have you talked to Doug?"

"Aye. And his mother. And the cleaning woman who was there. Like the three wise monkeys, they were. Hear nowt, see nowt, say nowt."

Martineau sighed. "Too bad," he said, and to Devery: "Come on. We'll go and have a word with Gus."

The sole occupant of Gus Hawkins' office was a middle-aged clerk who was doing his best to cope with four busy telephones. Gus was a strictly legal bookmaker. He employed no runners, and he did no ready-money betting except on the racecourse, where he did a great deal. His connexion in the city and on the course was considerable, and his reputation as a bookie was unspotted. On the telephone clients could make bets with him to win thousands of pounds, without a qualm about his ability and willingness to pay.

The clerk, Peter Purchas, seemed upset; even nervous. The effort and responsibility of running the office alone on a big-race day seemed to be too much for him. "I can't hedge none o' these bets," he found time to moan when he saw Martineau. "I'm too busy to balance. Gus'll have to stand 'em. We might lose a fortune."

Martineau remembered that it was St. Leger day. He had intended to back a horse called Empire Honey. Well, it probably wouldn't win.

"Where is Gus?" he asked. "Gone to the races?"

"Aye, he went. But police is going to stop him and turn him back. He should be here any minute."

"What time did he set off?"

"Just afore eleven. Just afore Cicely and the lad started for the bank. And here's me on me own. I don't know what to do about these bets."

Martineau could not advise him. He lit a cigarette and went to the window, and stood looking down into the street. His presence, and Devery's, seemed to worry Purchas, who kept shooting glances at him and muttering: "Wish Gus 'ud be quick."

Soon after one o'clock Gus arrived. He was followed into the office by Bill Bragg, the ex-wrestler who was his errand lad and 'minder'. His clerk, Lomax, father of Colin, had gone on to the hospital to see the injured boy.

Gus was a short, plump, bespectacled man of guileless appearance. His wit and acumen were not apparent until he opened his mouth. He was a good man, keenly aware but tolerant of the sins of the world; a hard man with a welsher and a soft man with anyone who was really down on his luck.

Bragg, the man who stood behind him looking over his head, had a face not only expressionless, it was incapable of expression. It was like the front door of a bombed-out house; the front door to nothing. He had a splendid physique run to seed, and a brain which retired in confusion from any problem too difficult for a fairly clever child of eight.

"Hello, Inspector," Gus said at once. "What a do! Those poor kids. . . . Poor little Cicely. . . . I shouldn't have sent 'em with all that money. . . . But, a lot or a little, it makes no difference to a thieving murderer."

A telephone rang. Gus stretched his short legs to cross the room. He snatched up the phone, listened a moment, and said: "Sorry, I can't take any more bets today. One of my

15

staff has died suddenly. Try Benny Solomons; Benny's all right."

As he finished speaking another phone rang. Zealously, Bill Bragg reached it first. "No more betting," he growled. "Somebody's dead." And he banged down the receiver.

"Bill, get away from that phone!" Gus shouted, and the big man backed off, looking hurt. The bookmaker spoke to Purchas: "No more bets. Leave the receivers off. I can't take bets with that poor lass lying dead."

He turned to the policemen. "Any clues, or anything?" he asked. "Any idea who did it?"

Martineau shook his head. Then he said: "What's the matter with your hands?"

Gus looked at his hands. The fingers and palms were stained bright green.

"I don't know what it is," he said. "I noticed it this morning when I got out of the bath. I suppose I handled that many pound notes at Doncaster yesterday, some of the green ink must have come off on my hands. I've never known it happen before, though." Then his mouth fell open in dismay. "Oh hell! Has somebody been passing me a lot of snide money?"

Martineau ignored the question. "Did you have a good day?" he asked.

"A marvellous day. Best in years. I never knew such a turn-up for the book. I don't mind telling you, I made over four thousand quid."

"And you sent four thousand to the bank this morning? Most of yesterday's winnings?"

"Correct. We celebrated a bit, after the races: Bill here, Stan Lomax and me. We got home late, and I was tired and maybe not just as sober as a driver should be. Anyway, instead of calling at the bank and putting the money in the night safe I dropped Stan and Bill and went straight home. Believe it or not, I left the money in the car and forgot to lock the garage door, and didn't remember it till this morning. I deserved to have the whole lot pinched. I wish it *had* been pinched, then those kids 'ud be all right now. Poor little Cicely! I wouldn't have had this happen for forty thousand, never mind four."

"Who counted the money this morning, before it was sent to the bank?" Martineau asked.

Gus looked slightly surprised. "Oh, there was four thousand all right," he said. "I counted it first, then Cicely counted it and put it in the bank bag. Then I set off to Doncaster, leaving her to see that it got to the bank."

"And you're sure it was money you got at the races? I want a serious answer, Gus. It's important."

"Every cent that went to the bank was won at the races. It came out of my bag all scrumpled up anyhow, just as I'd stuffed it in. My own money was still in bundles. I'd never had to use any of it, see? I set off to Doncaster with it today, and brought it back."

"And it's Saturday. The banks closed at noon."

"It'll go in the night safe. I'm sending Bill and old Purchas with it right away. I'll make sure *that's* not snatched."

Martineau reflected that everybody called Purchas 'old', though he was only in his middle forties. Probably it was because of the man's sunken, characterless face and his tendency to worry about broken routine.

"How was the stolen money made up?" he asked.

"Three thousand ones and two hundred fivers," Gus replied promptly. "And I hope it chokes 'em."

"Maybe it will," said Martineau.

"What a mess it all is," the bookmaker said. "Poor Cicely! Have her parents been told?"

The inspector nodded.

"I suppose I'd better go and see 'em," said Gus. "I don't know how I'll face 'em."

III

From a public telephone in Gaunt Street Martineau contacted the C.I.D. office and spoke to Superintendent Clay.

"I've seen Gus Hawkins," he said, "and his fingers are bright green. I think we've really got something there. Gus counted the money this morning, before the girl did. It was all cash he got at the races yesterday."

"Good," said Clay. "I've got something too. I put out an express and I've got a reply already, from Hallam City.

17

Hallam are *very* interested. They're interested to the extent of two hundred pounds."

"Not all in dusted notes, surely," said Martineau.

"Yes. Two hundred one-pound notes, all dusted. That shakes you, doesn't it?"

Martineau listened carefully to the story. When Granchester City wanted to know if any officer in any force had recently been dusting one-pound notes with malachite green, the Hallam police answered immediately. When they learned how serious was the Granchester case, their sharply inquiring tone changed, and they were ready with information. Their use of malachite green had ended a series of larcenies from the Hallam City Treasurer's department. Some sly person had been pilfering, in amounts rising from £2 to £10, from stacked money in the main collector's office.

The thief was clever, or lucky. He was never seen taking the money, nor did he leave fingerprints. He was fortunate in avoiding traps until an angry and determined detective took a camel's hair brush and a quantity of powdered mala-chite green, and painstakingly brushed the dry dye on to *all* the notes in two bundles of one hundred pounds. Until they could be carefully distributed as bait, the two hundred dusted notes were put in a safe place in a cashier's office, but the place was not safe enough. The thief—an elderly, unsuspected janitor—came upon the money while the cashier was out of the room for a moment, and in an access of greed he pocketed the lot. He immediately left the premises, telling a doorman that he was going home because he was ill. But he did not go home.

That was on Friday, the day before Cicely Wainwright was murdered. The police were waiting for the janitor when he returned home, morosely inebriated, late on Friday night. He had none of the stolen money in his possession, but the police knew that he was their man. He was betrayed by his green fingers. Without moisture the dye known as malachite green would not stain, but perspiration caused it to colour the fingers faintly but indelibly. Washing the hands in water made the stain much brighter. The janitor had been washing his hands, and to the expectant policemen they fairly shouted "Thief!"

Under pressure, the janitor said that he had taken the marked money to Doncaster, and lost it all at the races. The police were not inclined to believe him. They suspected that he had got drunk with a little of it, and 'sided' the rest. They 'worked on him', but he maintained that he was telling the truth.

"Well well!" said Martineau, when he had heard the story. "Aren't we lucky?"

"It seems so," Clay agreed. "But we'd better get weaving. before that dye starts to fade."

"Too true," said the inspector, making for the door. "Hallam first, to verify."

He rounded up Gus Hawkins, Stan Lomax, and Bill Bragg, and took them forty miles over the hills to Hallam. There, at his request, the police conducted an identification parade in reverse. The green-handed thief was brought out and introduced to Martineau. "Now," said the inspector. "Do you recognize any of these gentlemen?"

"Sure," said the prisoner. He turned indignantly to the Hallam detectives. "Happen you'll believe me now. That's the bookie I backed with yesterday. And that's his clerk. And that's his private bruiser."

To corroborate the statement, Gus himself remembered the prisoner as a man who had betted persistently and unsuccessfully at his stand on the previous day. He had even commented upon the man's ill luck.

"So the money went into a bookie's pocket," a Hallam detective bluntly commented.

"You can have it back," said Gus, "when you find the three thousand eight hundred that goes with it."

The bookmaker's attention had not been drawn to the prisoner's green fingers, but he had noticed them. On the way home he referred to them. "Is that the bloke who's been passing the snide?" he wanted to know.

"It's just possible," was Martineau's non-committal answer.

"It's poor stuff, if the ink comes off."

"It is, if that's the case," said the inspector with marked disinterest. That, he thought, was as much as Gus and his henchmen needed to knew about malachite green. And the sooner they forgot about the 'snide', the better.

With the Granchester police, of course, it was different. They were conducting a strictly secret search for green fingers in the city. Only the chemists in their shops would be informed, and they would not be told any more than they needed to know: that there had been a larceny, and that any person seeking a solvent for a green stain on the hands should be kept waiting until the police were called. There would be men standing by in readiness for such a call. They would be on their way almost as soon as the chemist who called them had put down his telephone.

IV

Gus Hawkins and Harry Martineau had two things in common; they were both married to handsome women and they were both unhappy about it. Gus's wife was, he suspected, occasionally unfaithful. Certainly she was far too gay for a normal married woman. He sometimes wondered if he gave her too much money.

It wasn't as if Chloe was accustomed to money. She had never had much of her own, and she was rather down on her luck when Gus met her. At least, he thought so. She had no money and no job, and she was running around with a shady crowd. Gus was attracted by her, and he was sorry for her. Nowadays, though he still found her attractive, he sometimes wondered how he had been induced to marry her.

At the time of the marriage, many people had remarked that it was strange how a wise guy like Gus could be snared and deluded by a dumb dame like Chloe.

As he left his office on the evening of that unhappy St. Leger day, Gus glumly remembered the night before. Last night was typical, he thought. Though he was late, she—depend on it—was later. It was annoyance and uncertainty about that which had made him forget about the four thousand pounds in the unlocked garage. When he arrived home, his comfortable suburban house was in darkness. When he saw it he swore, in a gust of helpless anger. He knew that Chloe would not yet be in bed. Not at home, anyway. She was out somewhere. Doing what? With whom?

He unlocked the front door and went into the house, and put the lights on successively in every room while he looked around. He searched with conscious suspicion, seeing everything. But there was nothing out of the ordinary: the house was in its normal state of moderately clean untidiness. Having switched off all the lights, he went into the front room. He knelt on the settee beside the window, with his arms on the sill. In front of the window was the short drive. The posts of the open gateway were silhouetted against the lighted road outside.

At a quarter to twelve Chloe came home. She turned in at the gate and hurried up the drive, but there was no sign of guilt or uneasiness in her haste. He stood up and moved back from the window so that she would not see him. As she opened the door with her key he stood silent, and, he hoped, forbidding. She came from the hall into the front room and threw her handbag on to the settee. Then she switched on the light.

When she saw him she jumped, and said "Oh!" Then she laughed and went straight to him, and hugged him.

"There," she said, petting him. "He got home first and no supper. When he's worked hard all day. Poor tired darling. Never mind, she'll have it ready in a minute."

She left him, and ran upstairs to put away her coat, because she was never untidy with her own clothes. She returned, pushing up the short sleeves of her pretty dress as if she were going to do all the work in the world.

"What would you like, dear?" she asked.

"What is there?" he inquired sulkily.

She giggled briefly. "Nothing much. I didn't get down to the shop today. Will you have an egg and some ham?"

"What, again?"

"You know you like ham and eggs, I'll have it ready in a jiffy."

He leaned in the kitchen doorway, watching her as she stood by the cooker. When the ham was in the pan he said: "Where have you been all this time?"

"I went to the Odeon," she said. "Then there was a terrific queue for buses. You know how it is, Friday nights. I just got on the last bus."

21

He remembered the film at the Odeon. "You said you'd seen it," he grumbled.

She nodded. "It was so good I thought I'd go and see it again. I enjoyed it twice as much the second time." Then suddenly she giggled again.

"Was it so funny?" he demanded sourly.

She turned and came close to him. She was a *petite* girl; slender, with a disproportionately heavy bosom. She had fair hair, brown eyes, and a pretty, pointed, elfin face. There was mischief in that face; maybe innocent mischief, maybe— well, Gus sometimes wondered.

"Did she stay out late then, and make him jealous?" she murmured, with her face hidden against his shoulder. She seemed to be contrite, and yet he thought that she might be secretly laughing at him.

"You're always out late," he growled, "and you always have an excuse. One of these nights your watch'll be wrong, and you'll miss that damned bus."

She smiled up into his face. His resentment did not worry her. So long as he did not actually *know* anything, she was sure of her ability to wheedle him into a good humour.

"Then," she twinkled, "she'll have to take a taxi."

She stood on her toes and pulled his head down and kissed him, and because he also had been drinking he did not smell the gin on her breath. Then she turned away and cracked an egg into the pan, and started to cut bread. He returned to the front room, and stared moodily through the window at the lighted gateway.

When the meal was ready she came to him, and hugged him again. "Now, go and eat his supper," she coaxed. "Then they can go to bed and she'll be nice to him. She'll love him, love him and love him, and he won't be jealous any more."

"If ever I catch her two-timing," he said to himself, "I'll break her neck." And yet he knew even then that it was a vain resolve. He had always had too much common sense to resort to violence.

She pressed closer, and as his arms went round her his mood changed as it had done before in similar circumstances. He thought that he *might* be wrong about Chloe. After all, he had no direct evidence.

22

That was last night. Tonight, he felt sure that if she had seen an evening paper she would be waiting at home for him. Even Chloe would stay at home to be with a husband who had just been robbed of four thousand pounds and had a valued and trusted woman clerk murdered. In the afternoon he had tried to speak to her on the telephone, but apparently she had been out. Later, when the evening papers had appeared, she had not phoned the office to ask for details, and so, perversely, he had not tried to reach her again. Now he thought: 'Let her wait. I need a drink.'

He went to the Stag's Head and had several drinks, but this time he did not conform to his own tradition of drinking champagne from a tankard to celebrate a thoroughly disastrous day. He had lost four thousand pounds, but, with poor Cicely lying dead, he could not drink champagne.

While he was in the bar, Ugo, the head waiter, passed through. Ugo, who was a sort of friend of his, informed him confidentially that he had some rather exceptional steaks. Gus was still slightly annoyed because his wife had not telephoned, and he thought again: 'Let her wait,' and ordered a meal.

Men *will* stay out when they should go home. That is probably the world's most common cause of domestic discord and unhappiness. Gus Hawkins should have gone home. Like other men who sometimes linger on the way from the office, he would have saved himself a headache if he had not done so. He would have saved himself a number of headaches.

It would have been much better if he had gone straight home. Certainly, on this occasion, it would have been much better for his wife.

V

Martineau and Devery ended a long day's work at ten o'clock. "Let's have an odd one at the Green Archer," Martineau suggested, because he did not want to go home. These days, he never wanted to go home.

His domestic trouble was not of the same type as Gus Hawkins'. Julia Martineau was not unfaithful, and it was impossible to suspect that she ever would be. She was only interested in fine clothes, social standing, attractive homes,

23

and the affairs of her acquaintances. The connubial behaviour of other people (as a topic of scandalous conversation) was more interesting to her than her own or her husband's. She was rarely aroused. The conjugal act was sometimes a duty, sometimes a favour to be granted, and always a ceremony which she allowed to be performed after it had been suitably prayed for. Lately, Martineau had ceased to pray.

At half-past ten, when the landlord of the Green Archer called "Time", Devery excused himself. "Sorry to dash off," he said, "I've got a supper date. With my girl."

"If you have to go a-courting at all," said his disillusioned senior, "supper time is as good a time as any."

"Exigencies of the service, sir," Devery replied briskly. "She seems satisfied if I show up *sometime* during the twenty-four hours."

He went. Martineau lingered, until he remembered that it was Saturday night. There would be queues of people waiting for outward-bound buses. He went to catch his bus.

He could not get on a bus before eleven o'clock, and it was eleven twenty-five when he arrived at his neat semi-detached house in suburban Parkhulme. A light was showing downstairs, at the back. Julia was waiting.

"Hallo," he said as he entered the living-room. His wife stared coldly at him and said: "What time do you call this?"

He looked at his watch and told her the exact time.

"What time did you sign off?" she wanted to know.

"Ten o'clock."

"And since then you've been in some pub."

"Correct," he said.

"You've been working on that murder, I suppose. Have you got anybody for it?"

He shook his head. "Anything for supper?" he asked, not very hopefully.

"There's your tea, if you want to warm it up," she said. "Other husbands can ring up their wives and tell them when they'll be home. Of course, I couldn't expect *you* to do that. You couldn't even phone and tell me you'd be working late. I had to make you tea whether you came or not."

He accepted the rebuke. He usually told her when he would be late. But today, when he had remembered that he should tell her, he had been in the middle of wild moorland on his way to Hallam.

He went into the little kitchen and looked at his 'tea' in the cold electric oven. Two small lamb chops, some tinned peas, chips. Gravy in a small jug, with a top layer of cold fat like a sheet of ice on water. It would all have been quite nice at tea-time. Even now, warmed up, it would be eatable because he was hungry. He closed the oven door and turned the switches. He went back to the living-room, which his wife called the dining-room. Also she called the front room the lounge, and he could always annoy her by calling it the parlour.

Julia sat upright on the edge of her fireside chair. As he had expected, a copy of *Vogue* was on the table within her reach. She was an extremely elegant woman, with an infallible taste in clothes. The plain, rather severe dress which she now wore was undeniably smart, and it certainly suited her mood and expression. She was thirty-three years of age, tall, dark-haired, clear-skinned. Her face and neck would have given pleasure to a sculptor. She had a perfectly natural model figure, and such a figure she had always had. It sometimes seemed to Martineau that her figure changed itself according to the demands of fashion. He was sure that her breasts had filled out since voluptuous busts became fashionable. If it became fashionable to be fat, Julia would quite naturally put on weight. If flat chests became the thing again, her breasts would seem to melt away.

"At least," she said, "one would think you could come home at ten, when you came off duty. You've been out of this house since half-past seven this morning."

'A girl had been murdered,' he thought. 'Four thousand pounds have been stolen. And behold, I have been out of the house since half-past seven this morning. Mercy on us, I didn't come home to my tea.'

"I was weary," he said. "I needed a drink."

"You could have had a bottle of beer at home."

"It isn't the same."

"I'm aware of that," she said. "You'd sooner be in a low pub than at home. With low women sitting around the bar, ready to go with you if you want them."

25

"I've told you before, you're all wrong about that." he said patiently. "I can't afford to spend my time in that sort of pub. In decent pubs nearly all the women are there with their husbands. They may not come up to your idea of society, but they're respectable."

"You didn't think about me, waiting here," she said.

Martineau admitted to himself that her last grumble seemed reasonable enough. It *seemed* so. But was she waiting with love or anxiety? He did not think so. He was beginning to believe that as a husband he was merely a property of some value to her. To women of her type all husbands were a nuisance, with their rough ways and physical demands, but they were a necessary nuisance. According to Julia's pattern of life a woman *had* to have a husband, the more successful the better. She had to have a husband to hold her head up in society, and to prevent other women from pitying her.

"It seems to me that my life is all waiting," she said. "Waiting for you to come in, or go out, or come to bed."

'She hasn't had enough to do,' he thought. 'She ought to have a couple of kids. Children in the house would make all the difference.'

His conception of a happy home had always included one or two children. He had married Julia under the delusion that children would arrive in the natural course of events. But from the beginning Julia had quite positively refused to have a child. She had never, at any time, allowed her husband's love-making to become uninhibited enough to produce one. Their sex life had always been artificial.

Martineau himself did not have a blind fondness for children, nor did he subscribe to the sentimental convention that all children were lovable. He knew that many of them were peevish little horrors who were only loved by their parents and grandparents. Still, a man sometimes met a gruff small boy or a dainty little girl who made him wish for a family of his own.

But Julia thought that life could be complete without children. She could barely simulate a mild affection for her friends' kiddies, and when they were in her house she was all the time on edge, afraid that they would kick the furniture or mark the wallpaper.

"My life's empty," she said now. "We never go out together, and you're never at home. I try to keep this place nice, and you treat it like a doss house."

It occurred to him that he was having to suffer because she had had an empty evening; no film she wanted to see, no book she wanted to read, nothing she wanted to hear on the radio, nothing to do. Probably she had been playing bridge all the afternoon, but that was a long time ago; seven empty hours ago.

"You haven't enough to do," he said.

She looked at him. "You're not suggesting that I should take a job, are you?"

"No," he said, "I'm not. If you take a job it's your own affair. But you want something to do. Something to occupy your mind."

"I'd look nice, the great Inspector Martineau's wife, hunting for a job."

"You're very particular about how things look, aren't you?" he said. "It'd look all right if you justified your exist-ence by having a baby or two. Your life wouldn't be empty any more. And we're both still plenty young enough. We could have some fine kids."

"Don't start that again," she said quickly. Then she said: "It would be different if I had Mother and Father here. At least I'd have company."

"No!" he said. "Definitely and finally, no!"

He went into the kitchen and returned with his supper. She watched him sulkily. He picked up the evening paper and glanced at the headlines while he ate, so she got up and banged off to bed without speaking. He said "Good night" but she did not answer. He shrugged and went on with his meal.

After supper he lit a cigarette, and went into the front room. He did not switch on the lights, but he could see fairly well by the light which streamed from the hallway through the open door. He stared through the window for a little while, then he turned to the piano and absently picked out a tune with one hand. He sat down and began to play. Wilfully he dropped his cigarette ash just anywhere on the carpet. He did not do it to annoy Julia, but he knew that it

27

would annoy her. 'Give her something to do,' he thought.

There was a sweet little tune which he had heard a youth whistling as he waited for his bus. He called it Hildegarde's song, after the singer who used it for a signature tune. He played it, softly. He was not a serious pianist, but he played well by ear. Almost everybody liked to hear him play. He played Hildegarde's song several times, getting it just right, putting his own emphasis where he liked it and letting the words of the part English, part French lyric run through his mind.

Julia knocked on the bedroom floor with the heel of a slipper. He played the tune once more, then got up and went to his own bed. Tomorrow was Sunday, but he had to work on a murder.

He lay in bed and thought about it. He tried to imagine the terror of Cicely Wainwright's death: crushed down by a heavy knee, among big feet on the dirty floor of an old car. She had been a bonnie girl. She would have married and made somebody happy, and had children.

Julia was asleep. She breathed deeply and evenly. He supposed, tolerantly, that there were faults on both sides. Then a new thought came to him quite suddenly. He wished she would leave him. There was no love in the house. He wished she would go. He wanted a fresh start.

She hadn't even asked him if Don Starling had been caught: Starling who had declared himself his mortal enemy. But perhaps she didn't feel afraid of what Starling might do. He didn't himself, for that matter.

He thought: 'I wonder if Starling has found himself a snug roost for the night?'

VI

When he parted from Martineau in the Green Archer, Devery did not go to a cold supper, or a cold welcome either. He went to a comfortable flat above an old-established furniture shop in Little Sefton Street, where he received a kiss from a girl, a nod from an old man, and a steak pudding from a warm oven. As he sat down to the meal he rubbed his hands and beamed his delight, because they were apt to do things by signs in that household. The girl smiled fondly

28

when she saw how he was enjoying the food. The old man nodded again and grinned.

The old man's name was Dick Steele, and for forty-five years he had owned and run the furniture shop—which had four floors and was big enough to be called a warehouse—in a reasonable and old-fashioned way, so that he was not rich and not poor. He was a small man, who had been sturdy. He was a little forgetful nowadays, and yet always ready to recall the past. Throughout that part of the city he was known as Furnisher Steele.

The girl was his only grandchild. Her name was Sylvia, but with the perversity of those who will speak as they wish and not as they ought, the old man had never bothered to pronounce the name correctly. He called her Silver, and so did everybody else.

Silver Steele was a natural blonde of Technicolor brilliance. She was a picture, And still following the movie blonde tradition she was beautiful but dumb. Unfortunately, she was deaf as well, and had been for all of her twenty-one years. She had never heard a sound in her life, and as an adult person she never uttered one. But her remaining senses were alert, and she had a brain in her head. She kept a well-run home for her grandfather, and made her way easily and efficiently in a soundless world. She had a sweet disposition. People liked her and said it was a shame, but she neither needed nor wanted pity.

"Marvellous!" said Devery as he put down his knife and fork. Silver read the word on his lips. She smiled, and began to clear the table. He went to his armchair—he was so much at home that he had his own chair—and presently she came and sat at his feet, leaning with an arm on his knee.

While Devery ate his supper, Furnisher Steele had been silent. Generally he was garrulous, rambling on about unimportant matters. And as a rule he was avid for information of the sort which can only be obtained from a member of the police force. Within the limits of discretion Devery usually indulged him in this matter, and tonight, with a murder case only a few hours old, he wondered a little because the questions did not come.

"I suppose you've seen the paper?" he said.

29

"Aye, I've seen it," was the short reply. Then: "Has Don Starling been caught yet?"

Devery shook his head. "Not yet."

"Then it's time he was!" came the sharp retort. "You're letting one man take the lot of you for a ta-ta. I thought the police reckoned to be so clever. Why don't they get crack-ing, and get him under lock and key again?"

Devery's surprise increased. The old man was usually more respectful than critical of the police.

"We're doing our best," he said. "Every policeman in England is on the lookout for him. We'll get him, all right. And before so very long."

He reflected that Furnisher's interest in Starling was not unnatural. He had followed the criminal's career ever since the night, some ten years before, when he had broken into the furniture shop. "He came here as nice as pie," the old man had said many a time. "He said he was looking for a sideboard, and he looked all around. He even looked at me antiques upstairs. Said he'd think about it. Then he came back at night and broke in."

"What's on your mind?" the detective queried. "Surely you don't think that Starling might come here again? He won't do that. He'll keep away from the places where he's known. He won't want to be seen."

"I don't like him being out," was the stubborn reply. "He's a dangerous man. He'll do somebody an injury."

When Furnisher made that remark he looked at Silver, and Devery wondered if in some queer way he imagined the fugitive could be a danger to his granddaughter. It was absurd. What possible motive . . . ? The ideas some of these old people got into their heads!

"What about Inspector Martineau?" the old man fol-lowed up. "Is he worried because you can't catch Starling?"

He was really inquiring about the state of Martineau's nerves, because Starling had declared—before judge, jury, Press and public—that he would kill Martineau. He had made the announcement at the Assizes two years before, after he had been given a fourteen-year slap in the face by the judge. Because of the long prison term, the threat had not been taken seriously. But now Starling was at large, and people were remembering it.

"Martineau isn't worried," said Devery. "He can handle Starling."

"Can he handle a bullet in his back?" asked Furnisher, and Devery smiled. To get close behind his enemy, unseen, the hunted man would have to spend a lot of time waiting around: more time than he could afford in a city where he was known to many people.

The two men talked a little while longer, but Furnisher did not regain his normal cheery mood. Soon he announced that he was going to bed. "Don't keep that girl up too long," he said.

When he had gone, Devery moved over to the settee with Silver. They sat close together. He squeezed her a little and kissed her, that was all. Though he desired her greatly—and he was no more straitlaced than the average young man—an unrecognized touch of chivalry prevented him from making importunate love to a girl who could only resist in desperate silence. And now he could afford to wait. They were to be married in a few weeks.

Apart from the times when her physical nearness affected him, Silver was peace. She did not need to be entertained with constant talk, either vocal or manual. She was content just to be beside him. Devery was aware of that, and he liked it. Her continued silence never bored or irritated him. In her company he realized how often normal people talk just to hear the sound of voices.

He had met Silver in unusual circumstances. It was one of those things which could only happen to a policeman. It occurred during his last tour of night duty, in uniform, before he was transferred to the detective staff. Finding the front door of a five-storey office building standing wide open after midnight, and seeing a light on the top floor, he went to investigate. As he ascended the dimly lighted stairs he heard a continuous strange noise, and he was unable to decide what made it. Swishuffle, swishuffle, swishuffle. A hundred women with a hundred brooms? Two elephants having a sparring match? Somebody dragging something very heavy?

As he climbed, each landing became progressively more

shabby and each locked office door less ornate. On the top floor, whence came the noise, there was only one door, labelled G.S.D.D.P. He knocked and received no answer. He opened the door and entered cautiously, and found himself in a large bare room, and in the presence of some two hundred people. They were dancing, in silence, in time to the movements of one man who stood on a dais, holding a conductor's baton.

The dancing stopped, and two hundred people stared at Devery in silent embarrassment, as if they had been caught acting the fool in secret. Only one person smiled. She was a lovely blonde girl who happened to be near the door. Devery was embarrassed too, and he returned the girl's smile with gratitude. He realized that he had stumbled upon a scene which was not for his eyes: a private revel of afflicted people. He said: "Oh, sorry," rather foolishly. Then he touched his helmet to the company, took one more good look at the smiling blonde, and hastily got out of there. As he went down the stairs he muttered: "Gad, what a smasher! What a beauty! What a pity!"

He was in that street again an hour later, when the Society for Deaf and Dumb People's dance was ending. He saw an old man meet the blonde girl. He watched them walk away. They walked past a taxi rank, so he guessed that they lived not far away.

The following day he commenced C.I.D. duties. His first inquiry was strictly unofficial. It concerned the dumb blonde. It did not take him long to find her.

That had happened about two years ago. "Just before the Underdown job," he remembered. That case was still very much on the agenda. Only one man—Don Starling—had been arrested, and the stuff had never been found. In connexion with it, Devery's mind dwelt on a coincidence. It was not a new thought, because the coincidence had been remarked by Martineau earlier in the day. Neither was it very important; simply a reflection that the Cicely Wainwright murder had occurred on the last day of Doncaster Races, while the Underdown job of nearly two years ago had happened on the last day of Granchester Races.

PART TWO

STARLING

I

UNLIKE Doncaster, Granchester was too big a city to have her economy seriously affected by an important race week. Nevertheless, during the Granchester November meetings, the last flat races of the season, there was a little more money moving in the town. And certain shopkeepers were acutely aware of it.

The tradesmen who mainly profited by the extra money were those who dealt in luxuries. Not only was the amount of their business increased by those who had been lucky at the races, but also by a number of tax dodgers who were quite happy to merely pretend that they had been lucky. By this subterfuge undeclared profits, hitherto an embarrassment, could be spent on furs and jewellery; and especially on diamonds, the favourite investment of all profiteers.

Nobody was more ready to exploit this human weakness for gambling and modified I.D.B. than Messrs. Underdown (London and G/chester Ltd.) of Castle Street. Theirs was the largest and most expensive jeweller's establishment in the city. To attract rich buyers to the even better gems inside the shop, the Underdown display during race week was as fine as any in Europe. It was so valuable that the bronze grilles, which normally protected the windows only at night, were put up in the daytime as well.

Naturally the police observed the splendour and value of the display, and they kept an eye on it. But no policeman can be in two places at once, and during the afternoons every man who could be spared was at the racecourse, trying to discourage the pickpockets and cornermen, the race gangs, the let-me-mark-your-card tricksters, and the crown and anchor, find the lady, pea and thimble, prick the garter, three-to-one-the-lucky-seven operators.

On the day of the Granchester November Handicap,

nearly two years before the Doncaster St. Leger day on which Cicely Wainwright was murdered, the temporary shortage of policemen inspired a few bright criminals with the notion of selecting a stone or two from the Underdown display without actually entering the shop. For this exploit they chose the starting time of the big race. They supposed that even the bobbies on the streets would slip in somewhere to see the race by television.

To the mobsters involved, the raid itself was not expected to be a great deal of trouble. They would use an old but effective method. It was the getaway to which the most thought and care were given. They knew that Police Head-quarters would be *instantly* informed of the raid, and they also knew that the police mobile cordon was well-nigh per-fect in rapid-alarm cases. Consummate guile, not speed, was needed for the escape. If the police could be induced to pursue the wrong man, or the wrong car. . . . Ah, that was the idea!

Unfortunately for several people, on the afternoon of the big race there was a young, newly-promoted sergeant of 'A' Division on duty in the heart of the city. Owing to his superiors' preoccupation with the traffic, the crowds, and the criminals at the racecourse, he 'had the town on his shoulders'. He felt the responsibility keenly, and he had no time to think about sport. At three o'clock, the time of the race, he was walking along Castle Street.

The sergeant was less than two hundred yards from Underdown's when he saw a three-ton lorry stop at the kerb near the shop. That was not strange, but neither was it usual: it was a very shabby lorry and a very smart shop. Then a man jumped from the cab of the lorry and *ran* to the rear of it. That was a mistake. The sergeant perceived that this might be a matter for the police. When he saw a black Ford car pull in behind the lorry he was certain. It was an old trick, the lorry and the car. He began to run towards Underdown's. To get along better he left the peopled sidewalk and ran in the middle of the road, and drivers of cars slowed and craned to see whom he was chasing; or, what would be more inter-esting, to see who might be chasing him.

The man who had run to the back of the lorry lifted from

it a crane hook, which was attached to the lorry by a strong rope. He ran across the sidewalk with the hook, and hung it on the bronze grille which protected Underdown's main window. Then he ran back to the lorry, and scrambled on behind as it jerked into motion. He lay flat on the empty load platform, and as soon as the grille had been ripped away from the window he began to saw at the tow-rope with a cut-throat razor. The lorry travelled a short distance with the grille skating and clanking behind, then the rope parted and the lorry sped away, leaving the grille lying in the road.

Before the lorry started, three men alighted from the Ford car which had stopped close behind it. They wore hats pulled well down in front, and scarves which masked their faces up to the eyes in a manner which seems nowadays to have gone out of fashion. One of them—the guard—held a pistol and an eighteen-inch length of lead pipe. He stood near the shop door, turning around watchfully, ready to deal with any person who might interfere. A second man ran to the window and swung a fourteen-pound sledgehammer at the 'unbreakable' glass. The glass broke, and its foundations had been so badly disturbed by the rough removal of the grille that the whole window fell out. The third man came up with an open canvas travelling bag. The hammer man dropped the sledge and began to sweep rings, brooches, bracelets, necklaces, pendants, earrings and jewelled watches from the shelves into the open bag.

An alarm clanged inside and outside the shop, and it also shrilled and showed a light on a panel at Police Headquarters. Inside the shop, the manager ran from his office and then back to his telephone and rather unnecessarily dialled 999. The senior assistant, a small middle-aged man, looked around helplessly for a weapon, and then dived away to the back of the shop to what he could find in the mop closet. A young lady assistant stood and screamed. Another assistant, an athletic young man, went out to do battle. He was momentarily stopped by the threat of the pistol, and while he was wondering if the mobster would dare to use it he was knocked out with the lead pipe.

No sooner had the assistant fallen than a little fat woman shopper waddled impetuously forward—probably she did not realize exactly what she was doing—and snatched at the guard's kerchief, pulling it down from his face. He cursed her briefly and bitterly, and gave her a back-handed swipe across the shoulder and chest with his leaden club. She fell down, and lay staring up at him.

The driver of the raiders' car had remained at the wheel. He had become aware of the approaching police sergeant. He was pounding the horn button, but the sound of the horn was mainly drowned by the din of the jeweller's alarm. Then, a little late, the guard saw the man in uniform. He shouted and beckoned to the men at the window, and started towards the car. But the sergeant had arrived, with his short, heavy truncheon in his hand. He stretched a long left arm to grab the travelling bag. He also hauled off with the truncheon, ready to strike.

The bagman resisted, but the policeman never struck the blow. The guard shot him. It was the third and fourth shots which hit him. The impact, in quick succession, of the two .45 slugs crumpled him as if he had received the thrust of an invisible battering-ram.

The three men tumbled into the car. It started immediately, and took the nearest turn to the right. It sped along the side street and turned right again at the next crossing. Then it followed a zig-zag pattern along quiet streets and finally stopped in an alley behind the Royal Lancaster Hotel. The four men abandoned the car and ran along the alley, one of them carrying the canvas bag full of plunder. They scattered, vanishing into other yards and alleys. Obviously the district was familiar to them.

A little while before the getaway car reached the alley, another black Ford saloon, which had been waiting along the route, started up and followed it. When the first car turned aside and stopped, the second one kept going along the street. With only one man in it, the car fled southward at a high speed. It had a long way to go before it reached open country.

At Police Headquarters, the alarm had resulted in a broadcast message to twenty Area Patrol cars which were prowling about within the city boundary. Two car crews were instructed to go at once to Underdown's, and the remainder were alerted. A second, more informative 999 call led to a message about a black Ford saloon, number not yet known. The mobile cordon began to operate.

The occupants of AP 18, going to Underdown's as ordered, noticed a black Ford travelling fast in the opposite direction. They were able to inform H.Q. of the position, direction, estimated speed, model and number of the car. H.Q. was also interested to hear that the occupant of the car was Edward Hooker, a man with a criminal record as long as a horse's leg.

A token representing Eddie Hooker in the Ford car was given a place of honour on the big table map at H.Q., and it was obvious that he was going to be the prey of either AP 4 or AP 27, both of whom were waiting for him. Two more cars were directed to cut across town and give additional cover, on the typical Headquarters principle that if you tell enough people to do something, it can't be your fault if it isn't done.

The fact that there was only one man in the car led to a strong suspicion that it was the wrong car, but that did not result in any alteration of plans. Eddie Hooker was worth turning up anytime.

The crew of AP4 were unlucky. They saw Hooker, and he saw them, but their intention of quickly overtaking him was baulked by an elderly lady in an elderly car. She pulled them up sharp by blithely signalling her intention to turn across their path, then she stalled her engine in front of them. Their motor horn blared pure hatred at her.

Hooker sped away from them, but two minutes later AP 27 came surging up behind him. He had known that he would be caught by the police—he was there, more or less, on the understanding that he would be caught—but so much police attention was too much for his nerves. He panicked, and pushed the accelerator down to the floorboard.

At sixty miles an hour he tried to go over a crossing against the lights. A big lorry loaded with carboys rumbled into the moving picture on the other side of his windscreen. Like other people, he always expected carboys to contain corrosive acid. Acid! He swerved blindly to avoid the lorry. The Ford jumped the kerb and ran head-on into the solid stone façade of the National Provincial Bank. No car ever built could have taken that impact. The Ford was a write-off.

Eddie Hooker was a shattered man, but he was still conscious when they extricated him from the wreck. Dazedly he remembered that he had a tale to tell. The two uniformed officers from AP 27 tried to make him comfortable while he waited for the ambulance. He looked at them expectantly, but they were traffic men with an accident on their hands, and for a while they were too busy to question him.

Martineau, D.I. of 'A' Division, had been hurriedly recalled from the races. On his way to Castle Street, he heard about the accident on the radio of his C.I.D. car.

"One man. It sounds like a fiddle," he said to Devery, who was at that time a newcomer in the detective department. "Turn off here. We'll see if Hooker has anything to say."

Devery took the first turning as instructed, and drove to the scene of the accident. He got there before the ambulance. Martineau knelt beside the broken man and said in a friendly tone: "Hallo, Eddie. Now what have you been doing?"

Hooker recognized Martineau. Here was a man who would most certainly ask questions. Well, there was a story all ready for him. The dying man was so anxious to tell it that he did not wait for the smash-and-grab raid to be mentioned.

"Nowt to do wi' me," he' whispered painfully. "I were just waiting for a judy. Lucky Lusk. I can prove it. While I were waiting I heard the winder go. Wi' my record I thought I'd better scarper before I got dragged into trouble."

"Where did you get your car?"

"Hired it for the day."

Martineau looked into glazed eyes which still could watch him cunningly, and he smiled. "Come off it," he said, with good humour. "Who were you stooging for?"

Eddie Hooker closed his eyes reproachfully, and at that moment the dark angel took him by surprise. Martineau waited some little time before he realized that the eyes would never open again.

That was one suspect who could never be cross-examined. And he had focused police attention on the wrong car. There were several alternative methods of escape for his accomplices. Martineau considered them all.

II

At first the police made rapid progress with the Underdown job. The wounded sergeant, when he could speak, stated positively that the man who had shot him was Don Starling. Also, the impulsive little woman who had pulled down Starling's mask could identify him from photographs.

The arrest and interrogation of Starling followed a familiar pattern. He was arrested at the home of his married sister, with whom he resided. He had no unusual amount of money, no jewellery, no gun, and no lead pipe; and he answered no questions.

Martineau had been put in charge of the case, and the negative interview took place in his office. The big policeman faced the less tall but almost equally formidable criminal. They were both about thirty-five years of age, they had known each other from boyhood, and they were sworn personal enemies. Neither was afraid of the other. Starling's brown eyes did not flinch from the searching grey ones.

The brown eyes burned in a not unintelligent face. The coarse dark hair was plentiful, brushed back from a low hairline. The man was virile and arrogant: he strutted. He could speak good English with a northern accent, and he was well dressed according to the style he favoured. He had been roughly reared in poor circumstances and yet spoiled. Lack of moral training and militant selfishness had resulted in criminal actions, and society's vigorous reprisals had pro-duced in him a pitiless steely intransigence. Some women thought him handsome, and those who were prepared to take him at his own value were impressed by him. He cared not a fig for any woman; women were prey. But he observed a point of honour with male associates. He would swindle an unwary accomplice, but he would never betray him.

As boys, at the same council school, in the nearby town of Boyton, Starling and Martineau had fought many a time. Martineau had been the bigger boy and the better fighter, but Starling had been tough, fearless and vengeful, and they had been not unevenly matched. Then Martineau had moved up to a grammar school, and Starling had moved down to a reformatory. After school, the big city had attracted them

39

both. Martineau had gone into a bank, and Starling had gone into a drapery establishment—after it had been closed for the day. That exploit earned Starling three years in a Borstal Institution, and it looked as if the two youths would not meet again. But at the age of twenty Martineau chose a more active life by joining the Granchester police. Soon afterwards Starling was released from Borstal. So, when they met, the two young men were enemies as naturally as wolf and wolf-hound.

In the fifteen years of Martineau's police service they met a number of times. The pattern of their encounters remained basically the same: Starling was usually, but not always, the loser. He grew to hate Martineau with a corrosive intensity. It was a truly murderous hatred.

The antipathy between the two men was well known. Once or twice, simply to injure the policeman, the criminal had claimed in court that he was persecuted. But the truth was that he was the last man in the world whom Martineau would have treated unfairly. Martineau would not give his enemy the satisfaction of being a wronged man.

This latest meeting was brief. Other detectives had—unsuccessfully—questioned Starling about the Underdown job, because there was not a chance in the world that he would ever 'sing' to Martineau. The inspector merely interviewed him as a matter of form. He gave him certain information. Eddie Hooker was dead. He had talked a little before he died. The police sergeant was not mortally wounded, but with a shattered pelvis he might be a cripple for life. He knew who had shot him. And there were several independent witnesses who could identify Starling.

"This is a bad do, Don," Martineau said. "Very bad."

There was a question in the air, which Starling would not ask. He had never served a longer prison term than three years, but now, if he were convicted. . . .

Martineau answered the unspoken question. "You'll get fourteen years," he said bluntly. "That's my considered opinion."

Starling did not even blink. "That'd be good news for you," he said. The inspector shrugged. "You *might* be able to save yourself a few years," he said mildly. "But that suggestion isn't an inducement. I can promise nothing."

The reply was a steady malevolent glare. The inspector's cool unconcern infuriated Starling. Unreasonable hatred mounted in him. "You're tickled to death because you think you've got me right," he said. "My oath, I wish there were just you and me here. I wish these other sods would clear out."

Martineau grinned at him. "Sure you do," he said. "And when I'd knocked you silly, you'd want to show your bruises to a magistrate." He changed his tone to a whine. " 'Please sir, look where the policeman hit me.' "

Starling stared fixedly at him. "My oath," he breathed. "My oath." Then he rushed. But Devery and another officer were watching him. They held him. He struggled for a moment, then steadied.

Martineau had not moved, or changed his expression.

The prisoner breathed deeply several times. "By God, Harry Martineau," he said. "I'll do you if it's my last act in life. I'll swing for you with pleasure. With the greatest of pleasure."

"Dearie me," said Martineau. "Threats! Take him away and shove him in a cell."

III

There was Lucky Lusk—Mrs. Lucrece Lusk—to be interviewed. Martineau took Devery with him, because it is customary for the police to go in pairs when they have to visit women who live alone. This discreet practice had been brought about by certain misunderstandings in the past. Solitary policemen and lonely ladies. . . . Allegations. . . . It is much more difficult for convincing allegations to be made against two officers.

Mrs. Lusk was a young, childless divorcee. She still lived in the four-roomed house, in a street of such small houses, which she had occupied for a time with the wandering and amorous Mr. Lusk. The street was in a sooty-brick district of factories and workers' houses which lurked in its own smoke not far from the plate glass and the coloured awnings of Castle Street. Mrs. Lusk was employed as a full-time barmaid at the Lacy Arms in Lacy Street.

41

The Lacy Arms was a busy, well-appointed pub which was patronized by many respectable people. But it was also a resort of some men and women who hesitated when asked what they did for a living. That was why Martineau occasionally went in there for a drink and a seemingly casual look around. That was why he knew Lucky Lusk. Most of the city's detectives knew Lucky.

It was 11 p.m. on the day of the Underdown job before he found time to call on Lucky, and she did not open her door until he had identified himself. Then she opened with a smile, but when she saw Devery she made a show of disappointment.

"Oh, come in," she said. "But why didn't you come alone?"

Martineau grinned. "It's your dangerous charm," he said. "They wouldn't let me come without a keeper. I suppose you know Detective Constable Devery."

She looked the tall young man up and down, and sighed humorously.

"Yes, but not intimately," she said, and Devery laughed. "Come in, lad," she invited. "Sit you down."

She accepted a cigarette, and a light, and said to Martineau: "Well, you're not here for the fun of it, and that's a shame. What else can I do for you, sweetheart?"

"Stop it," he said. "I know you're kidding, but others don't."

"Kidding?" She was wide-eyed and reproachful. "*I'm* not kidding, darling. You know I'm mad about you."

Looking into the clear brown eyes, he almost believed her. He could hardly be blamed for wanting to. She was handsome enough; a shapely girl whose shining auburn hair and smooth fair skin proclaimed her perfect health.

"Oh, give over," he said. "Where were you at three o'clock this afternoon?"

"Where would I be? Working! I got away about ten past."

"Then where did you go?"

"Here. Home. What's the trouble? Am I going to be accused of something?"

"No. Set your mind at rest. I'm after information, about

42

Eddie Hooker. He had an appointment with you at three o'clock this afternoon."

Lucky was coolly surprised. "He did?"

"He *said* he had an appointment with you."

"That little tea-leaf? Listen, Mr. Martineau, I don't make appointments with street sweepings. He came leaning on my bar last night. Tried to buy me a drink. He leered a bit. You know: 'What about it, baby?' He said something about borrowing a car and taking me straight out to the races when I came off duty this afternoon. I told him to follow his nose away from my bar and right out through the door, and not come back." .

"How did he take that?"

"He never turned a hair. He said he'd be waiting round the corner in Little Sefton Street at three o'clock. I said he could wait till he had a beard that long. He said he'd wait just the same, because I'd change my mind. He went out then, grinning like a Cheshire cat. I coulda threw a bottle at him."

"Had he any reason to think you'd change your mind?"

"Not that I know of. He used to live in this street, and I've known him since he had to reach up to steal from Woolworth's counter. But I never had anything to do with him. I always thought better of meself than that."

"Did you think it was strange he should approach you like that?"

"I didn't think about it at all. I get approached many a time. What *is* all this about Hooker? Had he something to do with that robbery at Underdown's?"

"He's dead, Lucky," said Martineau gently. "The evening papers just didn't get it soon enough, or you'd have heard."

She stared. "Dead? You mean—killed?"

He nodded. "In a motor smash. A police car was chasing him."

"Oh. Had he whipped something? The car?"

"No. The car was hired. The police were after him for something else. He mentioned you before he died."

"Was he going to use me for some sort of alibi?"

"We think so. You were his excuse for being there. Apart from last night, has he been in the Lacy much lately?"

She shook her head. "I haven't seen him."

43

"Did you see him with anyone else last night?"

"No."

"Do you know who his friends are?"

"No."

"Have you ever seen him with Don Starling?"

"Can't say I have."

"You know Don, don't you? Weren't you a bit thick with him at one time?"

Lucky nodded. "That was before I got married. I liked Don. He said he'd reform for me. The night he said that he went off and did a break-in. That finished me with him. I can't abear a thief."

"Do you ever see him nowadays?"

"Not often. I can't remember the last time."

"H'm," said Martineau. "Well, if you remember, will you let me know? Anything at all, about Hooker or Don Starling."

Lucky looked at him seriously. "You haven't told me the whole tale," she said. "It *is* that smash-and-grab raid, isn't it?"

"Yes," he admitted.

"A bobby was shot, wasn't he?"

"Yes."

"Then you won't hear anything from me, sweetheart. When they get mad enough to shoot bobbies, little Lucrece is going home to play with her dolls. Yes sir!"

Martineau grinned at her, and picked up his hat. "You're a waste of a good man's time," he said, still smiling.

Her own smile was mischievous. "Maybe you didn't adopt the right method of interrogation," she replied. "And besides, there's a witness. I might have told you all sorts of things if we'd been alone."

IV

The inquiries of Martineau and his subordinates revealed that at the time of the Underdown crime Don Starling had been working for a living. At least, he had been holding down a job. By means of forged references he had stepped into the humble position of assistant cellarman at the Royal Lancaster Hotel in Lacy Street, and he had worked there for three weeks. The fact that he was working at all was regarded by the police as a matter for suspicious inquiry. They found that he had slipped away from work to take part in the raid, and no doubt according to plan, had slipped back again after the crime without his five minutes' absence being noticed. They guessed that he had taken the job to provide himself with an alibi, and, maybe, with a hiding place for the loot. They searched the cellars of the Royal Lancaster from end to end, and back again. None of the stolen jewellery was found.

The stolen Ford used in the raid was found in the alley where it had been abandoned. The alley gave access to Little Sefton Street, and ran through into busy Lacy Street. The back of the Royal Lancaster was in Little Sefton Street, and so was Furnisher Steele's shop, where Starling had once 'done a job'. Remembering that, one or two detectives looked doubtfully at the furniture shop. But old Steele was known to be an honest man, and, moreover, young Devery had just started courting his granddaughter.

From the point where the car was abandoned, all trace of the thieves was lost until Starling was picked up at his sister's home. He resolutely continued to withhold all information, and in spite of patient and protracted inquiries, the police found no other suspect and no more evidence. They were beaten with the job.

The stolen jewellery was valued at £8,843, a sum large enough to upset the City Police recovery average. It also worried the insurance company who had to bear the loss. The company sent an investigator. He did no better than the police.

Since no accomplices were arrested, and none of the loot recovered, the obdurate Starling 'copped it for the lot'. He was tried and remanded in custody until the Granchester Assizes. At the Assizes his trial lasted less than an hour: the direct evidence was overwhelming. Before deciding on the sentence, the judge looked at Starling long and thoughtfully, seemingly unconscious of the truculent way in which the latter stared back. There were many things for His Lordship to consider, and these included a Browning pistol, a crippled police sergeant, the sum of £8,843 in property not recovered, the prisoner's record, and his unrepentant demeanour. At last he spoke, to inflict consecutive sentences in terms of years which the most illiterate old layabout in the public gallery could easily tot up to fourteen.

Fourteen years. Starling took the blow without wincing. But he may have thought it was rather severe, because he bowed ironically and said: "I thank you, my lord." This indomitable but silly gesture (by one who was normally ill-mannered) made His Lordship's lip curl. It also brought pleased expressions to faces in the Press box.

Then Starling really made the headlines by turning towards Martineau—who had given the details of his record —and coldly stating that he would certainly kill him at the first opportunity. Martineau politely smothered a yawn as he appeared not to hear the threat. It was all pie for the reporters.

Starling was sent to the Island, where he had never been before. There he found that he was among characters as tough as himself. He was sufficiently daunted to keep quiet and obey orders until he was familiar with prisoners, prison officers, and prison routine. When he had served some six months of his sentence he became aware that a big break-out was being planned. He also guessed that the prison authori-ties would hear about it, because some of the would-be escapers were too talkative. He declined to have any con-nexion with the matter.

In due time the conspirators were sought out by prison officers. They were punished and separated. Then someone —probably the real informer—started a rumour that Starling was the man who had 'come copper'. One day he happened to be alone in a prison workshop and four fellow-prisoners quietly entered and attacked him. He took a bad beating, but true to his code he did not complain. He waited, with the intention of taking his revenge in his own good time. He hoped to catch each one of his assailants alone, and he did not mind how long he had to wait. He could wait even longer than the length of his sentence. He would not forget.

A senior prison officer noticed his condition, and ques-tioned him about it. He refused to say who had attacked him, but admitted that he was suspected of having been an informer. The officer, who knew more about prison life than any old lag, took a serious view of the affair. His concern resulted in Starling's transfer to Pontfield Prison in Yorkshire.

The move pleased Starling. Life was easier at Pontfield than Parkhurst. It was also an easier place to escape from. And it was less than fifty miles from Granchester.

So Starling remained a model prisoner. He did as he was bidden, spoke civilly to one and all, and bided his time. He had no trade of his own, and he was put to work as a labourer on a building job; some new baths and showers for the prisoners. When the baths were completed, the gang started to lay the foundations of a big new office building quite near to the perimeter wall.

There is usually no great hurry in prison work: all the men—including the officers—have time on their hands. As the office building went up, Starling spent his second winter in prison without seeing an opportunity to escape. It was not merely a matter of getting out; he had to get away. It did not occur to him to get into contact with friends who would try to help him. When he escaped, he would do it alone. He would be beholden to no man.

From the second storey of the new building, the prisoners could see the trains go by on the London to Leeds line. One of Starling's workmates, a convicted mail thief who fretted about his wife, was disturbed by the trains.

"That bloody engine driver'll be able to wave to my Missis," he said once. "My 'ouse is right at the side o' t'line, not five miles from 'ere."

"Which way?" Starling asked casually.

"That way," said the man, pointing. "Nearly due north. Five mile, 'an the wife can only find time to come an' see me once every Flood."

"Well, who wants to come to this place any more than they're forced?"

"I'm 'er 'usband, aren't I? She would want to see me. Heck! If I could get outer 'ere I could be 'ome in less nor an hour. Me own fireside, an' a nice wife waitin'. Eh! I can't bear to think on it."

"They'd have you before you'd gone a mile, or else you'd

lose your way," said Starling, with just the right touch of derision.

"They wouldn't," snapped the mail thief. "An' 'ow could I get lost, follerin' t'line? I could walk 'ome in a fog. I could do it blindfold."

Starling carefully concealed his interest, but he was ready to listen whenever the man wanted to talk about his home and his wife. By adroit, seemingly uninterested questions he learned how he could literally find the little house in a fog. The first house in the first estate of council houses on the left of the line! Only five miles! A friend's house, with a young woman living alone! The very idea of it was an intoxicant. He also could hardly bear to think of it. He was almost suffocated by the pleasure of it.

"An' I can get in wi'out wakin' t'neighbour'ood," the mail thief boasted one day. "I've got a key 'id. I allus keep one 'id, just in case."

"You'll get your house broke into," said Starling. "Sneak-in men know just where to look for keys. On a string inside the letter-box, under a stone near the door, on a ledge above the door, hanging on a nail somewhere inside the shed. . . ."

He stopped, smiling inwardly. The sudden look of guarded anxiety on the mail thief's face told him that one of his guesses had not been far from the truth. The key would not be hard to find.

v

The year wore on, and the office building approached completion. In August some men from 'outside' began to put on the roofing slates. Towards the end of the month the mail thief complained that his wife had gone to Blackpool for a fortnight's holiday. He was afraid of whom she would meet at Blackpool. "She'll be danglin' it off th' end o' t'pier, tryin' to catch a feller," he predicted gloomily. "She'll forget she 'as an 'usband."

The news made Starling impatient. Now there was an empty house to walk into, and a man's suit in the wardrobe. The mail thief was about the same size as himself, being flabby where he was muscular.

When his chance came, it was one of the simplest escapes

that had ever been made from Pontfield. He had his eye on a ladder. At the end of every working day the ladders were taken away and carefully locked up, and brought out again in the morning. He had made himself useful in helping to put them up. It had become one of his jobs. He always put a long one around the corner of the building at the side nearest the perimeter wall, whether it was needed there or not. The men working on the building became used to that ladder in that position, and they seldom moved it. Often it stood there all day, unused and unnoticed.

With the ladder in mind Starling longed for a day of thick fog. Fog in August? What a hope!

The weather favoured him. There was no fog, but a morning of dull heat after a wet night. Distant thunder rolled, coming nearer and nearer like the growl of a moving battle. The earth steamed, making a faint mist. After the midday break, the storm reached Pontfield. Black laden clouds brought twilight in early afternoon, and torrential rain began to fall with a swishing roar.

The 'outside' men came down from the roof and gathered with the prison working party on the upper floor of a roofed section of the building. There was some camaraderie, and giving of cigarettes in the gloom. The two prison officers in charge pretended not to see the illegal gifts of 'snout'. The untimely darkness made them uneasy, and they did not want any sort of trouble.

Starling did not join in the talk and the cadging of cigarettes. He remained still and quiet, leaning against the door-frame of a toilet cubicle as if he were tired. He watched the prison officers. They kept looking through a window opening towards the C.P.O.'s office, as if they were expecting an order to take their prisoners to a safer place. They obviously debated whether or not one of them should go and make inquiries.

When *both* the officers' backs were turned for a moment, Starling slipped through the doorway into the toilet cubicle. There was no plumbing in the cubicle yet, nor any glass in the window. He climbed through the window frame, hung by his hands for a moment, and took the long drop to the ground. Nobody saw him go.

He ran round the building and got his ladder. Trailing the ladder, he hurried to the perimeter wall. He was concerned simply with the speed of his departure, and not with silence or concealment. The storm was noisy, and he did not expect to be seen in semi-darkness through steamed-up windows and pouring rain.

He reared the ladder against the wall, and climbed it. When he was straddling the top of the wall he pulled up the heavy ladder. It was so wet that it tended to slip in his wet hands. But he got it up and over, and reared against the outer side. He climbed down, and so great was his haste that he slid the last few feet to the ground.

"Good-bye," he said to the prison wall. "You can *try* and catch me now."

He took the ladder with him, and dropped it in long grass near the railway embankment, hoping that the absence of a visible means of escape would add a few minutes to the start he had gained. He climbed the embankment and, head down in the pouring rain, he began to run northwards along the line.

He settled down to a steady jogtrot. "I'll do it, I'll do it," he exulted to the beat of his own footsteps. His brown eyes peered watchfully from beneath heavy wet brows. His clothes were soaked, but he did not mind. He had a place to go: an unoccupied house with a key hidden somewhere around. There would be a clean, dry shirt and a decent civvy suit, and a raincoat, maybe. There would be shoes; shoes to wear instead of prison boots.

"There won't be any money, but there'll be something I can flog for bus fares," he reflected. "A nice portable radio, happen."

VI

In spite of the decent civvy suit and the raincoat, it was a perilous homeward journey for Don Starling. He was a man who never underrated himself, and he was fully aware of his own importance as an escaped fourteen-year prisoner whose main crime had been the shooting of a police officer. He knew that every policeman within a hundred miles would be given his description and later, his photograph. With a certain grim complacency he reflected that any policeman who succeeded in arresting him would consider himself to be a fortunate man.

In the mail thief's house he found twenty-two shillings—rent money, probably—in a small toby jug, and for 'flogging' purposes he selected an excellent little hand-sewing machine. After an anxious five-mile bus journey into Leeds (he alighted before the bus reached the terminus) he was able to pawn the sewing machine for five pounds. It amused him to give the mail thief's name and address to the pawnbroker.

With six pounds in his pocket, he decided how he would travel. Cross-country buses were too dangerous, he thought. He would go by train.

He studied a railway map which was pasted on a board outside one of the big stations. On the same long board there were half a dozen sheet time tables. He knew that this city of Leeds, so near to Pontfield, would soon be too hot for him, and he had to find an early train. He saw that there was one due to leave for Carlisle in fifteen minutes. He glanced at the map again, then walked boldly into the station.

In the station entrance he paused to buy an evening paper. He carried it folded. Near the ticket window he saw a railway policeman and an obvious plain-clothes man. Slapping the paper against his leg he walked briskly to the nearest window. He asked for a third-class return ticket to Hellifield, counted his change, and walked on into the station. By a great effort of will he did not so much as turn his head to see if the policemen were watching him. He thanked his lucky star because the mail-thief's brown shoes fitted his feet reasonably well. Prison boots would have betrayed him.

The train was waiting. There were not many people on it. He chose an empty compartment and sat with his back to the engine, so that he could look towards the platform barrier. It was as well for him that he did so, because just before the train started two more plain-clothes men walked along the platform looking into every compartment. Starling did not hesitate. He dropped to the floor and squeezed under the seat. He did not emerge until the train was out of the station.

He did not feel safe until he got out of the train at

Hellifield. At that quiet country junction there was not even a railway policeman in sight. After a further study of train schedules, he left the station and returned in time to catch a train to Preston. He booked single to Preston, and at Preston he booked single to Wigan. In Wigan he caught a bus, and approached Granchester from the west, instead of from the east as might have been expected.

When he reached Granchester it was dark, and still raining a little. He dropped off the bus as it turned a corner into Lacy Street—the less prosperous end of Lacy Street—and walked six yards to a darkened shop doorway. From the doorway he watched another doorway across the road. There was a shabby sign over it:

BILLIARDS.   SNOOKER.

12   TABLES   12

He had once been very familiar with that little Mecca of misspent youth. He knew that it would be exactly ten o'clock when the single light above the sign was switched off. The place always closed at that time.

In a little while the light went out, and he nodded with grim satisfaction. He had timed it well: no hanging about at the risk of being seen.

A few minutes later he heard the thud of feet on wooden stairs, and a half-a-dozen youths emerged from the billiard hall. Their attire ranged from nearly ragged to shoddy-smart. They parted noisily into two groups, and went their ways. Starling waited. Somebody always called at the toilet.

A minute later the expected lingerer emerged, still buttoning up, and hastened after his friends. Starling waited until there was no wayfarer near enough to recognize him, then he crossed the street and went through the doorway under the sign.

He climbed the wooden stairs carefully. There were three flights, because the billiard saloon was on the top floor of the building. He peered through a glass-paned door, and saw old Bert Darwin, who ran the place, busily pulling sheets over the tables.

He chuckled "Good old Bert," pushed the door gently,

and slipped sideways through the opening. He flitted unseen to the open door of Bert's office, and entered. There was a chair and a roll-top desk. He sat down, and lit one of the cigarettes he had bought in Leeds.

Bert finished covering the tables. He came into the office, whistling softly. He stopped whistling and his mouth fell open when he saw Starling. Starling grinned at him. It was a perfectly friendly grin, but somehow it made Bert unhappy.

" 'Lo, Bert," he said.

"Er, hallo Don. I never saw you come in."

"Neither did anybody else. I shall be staying here till morning."

"Nay, Don, you can't do that. Suppose——"

"Suppose nothing. You lock the place up safe, see? I'll stay here as quiet as a mouse. You'll leave me a key, and I'll let myself out in the morning. Nobody'll ever know I've been here. You won't know yourself if you choose to forget it. And you'd *better* forget it."

"I can't let you stay here. The police——"

Starling was on his feet. "You can and you will," he said.

"All right, Don, all right. But for God's sake be careful."

"I'll be careful. By the time the bogies get the rumour I'm here, I'll have been in five other places, all different. You mind you lock up safe, that's all. Then I can rest easy."

"I'll lock up, all right. H-here's my spare key."

"Thanks," said Starling, pocketing the key. He threw a florin on the desk. "You used to sell a few sweets. I'm hungry. Give me four bars of plain chocolate."

With fumbling fingers Bert unlocked a drawer and took out the chocolate.

"Right. That'll be all," said Starling. "Good night, Bert."

"Eh? Oh sure. Good night, Don."

Bert was at the office door when Starling spoke again. "Oh, and Bert," he said quietly. "Don't get any fancy ideas in connexion with coppers, will you?"

Bert was shocked, and hurt. "Nay, Don!" he reproached. "I'll admit I don't like having you here, but that don't mean I'll go running to the bogies. What do you think I am?"

"I don't think anything. I just want you to remember what's good for you. If the law finds me here tonight, you'll

53

be looked after. My friends'll look after you. They'll bash your crown in."

Bert went without further speech, and Starling quietly followed him down to the door to make sure it was locked. He tried the fire door too, and found it secure. Presently he would lie on the upholstered bench which ran around the walls of the big room, but at the moment he was content to sit in the dark and make plans.

The thing to do was to get some ready money—it never occurred to Starling that this was almost a universal problem —and then go after the stolen jewellery which he had hidden two years before. He had various schemes for raising money: he had had time to think about that. For what he had in mind he would need some mates. Arrangements would have to be made. Well, there was the telephone.

"In the morning, Don," he said to himself. "In the morning, just before you skip out of here."

VII

The billiards saloon was opened at ten o'clock every weekday morning. Having made a telephone call, Don Starling quitted the place at five minutes to nine, when the streets were thronged with hurrying city workers. He was keenly alert for the quick stare of sudden recognition, because today his picture was in the papers, but nobody noticed him as he made his way to Pasture Park. It was a fine, warm morning after yesterday's thunderstorm, and he sat in the sunshine on a bench in a secluded corner of the park. Life was good. He read about himself in a newspaper, but his hard glance was often raised to look above the paper. The price of freedom is eternal vigilance.

At half-past eleven, when the pubs opened, he sought surroundings better suited to his temperament. But by an exercise of his considerable will power he did not drink much, and the taverns he patronized were small places where neither he nor his friends had ever been customers.

During his solitary watchful drinking he considered his plans. His phone call had set the ball rolling. He had contacted the man he wanted and set him to work. Tomorrow he would meet the man, and in the meantime he would have to avoid the police. He had no illusions about the police: they would be very, very busy looking for him. That bastard Martineau would be running around like a scalded cat. Well, there was a number of possible hiding-places. The thing was, could he avoid boredom? Boredom made a man careless.

He needed companionship, and he needed a woman. "For two years I've been like a parrot in a cage," he reflected. He glanced around the small bar-lounge where he was sitting. It was not the place to look for his sort of woman.

The haunts of loose and lively women were the haunts of people who knew Don Starling. And they were the places where the police would be looking for him. Would he take the risk? A faint smile flitted across his face when he imagined the awed glances, the nudges and whispers, which his presence would cause. Maybe he would be able to pick up a little chicken who wanted some second-hand notoriety. Maybe he would find himself consorting with a red-hot young love-weed smoker. The thought stirred him.

He remembered some of the women he knew. Lucky Lusk would still be at the Lacy Arms. But he had never gone very far with Lucky, and now she would want to keep half the length of Lacy Street away from him. There were others with whom he had been more successful. Among them Chloe Barber, Gus Hawkins' wife. A wicked little piece, Chloe. It might be a good thing to get in touch with her. He would have to think about it.

Thinking about it, he had a substantial meal in a transport workers' cafe, and then he did not want any more drink. What now? The restful gloom of a cinema? A lovely day like this? Still undecided, he wandered back to the park.

He did not return to his original seat. He went to the other end of the park, to a quiet corner with a bench which had its back to the wall. A woman was sitting there, and he would have passed on, but she looked up and smiled. He sat down on the bench; not too near to the woman, not too far away for friendliness.

"Nice day," he said very casually, so that he did not risk a snub.

"Ooh, it's lovely, isn't it?" she replied, in the accent of

the working millions of Granchester and district. Her tone and manner put him immediately at ease.

He knew just how to impress her. Bringing out his cigarettes, he asked: "Do you mind if I pollute the air with tobacco smoke?" His assumed accent was rich and rounded enough to be described as fruity. Privately, he thought of it as 'Oxford and Cambridge'.

"I don't mind at all," she said. "I do like to see a man enjoying his cig."

"How about you? Will you try one?"

She hesitated. "Well, I don't smoke much. An' not out o' doors. . . ."

"Do have one. There's nobody to see you."

She accepted a cigarette and a light. She had already studied him as he approached, and now she puffed daintily at her Gold Flake and gave him a chance to look at her. A *hausfrau*, he thought. Typical. About thirty-eight years old. Not bad looking, not badly dressed. Not a bad figure, either. A bit hippy, but not bad. 'She'll do to be going on with,' he decided.

They talked. Her name was Dora Fenton. She had a completely ordinary mind. She was childless, and her husband was a steel erector. He was usually away during the week. He was away this week on a job at Morecambe. He would work overtime on Saturday, and get home in time to spend Saturday evening with his friends. Not with his wife who had been alone all week, mark you, but with his friends at the club.

"Really, you couldn't be blamed if you looked around for a bit of romance," said Starling, with sympathy.

"No, I couldn't," she eagerly agreed. "I've thought of it many a time."

She was politely curious about him. He had a good story to tell. His name was Danby Simpson. Mr. Danby Simpson. He was unmarried and unattached. (That pleased Mrs. Fenton.) He was a wine merchant's representative, and he travelled the country calling on big hotels and restaurants. "Only the very best places," he said with dignity. "Ours is a very old firm: Ascot, Wetherby and Company. We wouldn't dream of having anyone on the staff who wasn't a public school man."

"Are you a public school man, then?" she asked, with respect.

He coughed. "Winchester," he said modestly. "Yes, I am an Old Wykehamist."

She was impressed. "Where are you stopping?" she asked.

"I always stay at the Royal Lancaster," he said. "Tommy Sullivan, the manager, is an old acquaintance of mine. As a matter of fact, I've just had lunch with him. I had no business this afternoon, so I thought I'd take a walk down this way. I know the town fairly well. Been here many times."

He aired his superficial knowledge of wine for her benefit. She knew nothing about wine, so he was in no danger of making a mistake.

In a little while she said that it was hot in the sun, but such a shame to go indoors.

"How about a sojourn in a nearby hostelry?" he suggested. "A little wine, perhaps? A little sherry? An Amontillado or a dry Tio Pepe?"

She was willing. They went for a drink. He came to the conclusion that she was a fool, but she enjoyed herself tremendously. At three o'clock, closing time, the sparkle of adventure was in her eye.

"Where now?" he asked. "Must we part so soon?"

"It seems a shame," she said.

"I could take you somewhere for afternoon tea," he said, "but I get so weary of hotels and restaurants. I long sometimes for a bit of home comfort."

The gin and Cointreau in two five-shilling White Ladies had quickened her. She did not miss the innuendo. She was both relieved and excited when she made her decision.

"Why not 'ave a cup o' tea at my 'ouse?" she suggested.

"Oh, I'd love to," he replied. "But . . . won't the neighbours talk?"

"They won't see you," she replied, so quickly that he knew she had been arranging the matter in her mind. "Our 'ouses 'ave 'igh backyard walls. You stroll round to the back an' keep close to the wall; I'll go the front way an' let you in."

"That's an excellent idea," he said, and reached under

the table. A small hot hand met his half way, and squeezed it. He thought that the woman's excitement made her quite pretty. Not bad at all.

It was an excellent idea. It gave him the best sort of cover for at least several hours, and perhaps for the night.

VIII

The following day, by arrangement, Starling met a man called Laurie Lovett in a crowded department store. Lovett was late, so Starling made one or two small purchases. Neatly wrapped in the store's distinctive wrapping paper, the purchases were intended to remove suspicion from the roving eyes of store detectives. Starling hoped that he looked like a man who was waiting for his wife.

When Lovett arrived, he quietly called him a bad name. Lovett took no notice of the name. He was a broad, strong man with a thin white face and a hard, surly stare. His mouth was a tautly held slash with lips almost as pale as his skin. He looked around all the time he was talking, and he talked with an odd shifty manner.

"What's he say?" Starling demanded.

"He was scared at first. He's still scared, if it comes to that. But I said you being in it made it all the safer, 'cause you'd never soften for the cops. I said you'd proved that by taking all the humpy for the Underdown job. Anyway, he's in. He says he'll give us the office if he can. He can do it easy: I told him so. If there's a worthwhile amount of cash to go to the bank, he can wait till it's nearly ready for moving, then stand near the window for a second or two and scratch the back of his head with his right hand. He's a scruffy old geezer nobody'll think anything of it. It'll be easy."

"Okay. Now he's in, tell him he knows what he'll get if he drops a wrong word. If he spills anything, he's had it. Are your cabs all right?"

"Sure. I had to turn down a good Doncaster job. Doug Savage."

"That loafhead! Does he still fancy himself as a big racing man?"

"He sure does. Now the old man has cocked his toe he's

58

running the Prodigal Son for the old lady. You'd think he was manager of the Royal Lancs, no less."

"He'll lose his mother her pub if she don't watch it. How's Gordon?"

Lovett stared at a revolvable stand of brilliant ties. He seemed to be intent on selecting one.

"The kid's game," he said seriously. "Don't worry about him. I want him to be in the clear if owt happens, though."

Starling looked at him. "He can't help but be in the clear if he keeps his trap shut. Anyway, you know *I* won't drop him into anything, whatever the others do."

Lovett nodded, looking slightly worried. Then he said: "Where you hiding, Don?"

The other man smiled. "Oh, here and there. Keep moving, that's my motto."

"You don't give much away, do you? When are you going to share out the sparklers? You been cagey about them. Where are they?"

"I told you where. In the cellar. I can't tell you more, because the stuff's so well hid there's nobody but me can find it. Do you think the cops haven't searched that place time and again? There's nobody gets that without me. You'll get your share, but it was me got the fourteen years. Remember?"

"That's true enough, Don. And you never gave your pals away."

"And never will. So it's all fixed then. What about this new bloke—what do you call him?—Clogger? Sure he's all right?"

"He's right enough."

"And Lolly, is he ready?"

"As ready as he ever will be. Eigh up! This chap coming off the escalator knows me. Let me be away. Cheerio."

"Cheerio," said Starling, and he also turned away, walking erect and keen-eyed. His stiff, sturdy but by no means short figure moved with something of a terrier's bounce.

IX

Starling slept that night in Boyton, in the frowsy bed of an old bachelor night watchman whom he had known from childhood. In the morning he moved out at his usual time, between eight and nine, though the streets—except those in the centre of the town—were not so crowded because it was Saturday.

Not only was it Saturday, it was St. Leger day, and a small percentage of the population were setting off to see the races at Doncaster. It was a royal occasion. The Queen would be there. Well, today Don Starling could also go to the races. Moreover, if no mistake were made this morning, he would have some money to put on the horses. The amount depended on how much Gus Hawkins sent to the bank.

The next two hours were the most trying for Starling since his escape from Pontfield. He had to make his way to a quiet yard behind a row of shops in Highfield. A greengrocer kept one of the shops, and he garaged his small van in the yard. He used the van very early in the morning to bring his supplies from the wholesale market. Afterwards, while he was busy in his shop, he left the van standing in the open garage in the yard. In all probability he would not look at the van again until evening, and perhaps then only when he locked up the garage.

Starling had a rendezvous at the van, at nine forty-five. He was there at nine-thirty, reconnoitring cautiously. Everything was as he had been told it would be. He chose his moment, and slipped into the garage. He entered the van and sat in the back of it, in darkness which smelled of apples, celery and cut flowers. To ease the tension he broke one of his own rules for concealment: he smoked a cigarette, holding it cupped in his hand.

At nine-fifty Lolly Jakes arrived. Starling had not seen him for two years. Lolly slipped casually into the driving seat of the van, then he half-turned his head and said softly: "That you, Don?"

"Yeh. All in order?"

"Sure. The greengrocer's as busy as hell. Coining money. We shall have finished with this thing before he knows it's gone."

"You're late."

"Plenty of time," said Lolly comfortably. "The banks don't open till ten. We'll be there. We'll collect too. There should be plenty. It was a proper day out for the bookies yesterday. All the favourites stopped to cough."

Lolly had a broad face, with a very small hooked nose and dull, prominent eyes. He had meaty shoulders, and the back of his neck was like a section of Irish bacon. He was incurably lazy, but sudden, treacherous and dangerous in the use of razor and knuckleduster. For their purposes, both Starling and Lovett considered him to be reliable. The local knowledge required to 'borrow' a van without trouble had been his initial contribution to the operation which was beginning.

Lolly drove the van into town and parked it at the junction of Higgitt's Passage and Back Lacy Street. He remained in the driving seat, and Starling continued to lurk in the back. From the small rear window the fugitive could see the Prodigal Son, the little pub which Doug Savage managed for his mother. The door was closed, and the place seemed to have a sly, secretive air. Whatever the occupants saw, they would not tell the police. Doug Savage was a loud-mouth, but not when the constabulary were within hearing. Starling dismissed the Prodigal Son from his mind.

The forty minutes' wait was a bad time for him. It seemed that the signal for action would never come. And all the time he was in danger, here in the centre of the city, where he had not dared to venture since his escape from prison. Here were more policemen to the acre than anywhere else in the north of England, and they all knew Don Starling.

The heart of a great provincial city is a small place, and its denizens know each other. It is the centre of circulation, and the anonymous flowing crowds are its life-blood. But among the swarming thousands certain people are, in a manner of speaking, stationary. A few hundred barmaids, publicans, waitresses, caretakers, doormen, bank messengers, newsboys, barrow boys, businessmen, postmen, taxi drivers, shopkeepers, bookies' runners, spivs, layabouts, thieves, whoremongers, prostitutes and policemen know each other by contact, by name, or by sight. It was so in Granchester, and Don Starling was aware of it. He had spent his time and his money in the heart of the city, and now he dared show himself but briefly, at the moment of action.

While he waited, he naturally wondered what his accomplices were doing. What about Clogger Roach, whom he had never seen? And Peter Purchas, that weak and timorous man? All *he* had to do was scratch his head, and no doubt his hand would tremble when he did it.

The signal would mean that a worthwhile sum of money would soon be on its way from Gus Hawkins' office to the bank. If Gus had banked his race money and winnings last night, there would be another simple signal to indicate that money would be taken *from* the bank. This errand had been accomplished many hundreds of times before by a girl cashier and a man—or a boy. There had never been any sort of interference. No trouble would be expected this morning.

At last it became evident that Purchas had given the signal. A Buick car reversed into the archway at the end of the back street, and Lolly Jakes said: "Here's Laurie." And a minute later Clogger Roach sauntered past the rear of the van.

Clogger was the lookout. He had been 'given the office' by Purchas. He was comparatively a stranger in town, but Laurie Lovett had known him a long time, and he guaranteed him. Through the van window Starling studied the wiry figure and the narrow head. Clogger turned to look back, and revealed the dark, fanatical face of one who would always be passionately sure of his rights in the world, and equally passionate in denying his obligations. An envious, ill-humoured man. Starling disliked him on sight.

Then there was no time to study character. Clogger was walking back briskly, just as if he were going somewhere. It had been arranged that he would pass the girl and her escort when they were close to the van. The moment had come. Starling pushed open the door of the van. Jakes got out of the driving seat. Laurie Lovett reversed the Buick along the back street.

The youth and the girl with the money were there, just passing the van. No one else was in sight.

The lad was plucky. He said: "Run for it, Ciss," and squared up to Jakes and Starling. But Clogger was moving silently behind him. He swung a loaded cosh at the full

62

length of his arm and felled the boy. It was an unnecessarily hard blow. He swung at the girl, too, but she was away, screaming as she ran.

In two strides Starling caught her. Terrified, she screamed louder. He struck hard with his fist at her exposed throat, and the scream ended abruptly. Jakes came up, and the two men dragged her to the Buick at a run. Clogger was holding a rear door open. They threw her into the car, and tumbled in after her. Clogger got into the front seat beside the driver, and the car sped along the back street, through the archway, and into the open street.

The girl lay knees-up on the floor of the car and Starling crouched over her. She was evidently hysterical, because she was screaming again; a thick, painful scream. The noise alarmed everybody in the car. "Shut her up!" Clogger snarled. Starling knelt heavily on her chest. He put his left hand over her mouth and nostrils and hammered savagely at her throat and jaw. The scream became a muffled moan. "Here, stroke her with this," said Clogger. Starling struck once with the cosh foreshortened. But the car was swinging round a corner and, instead of the skull, the bruised, tender throat received the blow. The girl went limp, and her eyes closed.

Starling and Clogger had no more time for her. They were watching Lolly Jakes, who had started work with a razor on the locked money bag which was chained to the girl's wrist. "It'll ruin the edge," he grumbled, as the keen blade sheared through tough leather. Soon he opened the ruined bag, and shook bundles of notes on to the seat between himself and Starling. "Cripes, there's a fortune here!" he exclaimed.

"There sure is," said Starling. "This is a better job than the other one. Keep 'er rolling, driver, we don't want to lose this little lot."

Laurie Lovett was following a prearranged route, selecting long streets which ran roughly parallel to a main road, avoiding traffic lights and point-duty policemen. He was getting along fast. He had fifteen miles to go, and he meant to cover the distance before the police knew what kind of a car to look for.

Starling had been counting money. "Bundles of a hundred," he announced, and Jakes said: "Thirty bundles. Then there's these fivers."

"Two hundred fivers," said Starling.

"Hell's bells! There's four thousand nicker here!" cried Jakes, after a little sum in the quick mental arithmetic of the inveterate follower of racing.

In the front seat, Clogger rubbed his hands and chortled. "Nearly a thousand apiece, when we've paid out the chicken-feed," he said.

"Nine hundred apiece," Starling amended. "And two hundred apiece for the old 'un and the young 'un."

"The kid?" Clogger objected. "But he's only——"

Starling held up his hand. "He's in it," he said. "We've got to keep him happy."

"Don't get me wrong," said Clogger, after a quick glance at Laurie Lovett. "I don't want to do anybody out of his share. I'm just thinking he might start flashing his wad and get noticed."

"He won't," said Laurie, with his eyes on the road. "I'll see he behaves."

Starling was sitting with one foot on the girl's chest. She had been struggling feebly, and panting and gasping. As she had not been making much noise, he had ignored her while he counted money. Now she lay still. He looked down, and saw that her eyes were open.

"Mention no names," he said. "The filly's listening."

Then, uneasily, he looked again. The girl's eyes were open in a fixed stare. The blood receded from his face, then rushed back in a red tide. He looked at the others. They had not noticed. They could not see the girl's face, and they did not crane to look. They did not want her to see too much of them. But it did not matter how much she saw of Starling, in their opinion. He was already on the run. When he was caught, as they knew he would be sooner or later, he would take his punishment without betraying them.

Now they were safely out of the city, but they still had to pass through the town of Boyton. They were also forced to keep to the main road to maintain their speed, and there was some danger that they might meet a police car whose crew had been warned to look out for them. They hoped fervently that it would be at least half-an-hour before the police learned about the Buick.

At last they were through Boyton. They left the houses behind, and began the long climb up to the moors. Starling gnawed at his left thumbnail.

"When are we going to dump the dame?" Clogger wanted to know.

"The first bit of quiet road," said Jakes.

"We won't take her too far," said Clogger, almost gay now. "Don't forget she's got to walk back."

For the last ten minutes Starling had been getting used to the idea that he was riding with death. 'So what?' was his attitude. The world outside the car was still rolling. The bees were still busy in the heather. The same clouds were in the sky. The girl was dead, so what?

Of that other death which, now, would always be a probability of the near future he tried not to think. He tried to shut a door of his mind against it. When it would not be shut away, he tried to be disdainful of it. 'So what? We've all got to die sometime.'

He wondered how the others would react. This Clogger Roach, for instance. He was looking very pleased with himself. Now watch him grow white in a night.

"She's done all the walking she'll ever do," he said quietly.

Clogger and Jakes turned their heads quickly, their smiles fading. They stared. Then Jakes pulled Starling's knee aside and looked down at the girl's face.

"Cripes!" he said unhappily. "She's croaked."

Starling nodded. "Some time ago," he said.

"You bloody fool," said Jakes, his voice rising with panic.

"Hell fire!" Clogger whispered, and he had indeed turned pale. "You didn't *have* to do that, did you?"

Laurie Lovett was silent. He kept his eyes on the road as if nothing had happened. But a muscle of his jaw had started to twitch.

The same fear was upon them all. They were reminded of a man they all knew by sight. He kept a pub in Hollinwood. The name of the pub was Help the Poor Struggler. The man's name was Albert Pierrepoint. He was the public hangman.

"Thank God, I never laid a hand on her," said Clogger fervently.

Lovett was taking a bend at high speed. He did not look at Clogger, but from the corner of his mouth he said: "You lent Don your knobkerrie, remember?"

"Murder. We're all in it," Jakes mumbled.

"I think you'd better pull yourselves together," said Starling sombrely. "You thought of getting away with the robbery, didn't you? Why not this job as well? It's one witness less, isn't it?"

"Yes, but murder . . ." said Jakes. "You know how they are with that. They'll never give up."

"That may be," said Lovett. "But they'll never know it's us if we behave right in our heads."

"Oh, give over," Starling growled. "We're not here to cheer *him* up." He looked back through the rear window of the car. The road was deserted. "This'll do," he said. "Pull up, Laurie, and we'll get rid of her."

The car stopped. Starling reached over and opened the door beside Jakes. He pointed. "Drop her behind that hummock," he said.

"Not me!" was the objection. "Why not you?" You did her in."

Starling moved, and Jakes's hand went to his razor pocket. But Starling had produced a big automatic pistol. His companions stared at it.

"All right, I did her in," he said. "And I can do you in. One murder or two, what's the difference?"

"Where did you get that?" Clogger asked, in astonishment.

Starling allowed himself a faint grin. He had found the pistol fully loaded in a drawer in the Fentons' bedroom. No doubt it was a memento of World War Two, highly prized by steel erector Fenton. Well, he was returning home today. If she had discovered the theft of the gun, Mrs. Fenton would be in a panic.

"Never mind where I got it," he said. "I'm a dangerous gunman, didn't you know? Lord Justice D'Arcy said so when he sent me down for fourteen. Now then, we're wasting time. Get this thing out of my sight!"

Jakes knew Starling very well. He knew that Lord Justice D'Arcy had not exaggerated. Watching the pistol, he stepped backwards out of the car. Grunting with effort, he pulled the body from the car and carried it over the rough ground. The slashed bag dangled from the chain attached to the slender wrist.

At that moment another car appeared on the crest of the eastward slope. It approached rapidly.

Jakes dropped the body behind the hillock. He ran back to the Buick and scrambled in as it began to move. "What do we do with this feller?" Clogger was asking in an agitated voice.

Apparently nobody knew what to do, nor was there time to decide. Starling said: "Cover your faces," and hands with outspread fingers were held up to mask identity. As the strange car drew near, Lovett made the Buick swerve towards it. But he dared not risk a crash, and it was only a half-hearted attempt to force the other car off the road. The other driver sounded his horn and held his course, and went on towards Granchester.

"Think he saw me carrying the girl?" Jakes wanted to know.

"Very likely," said Clogger gloomily. "He'll stop at the first phone."

"It makes no difference," said Starling. "We've got to keep moving fast, that's all. We've only a mile or two to go, then we're through with this car. Here, stow this money in your pocket. . . ."

x

At fifteen minutes past seven that evening, Furnisher Steele answered the telephone. "Hallo, hallo," he said, which is not the proper way to answer a phone call.

"Hallo yourself," said a man's voice. "I want Furnisher Steele."

"Speaking."

"You may remember me, I'm Don Starling. You once got me sent down for a stretch."

The old man did not like Starling's tone. Also, he believed

in looking squarely at men and affairs. "I got you nothing," he replied. "You got yourself sent down."

"I've got you in my book, anyway; but I'm going to give you a chance to put yourself right."

"I'm right as I am," said Furnisher. "To hell with you."

"You won't be so right when I've done with you, unless you do what I want. *I* don't mind having an old man bashed, you know. You'd better be sensible."

"I'll be sensible. There's a young man comes here who's a detective. I'll tell him about you."

"I don't think you will. I haven't finished yet. What about that deaf-and-dumb kid of yours? She's lovely. Something not so nice could happen to her, and she wouldn't be able to scream. Better do what I want. It's only a small thing. It won't take you five minutes."

Furnisher had not heard the last few words. The monstrous suggestion of the main statement astounded and horrified him. He could scarcely believe that he had heard it. For some little time he could not answer, but when he did speak he had none of an old man's bluster. There was a cold fury and firm resolve in his voice.

"Listen, Don Starling," he said, reverting to his native dialect. "Anybody round 'ere 'ull tell thee I'm a man o' my word. I 'ave a gun, an' I'm not too old to use it. If thee or thy pals comes anywhere near my gran'-child BY GOD I'LL SHOOT YER! I'll be right close beside 'er till tha's bin caught, an' that won't be long."

There was a long silence, and Furnisher wondered if the other man had gone away and failed to hear his words. But Starling answered at last, and his tone had changed.

"So you won't frighten, old man," he said. "I like a fellow with some guts. Since you're a man of your word, I'll make a bargain with you. Say nothing to *anybody* about this phone call, and I'll leave you and the girl alone. What about it?"

Furnisher thought about that. Starling was a vicious man and a resourceful man. Look how he was still eluding the police! It was no use asking for trouble, and the information wouldn't be a great deal of use to Devery.

"All right," he said. "It's a bargain. I'll say nowt. I'll keep my word, and I'll have my gun handy in case you don't keep yours."

"Fair enough," said Starling, and rung off. Later, Furnisher was plagued with curiosity. What had Starling wanted him to do? Now he would never know. "Aay dear," he sighed. "I talk too much."

XI

At half-past seven the manager of the Lacy Arms answered his telephone. "Central, double three double five," he said efficiently.

He heard a curiously hollow voice: "Is that the Lacy Arms? Sorry to bother you on Saturday night, but I'd like to speak to one of your barmaids, Mrs. Lusk. It's rather important."

"Who's that speaking?" the manager demanded.

"This is *Mister* Lusk, her ex-husband. On urgent family business."

"Oh, all right," said the manager. "I'll get her."

"That article!" said Lucky Lusk, when she was informed of the call. "I haven't heard of him for three years. I know what his urgent business'll be. He's hard up!"

"Shall I tell him you're too busy?" the manager suggested.

"No, I'd better speak to him," she said, and in spite of her harsh words she approached the telephone with feelings of curiosity and mild anxiety. "Hallo Chris, you there?" she asked.

She heard a chuckle, and a voice she knew. "Mention no names, honey, because this is Don, your dream man."

She was taken aback. "Wha-what do you want?" she stammered.

"First of all I want to tell you I'm a desperate man. Old friends who won't help me in my hour of need will get carved up. I mean carved up. Around the face and the swan-like neck, you know."

As plainly as if he were there she could see Starling's curiously hot brown eyes, and the slight sneer which would be on his face when he talked in that manner. He was like some corner boy acting tough. Except that he *was* tough.

69

But she had recovered her poise. **"You've been drinking,"** she said.

"Not a drop." The tone changed slightly. "I mean what I say. I want you to do me a very small service, and then keep quiet. You know Gus Hawkins?"

She did. And she had also read the evening paper.

He accurately guessed her thoughts. "Oh no," he said convincingly. "Don't mix me up with a murder. I have enough to do keeping away from the coppers as it is. I'm on the run, Lucky."

"A man like Gus Hawkins wouldn't have anything to do with the likes of you," she said. "What do you want with him?"

"He can help me. He won't be feeling so good about things, but he can still help me. I don't want to go to his house till I know he's at home, and just now I think he might be in the Stag's Head, celebrating the bad day he's had. I daren't go there myself, but it's only three minutes walk for you. If you'll go and look, you'll save me a journey."

She was doubtful. It was all rather pat, rather specious.

"I can't leave here on a Saturday night," she said.

"I meant what I said about being desperate," he reminded her. "I'm not going to argue with you. If you won't do it for old times' sake you'll do it to save your bonny face. Now go on, you bitch, ànd do as I say! I'll ring again in eight minutes. When you get back from the Stag you wait right there by the phone, so's I don't have to talk to your boss again. Understand?"

"Yes," she said.

"Then get on with it!" he snarled, and rang off.

Almost blind with rage, she went back to the bar. The pig, the dirty pig, to talk to her like that! She hoped the police would catch him and flog him! She had half a mind to go back and dial Central one-two-one-two, and tell Martineau. He wasn't afraid of Starling.

In the bar, the manager looked at her with concern. "Bad news?" he asked.

"I've got to slip out for five minutes, Mr. Rose," she said. "I won't be longer than that." For in spite of her anger she was afraid. Don Starling had threatened to slash her face.

She did not think he would do it, but he *might* do it. He really was desperate: she knew that. He had not spoken like the Don Starling she used to know.

The Starling of two years ago would have tried normal persuasion first. He would not have spoken roughly until she had definitely refused to help him. But today he had started with a threat, even though it was such a small favour that he asked. A ridiculous thing, really. Go along the street on a trivial errand, or I'll disfigure you. The man had lost all sense of proportion.

He distrusted everybody, that was it. He wanted to frighten everybody so that they wouldn't dare to tell the police. Well, he'd frightened her, all right. She wasn't going to tell. She had troubles enough.

Lucky's thoughts carried her along Lacy Street. Daylight was just beginning to fade, and the street with its lights, its coloured signs and its shop windows glowed up into the darkening sky. The roadway crawled with traffic. The sidewalks were crowded with Saturday night strollers, and she threaded and dodged through them automatically. A policeman standing on a corner nodded and spoke to her. A cinema doorman, looking slightly seedy in a brilliant uniform as cinema doormen often do, stopped shouting the price of seats to say: "Hallo Lucky. Thirsty work. I could do a beer right now." She smiled and answered, without listening to his words or knowing what she had said to him. She felt sick and worried. Suppose something went wrong, and Don Starling thought it was her fault? He wouldn't wait to ask questions about that. He would slash her face before she had time to say anything. He might blind her! She trembled at the thought.

She went into the Stag's Head, looked around, and came out. And it almost seemed as if Starling had been watching her movements, because the Lacy Arms' telephone rang as soon as she got back to it.

"Well?" Starling asked.

"He's in the grill, just sitting down to a meal," she said.

"You're sure of that?"

"Well, he's eating cantaloupe, and all the cutlery is still on the table. So I suppose he's just starting."

71

"No champagne?"

"I never saw any."

"Is he alone?"

"Yes."

"Thanks, Lucky. Sorry I had to get rough with you. I was on edge, I guess. No hard feelings?"

"You keep your distance in future, that's all," she said. "I'm not your woman, and I never was. Just keep away from me, that's all I want."

Starling laughed. "Bye-bye," he said, and rang off.

XII

Ten minutes after he had stepped out of the telephone box, Starling walked boldly up the little drive of Gus Hawkins' house. He had been there many times before. He went round the house, and smiled when he found that the back door was unlocked. He entered quietly, and looked around, and listened. He heard somebody moving upstairs. "She's getting ready to go out," he decided.

He waited near the foot of the stairs. There was an evening paper on the hall table. It looked as if it had not been opened. He did not touch it. He had already seen a copy, and he had not liked what he read. But, fortunately, his own name had not been mentioned in connexion with the murder, even in a speculative way.

Chloe Hawkins came running down the stairs, in a hurry, evidently. Her reaction, when she saw him, was normal in the circumstances; a little startled shriek, and the look of consternation to which the intruder was becoming accustomed.

He smiled. "Where are you off to?" he asked. "My, you look nice!"

"Don," she faltered. "Why did you come here?"

"To see you, of course. Don't you remember? We're—friends."

"But the police are after you. And suppose Gus comes home?"

"I don't think he'll come yet, Chloe. He's just sitting down to a meal at the Stag's Head."

"Oh, but you can't stay, Don. It—isn't fair to me. What do you want? Money? I haven't much."

He put one arm around her tiny waist and squeezed her, lifting her on to her toes. "I don't want money," he said. "At the moment I want you. I've been in a monastery for the last two years, you know."

"Oh. And then will you go?" she asked, slightly relieved.

"What is this? Am I a leper or something?" he demanded with assumed irritation. "Everywhere I go, people want me to keep going."

"Well, the police are seeking you everywhere. It's in all the papers. You won't stay long, will you?"

"Not more than a fortnight. And now, how about something to eat, my dear? Just a snack: I don't expect you to cook anything."

He had gone all through the eventful day, since morning, without a wash. He had not touched Cicely Wainwright after she had so inconveniently died, but nevertheless he could not eat until he had cleansed his hands. He had a wash in the kitchen, so that he could keep an eye on Chloe. Then he drew a chair to the kitchen table and had a factory-made pork pie with pickles, followed by two cups of tea. Chloe watched him uneasily, smoking all the time. She noticed that his hands were stained green, just as her husband's had been at breakfast that morning. She was too worried by his presence to make any comment about the stain.

Starling also noticed the stain, and wondered about it. Something on Chloe's towel? He could not see that it was important, and he did not speak about it.

After eating, he watched her remove the evidence of the meal. As she was passing near to him he caught her hand. He rose and embraced her. He fondled her and became excited. In a little while, though she still wished that he would go away, she responded to his urgency. When he suggested that they should go to her bedroom, she was not unwilling.

They went upstairs together. On the broad landing at the head of the stairs he stopped. He looked up at the ceiling.

"Is the old gadget still working?" he asked.

"Of course," she replied, surprised that he could remember the loft ladder at such a moment.

"Is it used much?"

"Nobody's been up there for months."

"Do you remember the time I had to hide up there when Gus came home too soon? I stuck it twelve hours for your sweet sake."

She smiled faintly. "It was awful. All the time I was scared you'd make a noise."

"It could happen again," he said as they went into the bedroom.

Twenty minutes later, he walked out on to the landing and again looked at the ceiling, at the part where there appeared to be a long trapdoor. He went to the stairhead window, where the cords which controlled the loft ladder were hidden by a draw-on curtain. He found the cords, and operated the nicely counter-balanced mechanism. The trapdoor dropped open gently and noiselessly. He reached up and pulled at the step-ladder which was revealed. It slid down smoothly until one end of it was resting on the landing.

Chloe came out of the bedroom and saw that he had let down the loft ladder. "What have you done that for?" she demanded in alarm.

"I've got to sleep *somewhere* tonight," he said. "Your attic will do me nicely."

She stared at him in dismay.

"Don't worry, I shall only stay one night," he said. "Keep moving, that's me. Mr. Bloody Martineau won't see me till I want him to see me."

She did not speak. He grinned at her.

"I believe I noticed an old chamber pot among the family heirlooms stored up aloft," he said. "You know, the one with pink roses on it. So all I need is a couple of blankets and a jug of water. Go get 'em."

"You *can't* stay here, Don," she whimpered.

"Sure I can," he said confidently. "I'll be as quiet as a mouse, and I don't snore. I'll clear off tomorrow as soon as Gus has gone out, and you won't have a thing to worry about. Now go get my blankets, I am about to retire."

She brought blankets and a jug of water. He took them from her. "And so to bed," he said lightly. "Cheer up, Chloe. Don't worry about me. Go out and enjoy yourself."

She shook her head. "I'm not going out. I daren't, now."

"Please yourself," he said. Then he paused with one foot

on the bottom step. "Don't entertain any notion of calling the coppers," he warned her. "If I'm caught here, Gus will get to know about the good times you've had with me. And not only me, a few more fellows as well. Doug Savage for one. So keep your cute little mouth buttoned up. Good-night, sweetheart. Pull the stairs up after me."

XIII

It was nearly ten o'clock when Gus arrived home. There were lights in the house. When he saw that Chloe was waiting he felt somewhat repentant, wishing that he had not stayed for a meal at the Stag's Head. He apologized as he embraced her.

"That's all right," she replied. "Nobody can blame a man if he stays for the odd drink after a hard day."

But she could not quite meet his glance, and he wondered if she were hiding resentment. Then he saw the evening paper, unopened, on the hall table.

"Haven't you looked at the paper?" he asked. "Haven't you heard the news?"

"No. What news?" she queried, rather absently he thought.

He told her. She seemed to stop breathing when she heard the word 'murder'. She held a button of his coat, and looked at it as she listened.

"Oh dear, that's dreadful." she said when she had heard it all. "Dreadful!" she repeated.

He noticed that she was very pale. "Now don't get upset," he said kindly. "The four thousand is a smack, but I can stand it. It's Cicely and the boy I'm bothered about."

"Of course," she said quickly. "How is Colin?"

"He's got a bad concussion, but the doctor says he'll be all right. I hope so. You can never tell with a bang on the head."

Her attention seemed to be straying. Then she became aware of his scrutiny, and she said: "I do hope he'll get better, darling. Shall I make some supper?"

"Not for me, thanks. I've just had a meal."

"I'll make a drink of coffee," she said, and hurried away to the kitchen. He frowned after her, observing uneasiness in her; uneasiness which was additional to the shocked con-

75

cern which he had expected. It was as if the murder of Cicely had aroused in her some fear for herself. He shook his head. Unpredictable creatures, women.

After drinking his coffee, he felt extraordinarily drowsy. He was immediately suspicious, because he was never sleepy before midnight. "Did you put one of your sleeping pills in my coffee?" he demanded with heavy-eyed sharpness.

"No," she denied.

"You have!" he insisted. "I can tell. Damn it, I'm not so worried about Cicely that I have to be put to sleep."

She looked down at her hands, and the expression on her small face was hidden by fair hair and long dark eyelashes. He considered her, and reflected that the sleeping tablet showed practical sympathy, at any rate.

"Never mind," he said. "Let's go to bed."

XIV

That was Saturday, St. Leger Day. The day Granchester was shocked by the murder of Cicely Wainwright. The day her murderers' guilty hands were stained green instead of red. The day Furnisher Steele was made to worry about his grandchild and Lucky Lusk about her face. The day Martineau, for the first time, actually wished that his wife Julia would leave him.

PART THREE

MARTINEAU

I

THE stolen Buick used in the Cicely Wainwright murder was not found abandoned on the same day. This was rather a surprise for Martineau, and on Sunday morning, when the car was still missing, he began to entertain a cautious hope that it had been hidden in some place which, when found, would provide a clue to the identity of at least one of the felons.

The search for the Buick was an issue second only in importance to the search for green fingers. Martineau phoned Detective Inspector Vanbrugh of the County Police and talked the matter over with him.

"I'm strictly ethical today," he said finally. "I'd like to make some inquiries in the county area, and I'd welcome the co-operation of one of your officers."

"Will I do?" asked Vanbrugh. "I'm working on the job from this end."

"Thanks very much," said Martineau. "I've got a car. I'll pick you up in five minutes."

In a Jaguar, with Devery driving, Martineau and Vanbrugh took the road to Boyton and the moors.

"Have you any particular place in mind?" the County man wanted to know.

"No," said Martineau. "I want to follow the road past the place where we found the girl, and see what there is."

"I'll tell you what there is. Miles and miles of damn all. Except the Moorcock. That's a pub, in case you don't know."

"There'll be a few isolated farms, I suppose."

"Just a few. And some even more isolated reservoir keepers' cottages. It won't take us long to visit the lot, if the farm roads are good enough for this luxury wagon of yours."

"I've heard about the Moorcock. Maybe we can call there."

"Sure we'll call," said Vanbrugh. "Our men have been there, of course, but it won't hurt the Moorcock people to have another visit."

Soon the car was climbing towards the place where Cicely Wainwright's body had been found. It was a fine morning, but there was a strong cool wind blowing across the hills. Traffic was sparse. In four miles the men in the police car saw only three cars, one bus, and two taxicabs. The cabs, and two of the cars, were packed with men, and the men were not of a type which would normally be seen riding in taxis. Vanbrugh frowned when he saw them.

"They're going the wrong way," he said. "There's no place for a gaming school nearer the city than this. Not that I know of, anyway."

"The schools move around, don't they?" Martineau remarked. "A different place every Sunday."

"They profane the Sabbath in a number of places, and they use them on an irregular rotary system. The don't often use the same place twice running."

"Who decides?"

"The organizer. A man called Broadhead, we think. He gets a small commission for keeping the ring and paying the crows. He's supposed to keep out welshers and twisters, too, but I imagine that's impossible."

As a city policeman, Martineau had no experience of big open-air gambling schools. But, among policemen, he had heard some talk of them. Now he wanted to hear more.

"Big money changes hands, doesn't it?" he asked.

Vanbrugh explained that in the game where a man spun two halfpennies and tried to make them both alight 'heads' upward on the ground, hundreds of pounds were often wagered on one throw of the coins. As in the more socially elevated game of Baccarat, winning players were inclined to leave both stakes and winnings in the ring, 'doubling up' again and again in the hope of achieving the well-nigh impossible, a run of 'heads' which would win all the available money of fifty or sixty gamblers in the ring. Starting with a one-pound stake and leaving all winnings on the ground, players had been known to 'head 'em' eleven consecutive times in their efforts to 'skin the ring'. And not all these nervy players were eventual losers. More than two thousand pounds lying in the ring was sometimes too much for the collective gambling spirit of the school, and the challenge would be only partly met. When the nervy one finally 'tailed 'em', he might not lose more than a quarter of his winnings.

"What about the sharps who can palm the coins and throw with two-headed ones?" Martineau queried.

"All that is taken care of," Vanbrugh replied. "There's a paid man called a putter-on. The man who's making the toss holds two fingers out, close together, and the putter-on lays the coins on his fingers. After that, he simply throws them up. They spin together in the air, and they usually land showing two heads or two tails. If there's one head and one tail, it's a void throw, and the money stays down."

"How often do you raid a tossing school?"

"Very seldom," said Vanbrugh. "You need a lot of men for that. Besides, those types *will* gamble somewhere, so they might as well be up on the moors out of harm's way. We don't bother much unless a school gets too big, or unless we get complaints of disorder and annoyance to people walking on the moors." He pointed to some rising ground on the left of the road. "There's a little disused quarry up there. It's one of their places. It's like all the others, very hard to approach without being spotted by the crows. There's usually four or five of 'em, spread out in a wide circle. They pick the high places where they can see all around, and they have field glasses."

"You'd need fifty men to surround the place and close in," said Martineau.

"Yes, and you've also got to prove that they were gambling," the County man agreed. "More trouble than what the job is worth."

The road became level at the height of the moor, and Martineau saw a little inn standing lonely on the edge of a desolate plateau.

"That's the Moorcock," said Vanbrugh, "and I see they've got customers." He indicated three taxis and one old car which stood beside the inn.

Devery stopped the car, and the three men alighted and gazed around.

"It'll be a bit bleak in winter," Martineau commented. He looked at a narrow, sandy moorland road which crossed the main road at an angle. "Where does that go?" he asked.

"To the north, nowhere," answered Vanbrugh. "It peters out at a farm. To the south, it passes a couple of ruined farms and finally joins the Huddersfield road. It's only used by farmers and such."

He returned his attention to the taxis. "I don't understand this," he said. "These people wouldn't be here at this time if they hadn't come to toss ha'pennies in the old quarry. And yet we saw those other clients going *away* from it."

"Happen there's been a change of plan," Martineau guessed.

"You mean, some of 'em came here, then found they'd come to the wrong place? It could be. This lot here could be a few more of 'em, just having a drink before they move on. I think I'd better take down their numbers, just in case."

"I've got the numbers, sir," said Devery.

"Good man!" said Vanbrugh. He looked at his watch. "Five past twelve. The place is officially open. We'll try an odd glass of ale, shall we?"

They entered the Moorcock, passing through an inner doorway into a small bar. Nearly a score of men crowded the place, and there was a hubbub of talk. The talk ceased as the newcomers were observed, and there were some furtive glances at the clock behind the bar. Some of the men knew Martineau, others knew Vanbrugh. Others, gamblers, living on the fringe of the criminal world as gamblers often do, sensed immediately that they were policemen.

They made their way to the bar and Martineau ordered half-pints of beer. Vanbrugh saw a man he knew, and he said: "How do, Tinker. No school today? Or is it a break for refreshment?" The man grinned and said: "What school, Inspector? If you mean Sunday School, I give over when I was twelve."

While this brief conversation went on, men were finishing their drinks and leaving the premises. As the door swung behind each departing group. cars could be heard starting up. Martineau smiled. "We're ruining trade," he said.

The landlady left the bar and went through into the

kitchen. The landlord remained, watching the exodus of customers with an expressionless gaze. He was a small, thin man with a sharp, high-coloured face. He looked as if he might have been a retired jockey—retired or warned off.

"I'm sorry we've driven off your customers, Alf," said Vanbrugh, though he did not look sorry.

Alf shrugged. Operating outside the licensing laws as he often did, he could not afford to quarrel with Vanbrugh. "It can't be helped," he said without rancour. "It was only passing trade, anyway. They'd soon a-been going."

"This is Inspector Martineau of Granchester City force," said the County man. "We're making inquiries about that murder yesterday."

Alf's glance shifted. "Ah, a bad do," he said. "A bad do for Gus, too."

"You know Gus?" Martineau interposed.

"Sure, I know Gus. He always calls when he passes this way."

"Did you see anything of an old Buick car yesterday morning? About opening time, maybe."

"I saw in the paper they was looking for a Buick," said Alf, and again his eyes shifted. He seemed to be trying to signal a warning. Martineau turned casually to look at the remaining customers. There were only four of them. Three of them were beery, raffish types; the fourth was a young taxi driver, not much more than twenty years old. The driver was drinking lemonade, the other three were drinking pints of ale. Martineau could associate the pint-swillers with gambling, but not with yesterday's crime. They were too bloated and flabby and, he thought, too old. Probably Alf's alarm was due to his own fear of being heard telling the police anything at all.

But Alf had something to tell. "Excuse me," he said. He dodged quickly out of the bar, and went into the kitchen. He returned in a very short time. "Just something I had to tell the wife," he apologized. Then he winked at Vanbrugh.

"There was nowt much stirring up this way yesterday," he said. "You'll be lucky if you find owt." Then rather pointedly he turned away and began to collect empty glasses.

The three policemen drank their half-pints of beer. They

said "Good day" and went outside. Now on the parking ground of the inn there was only the police car and one taxi. There was also the landlady standing at the side door. She beckoned, with an air of haste and secrecy. Vanbrugh and Martineau went to speak to her.

Breathlessly she said her piece: "My husband says to tell you summat's scared 'em away from t'owd quarry today. He doesn't know what it is, except they're keeping away. They've nearly all gone some place else."

They thanked her. "We'll go and have a look at the quarry," said Martineau to Devery as they got into the car.

When Vanbrugh said: "About here somewhere," they left the Jaguar and climbed the rough rising land. The place they sought was carved into the side of a little hill, and had been left in the form of a small basin with half of its rim broken away. It had never been a commercial quarry; it was merely a place where in the past, upland farmers had quarried stone to build barns and drywalls. Beneath the little cliff which had been made, there was a flat sandy place. It had been trodden hard, and it was littered with old used matchsticks and cigarette ends. But, when they found the place, they did not immediately notice the tell-tale rubbish. The first thing they saw was a pre-war Buick Roadmaster, dark grey in colour like city grime. The car looked as if its present owner had not washed it since he acquired it.

"Ah," said Martineau. "So this is what scared the gamblers."

"Yes, and how the devil was it brought here?" Vanbrugh demanded.

While they looked at the car, Devery walked on. He returned and reported that there was an old cart track on the other side of the quarry.

"It runs into the lane which comes out near the Moorcock," he said.

He was sent to find a telephone, and the two inspectors followed the cart track down to the lane.

"I expect they switched cars somewhere around here," said Martineau.

Vanbrugh's glance swept the deserted lane. "A right place

to do it," he said. "But some country body might have seen something. We'll have further inquiries. I'll see to it."

They went back to the quarry, to the abandoned Buick.

"Well," said Martineau. "It's a start. This'll give the fingerprint boys a bit of something to do."

II

Chloe's sleeping pill did not prevent Gus Hawkins from awaking at his usual time on Sunday morning. He opened his eyes and became aware of the stiff breeze out of doors. The trees in his garden were waving to him.

He yawned and stretched. "It looks like a cool wind," he said, comfortably aware that he did not have to get up and go to the office.

Chloe did not hear him. She had lain awake a long time listening for noises overhead, and now she slept heavily. It was Gus who heard a noise; a faint tinkling sound. He frowned. It occurred to him that the wind had loosened a tile on the roof.

He got up and had a quick bath, and put on some old flannels and a sweater. He went downstairs and put the kettle on, while he waited for it to boil he went outside and walked to the end of his back garden. He looked up. The roof tiles appeared to be in regular pattern; none displaced. He walked to the front gate. The tiles on that side too were quite in order.

There was a very small skylight window in the roof. While he was looking up, he saw—or thought he saw—a brief flutter of movement behind the glass. He smiled. That was it. Another small bird had got in. Once he had found a dead starling in the attic. He never knew how it came to be there, but the poor thing had got in somehow and, unable to get out, it had starved to death. Well, a bird in the attic was better than a loose tile on the roof. He had only to go up and open the skylight, and it would fly out.

He went back to the house and brewed the morning tea. He carried a cup upstairs for Chloe. She awoke when he entered the bedroom. She lay still, looking at him drowsily.

"Cupper tea, love," he said. Then: "I think there's a starling in the attic."

83

She sat bolt upright, staring open-mouthed. Her face was sickly white. The cup rattled in the saucer as she mechanically accepted it, and some of the tea was spilled. "Wha-what?" she stammered.

He grinned. "There's another starling got into the attic. You're not frightened of a bird, are you?"

She achieved a weak smile. "Well, they flutter around, don't they?"

"I'll go and let the poor thing out," he said.

"No, don't bother just now," she said quickly. "Come back to bed, darling."

He seemed slightly surprised. She guessed that she was not looking her best. She pouted, and stroked and patted his pillow, and wriggled impatiently.

"She wants him to come back to bed right now," she whispered.

"You haven't got the sleep out of your eyes," he said, and went out on to the landing.

"Gus! Come here!" she called, in a panic.

"All right," he said. "In a minute." He was holding the cord and letting down the loft ladder.

She sat listening, speechless with apprehension now.

Gus climbed the steps. When his shoulders reached the level of the attic floor he received a hard blow on the head, from above and behind. He fell forward on to the steps, slithered down them, and lay crumpled at the foot.

Don Starling hurried down the steps with steel erector Fenton's gun in his hand. He leaped over Gus, and ran into the bedroom. "You little cow!" he accused. "I've a good mind to belt you one, too. You told him! Has he phoned for the cops?"

III

Gus Hawkins was knocked on the head at about ten o'clock. The police were informed at half-past, by his doctor. At two o'clock, four hours after the incident, Martineau was casually told about it by a C.I.D. clerk when he returned to Headquarters from the old quarry on the moors.

"Hawkins?" he said, immediately interested. "What happened?"

"His wife called the doctor and said he'd fallen down the attic steps. When the doc got there he found she hadn't done a thing for Gus except try to pour brandy into him while he was still unconscious. I understand she's one of the help- less type; a charming nincompoop."

Martineau nodded. "She's a bad egg," he said.

The clerk, being a policeman, was neither surprised nor shocked. "Is zat so?" he said. "Well, the doctor lives just across the road from Gus, and, from upstairs, the doctor's wife saw a man leave the house rather hurriedly while the doc was actually taking the phone call. She told the doctor, and he mentioned the man to Mrs. Hawkins. She said she never saw any man. She was in bed when the accident hap- pened, she said."

"So the doctor thought Gus might have had a burglar, and he advised calling the police."

"Something like that, sir. But Mrs. Hawkins didn't want the police. She said she didn't think there'd been a man in the house."

"So?"

"So the doctor called the police himself. Gus was still unconscious, and the doc couldn't quite figure how a simple tumble had so well and truly laid him out."

"You mean, the doctor thinks somebody crowned him?"

"He admitted that it was a possibility, sir."

"Who went on the job?"

"Harmon and Cassidy."

"What did they get?"

"Nothing but a lot of prints."

"Where are they now?"

"Gone to have a bite of lunch, sir."

"What about Gus? Is the injury serious?"

"I don't know. They took him to the Infirmary."

"Poor old Gus," said Martineau. "I think I'll go and see how he is."

But at that moment Detective Constable Cassidy entered the office. "I want you," said Martineau. "Give me the griff on this Hawkins' job."

"There's very little to give, sir," said Cassidy, with sorrow in his Irish voice. "We've made neither head nor tail of it.

85

There's nothing been stolen, that we know of. But somebody was in the attic, or has been there lately. For what reason, it's hard to say."

"Happen he just ran up there to avoid Gus?"

"No sir," said Cassidy. "You haven't got the picture." He explained how the loft ladder worked.

"I see," said Martineau thoughtfully. "What do you think of Mrs. Hawkins? What did she tell you?"

"Ah, she was very jittery, sir. Didn't seem to know what she was saying half the time. She said she ran out on to the landing as soon as she heard Mr. Hawkins fall, but she neither saw nor heard anybody else. I asked her if he had any reason for going up the steps and she said he'd heard a noise, but she'd already told the doctor she didn't know why he went up."

"Not quite truthful, you think?"

"I wouldn't like to give me expert opinion on that, sir. She was a mite confused, maybe."

"She was confused, all right, but not the way you think," said Martineau. "I'll go and hear what Gus has to say, if he's conscious."

He took Devery with him to the hospital, and as they entered by the main doorway they passed a young woman who was going out. She did not know them, or recognize them as policemen. Martineau turned, and watched her get into a waiting taxi.

"There, very much in the flesh, goes Mrs. Hawkins," he said as the taxi moved away.

"I thought you only knew her by reputation," said Devery.

"I don't have opinions about people I know by reputation," was the crisp reply. "I know her by sight. I've seen her around, before and after marriage. If she's an honest wife, you can call me Morgan Unwin Gassbury."

At the inquiry desk Martineau introduced himself. A call was put through to a private ward. Yes, the police could see Mr. Hawkins.

Gus had a sunny room to himself, and somebody had already provided flowers. His head was bandaged, but he was propped up by pillows.

86

"Ten minutes. And don't get him worried or excited," said the ward sister.

"What the devil do you want?" asked Gus.

"We heard you were poorly, and thought we'd come and see you," said Martineau, grinning.

"I notice you didn't bring me any grapes. I never saw a copper part with anything yet. Nobody ever comes off best with you fellows."

"Tut, tut, he's peevish. He must be getting better already."

"Give over," said Gus. "You can't kid me. What do you want?"

"Did you see what hit you?"

"No. Never saw a thing. It was like the house falling on me."

"Why were you going into the attic?"

Gus told them how he had gone outside to look at the roof. "I saw something move," he went on, "and thought we'd got another starling trapped up there."

Martineau jumped. "A what?"

"We once had a starling got into the attic. It couldn't get out and it died."

Martineau glanced at Devery, and received a look of bright surmise. Then he heard Gus asking a question: "Now *you* tell me what hit me. My wife said the police hadn't told her anything. Was it a beam or something fell on me?"

Martineau had been warned not to worry Gus. There was nothing more likely to do so than a suspicion that somebody had been hiding in the attic. "It was an accident of some sort, Gus," he said. "It isn't my inquiry, but I'll get the details for you. Tell you what, I'll send one of the officers concerned to talk to you."

"Yes, please do that," said Gus, but he was watching closely.

Martineau knew that he was a hard man to deceive. Probably he already had his suspicions. It was time to be going. "All right, Gus. I hope you're soon better," he said, and took his leave. Outside, he said to Devery: "Now we'll go and see his missus. She'll tell us more. I don't mind worrying her at all."

Soon, unhampered by traffic, they were speeding across the city. They did not talk, until Martineau suddenly exclaimed: "Oh confound it! I'm in the doghouse again! I forgot to phone and tell my wife I wouldn't be home for dinner."

Sunday was the one working day when the inspector went home for the mid-day meal. Now that it was mentioned, Devery felt annoyed with himself. He also had forgotten, and he had intended to increase his reputation for reliability and helpfulness by reminding his superior.

"It's hardly your fault, sir," he said. "You couldn't know how things were going to develop."

"It's too late now, anyway," said Martineau. "I'm apt to forget the domestic side when I'm busy; especially when I hear of a starling with a capital S fluttering around. We're supposed to be on the Cicely Wainwright job, but I'd take time out from hunting the devil himself if there was half a chance of picking up Don Starling."

"It's an odd coincidence, if it was Starling in the attic."

"In the mention of his name, you mean? The other thing is no coincidence at all. I don't know why I didn't think of it before. Mrs. Hawkins was knocking about with a queer crowd when she met Gus. She used to go to the places where Don Starling spent his time."

"You think she knows him?"

"Of course she knows him. I've seen her with him, before Gus started courting her. She's a little strumpet and she's probably been with him since she was married. He'll have been in that house before, when Gus was out. He'll have been upstairs too, if I know anything about the social behaviour of riffraff. I'll bet he knew all about that loft ladder."

"It all ties in," said Devery. "You could be right."

"We have means of making sure," his senior replied. "Cassidy found plenty of dabs. But first we'll hear what Mrs. Hawkins has to say."

They found Mrs. Hawkins alone. When she answered the doorbell, Martineau introduced himself unsmilingly. "And this is Constable Devery," he said tersely. "May we come in? I want to ask you a few questions about your husband's accident."

When they were in the front room, he did not wait to be asked to sit down. "Who was the man in the attic?" he asked abruptly.

She gulped. "I—man in attic?"

"Yes. We think we know. We want you to tell us."

She stared at the carpet. "I never saw any man," she said in a low voice.

"May I use your phone?" he asked. She looked at him dully, and nodded. He went to the telephone in the hallway, leaving the room door open. He dialled CENtral 1212, and then, loudly enough for her to hear, he said: "Martineau here. Give me the C.I.D."

When the C.I.D. clerk answered, he said: "I want Cassidy, if he's in," and when Cassidy came on the line he asked: "What have you done with the fingerprints you found in Gus Hawkins' attic?" ·

"Sergeant Bird has them, sir. We——"

"Listen. Get out Don Starling's prints and compare, will you?"

"Starling!" Cassidy echoed. "Well of all—I'll do that at once, sir. Give me your number and I'll ring you back."

Martineau gave the number, and went back to observe Chloe Hawkins' consternation.

"It's a very serious offence to harbour an escaped convict, Mrs. Hawkins," he said.

She did not look at him. He could see that she was trembling, and he advised her to sit down.

"Of course," he went on, suddenly gentle, "if you had been intimidated or blackmailed, and you told us the whole story, it would put a different complexion upon the matter."

She remained silent, but she was obviously in a torment of doubt.

"Without help," he pursued, speaking nothing but the truth, "we shall have to make persistent inquiries. When we do that, it is often embarrassing for the people concerned. We find out all sorts of things."

She had found a handkerchief somewhere. She twisted it in her hands. Martineau waited for her to speak.

"I didn't do anything. I didn't harbour him," she said at last. "He came here and just walked into the house."

89

"You are referring to Don Starling, of course?"

"Yes. He said he was going to stay here for one night, and if I didn't hide him he'd tell Gus all sorts of lies about me. I—I was afraid of him, so I hid him in the attic, and this morning Gus heard him."

"He slept in the attic? On the bare boards?"

"I gave him two blankets, but I moved them this morning before the detectives came. I put them in the laundry basket."

"Did you see him hit Gus?"

"No. I was in bed. He came into the bedroom, and accused me of having told Gus. I told him he'd done it himself with making a noise. I said he'd better go quickly, in case the police came to see Gus about the murder. So he went, and Mrs. London—that's the doctor's wife—saw him going away from the house."

"What time did he come, last night?"

"About five to eight."

"Was he very hungry?"

"He made me give him a meal, but I wouldn't say he was starving."

"Was he dirty and unshaven?"

"Not particularly. He had a wash before his meal, but—" She remembered something. "Yes, he did need a shave, but not too badly."

"What was he wearing?"

She described Starling's clothes as well as she could.

"Did he ask for money?" Martineau pursued.

"No. At first I thought he'd come for money. He said he didn't want money."

"You mentioned money and he said he didn't want any?"

"That's right."

"Well, well!" said Martineau. "A man on the run. . . ." He looked thoughtful. He began to pace about.

One quality of a good policeman is the ability to remember to ask all the questions which should be asked. Martineau had his share of that ability. Now he remembered to pose two pertinent questions before he asked the one which, now, might be the most important. But Mrs. Hawkins could give him no clue as to where Starling had been when he came to her, nor where he went when he left her.

"Too bad," said Martineau. "Now, did you notice anything unusual about his appearance?"

"I don't think so. What do you mean?"

"You saw him wash his hands. Did you watch him eat his meal?"

"Yes."

"Did he have dirty, broken fingernails?"

"I didn't notice his nails."

"So his hands seemed to be quite clean and well cared for? As clean as mine, for instance?"

"No, not as clean as yours. His fingers were sort of stained."

"What colour?"

"Green."

"You're sure about the stain, and the colour?"

"I'm quite sure. They weren't as green as Gus's, but I remember noticing them and wondering if it was the same sort of stuff he'd got on his hands."

"Thank you, Mrs. Hawkins. Now I'm afraid I'll have to use your phone again. Do you mind?"

She did not mind. She heard him giving the new information to Headquarters. He put some emphasis on the matter of green-stained hands. He wanted her to hear him, so that she would not forget.

IV

When he had taken Mrs. Hawkins' statement and left the house, Martineau remembered to telephone his wife. Though he had failed her with regard to dinner, he could at least tell her he would not be home for tea. He stopped at the first public telephone, but there was no answer to his call. So she was out, somewhere. He sighed. He would have to call later.

He forgot to call later.

V

About the time that Gus Hawkins was taken to hospital, his enormous but dim-witted henchman, Bill Bragg, strolled from his home to the Brick Lane Working Men's Club. There it was his practice on Sunday mornings to have a pint or two of beer before the normal opening time, to engage in conversation with friends, and to acquire certain information.

Bill talked a lot that morning. Because of his connexion, through Gus Hawkins, with yesterday's crime, his friends were interested in what he had to say. But at eleven forty-five he got up to go home. His Sunday dinner would be on the table at twelve noon, and he did not want to be late for the best meal of the week.

On his way out of the club he paused at the bar and quietly asked the steward a question.

"It's a good job you didn't ask me five minutes since," the steward told him. "They've just been through on the phone. Moorcock is off. They've changed it to Fly Holler."

"What's up wi' the Moorcock?" Bill wanted to know.

"That's what I said, but I were told I'd fare better if I ast no questions," the steward replied. "Are you going to the Fly?"

Bill looked through a window at a patch of sky. "I'll see how I feel when I've had me dinner," he said. "I might go, if it keeps fine."

After dinner he was still undecided, but he made up his mind quickly when Mrs. Bragg suggested going out to tea and spending the evening at the home of her sister. The sister's husband was a teetotaller whom Bill despised.

"No, I'm not going," he said flatly. "I've got a bit o' business on. You go, an' I'll call for yer tonight. My word, it's time I were off. I'll be late."

So he went to Fly Hollow, which was a place named by gamblers, being about a mile away from the moorland hamlet of Fly End. He alighted from a cross-country bus at the little cluster of grey stone houses, and soon he was out of the place, walking along a narrow lane between banks of dark moor grass topped by low drystone walls. On both sides of the road were dark sloping fields, so poor that they only made the roughest of grazing for sheep.

He had walked about a quarter of a mile when he heard a motor vehicle coming along behind him. He looked round and saw that it was a taxi, with only one passenger. He was enjoying his walk and the air was bracing, but he was never a man who would walk when he could ride. He guessed that the taxi would be going to the gaming school, so he gave the hitch-hiker's sign.

The taxi stopped, and Bill observed that it was a Silverline, and that the passenger was Lolly Jakes. He was mildly surprised, because Lolly was a poor man like himself, and he usually went to the gaming rendezvous in a bus.

Lolly's smile of greeting was rather sour as he made room for Bill in the taxi. Just now, he wanted to have nothing to do with anybody who was connected with Gus Hawkins. But neither did he want to incur the dislike of any such person. He had decided, reluctantly, that it was better to bear Bill's company and have him be grateful for a free ride than to have him annoyed by being left to walk.

Bill thought nothing of Lolly's lack of cordiality. He knew that he took up a lot of room in a taxi, and people usually winced when he sat down beside them. "How are yer, Lolly?" he asked. "You at Doncaster yesterday?"

"Yer. I went," said Lolly.

"Who'd yer go with?"

"The Duke of Edinburgh and his party."

Bill grinned, not at all offended. "How'd you go on?" he asked. He did not really want to know. He was just making conversation.

At Doncaster Lolly had worked out an imaginary list of winning bets in case the police caught him in possession of his share of the stolen money. He had memorized the list until he had almost come to believe it himself. Now he nearly said: "Five winners," but stopped himself in time. He did not want Bill Bragg to be gossiping enviously about him, or even thinking about him at all.

"I didn't do so bad," he said.

To Bill, the brief half-surly answer was natural enough. Sometimes fellows bragged about their winnings, sometimes they had reasons for not letting anybody know they'd had a win. It occurred to him that a shiftless character like Lolly might owe money to several men who would be at the gaming school. If they heard that he had been lucky at the races they would demand repayment.

"*We* didn't get any racing yesterday," said Bill heavily. "The murder, yer know."

"Aye, I heard," said Lolly, trying to be casual.

"We was on our way," Bill continued, "but the coppers looked out for us and turned us back when we was halfway there. They didn't make no mistake. Picked us out of a proper procession of motors. The cops can gen'rally find yer when they want yer."

"Yers," Lolly agreed, though he did not like the last remark at all. This talk of murder and the police was depressing him. If it went on, it would ruin his day.

Bill thought that he was receiving willing attention. He warmed to his subject. Opening his huge hands he said: "See these? If I could get hold o' one a-them murderers he wouldn't live ter stand trial. I'd throttle the sod."

In spite of his size and his immense strength, his expression—if it could be called an expression—was like that of a small boy trying to be fierce. But Lolly was not studying his face: he was listening to the very real anger in the rough growling voice.

"I'd like ter take all the four of 'em an' pull the'r necks out like cock chickens at Chris'mus," said Bill. "Cicely were one 'o the nicest, straightest lasses in Granchester. An' young Colin is a real good lad."

Lolly swallowed rather noisily. "It makes yer feel that way," he admitted, and inwardly he also fumed with anger against the man who had actually killed Cicely Wainwright. But for that, he thought, everything would have been lovely: nothing at all to worry about. But murder. . . . The police never gave up on a murder.

"Pickin' on a young filly like that!" Bill went on. "Gus should a-sent me wi' the money. I'd a-showed 'em. I'd a-paralysed 'em."

Lolly looked sidelong at those hands with fingers like bananas and shuddered slightly. Surreptitiously he felt in his pocket to make sure that his razor was readily accessible. It was a purely nervous move, because he knew that Bill could never be subtle enough to make an indirect accusation. Bill did not suspect him.

The taxi stopped at a place where there were no banks on

each side of the road. The rough grass verge gave the driver room enough to reverse his vehicle and turn back to Fly End. The passengers alighted, and Lolly paid the fare. He graciously waved an acknowledgement of the driver's thanks for the tip, and followed Bill over the drywall on to the open moorland.

The two men climbed gradually as they walked over the rough ground, making their way around a hill which was shaped like a flattish cone. As they went they were observed by a man who sat in the heather at the apex of the cone. He might have been there to enjoy the fresh air and the view. He had a pair of binoculars.

On the other side of the hill, Bill and Lolly came to an outcrop of huge black rocks, a common enough feature in that district. Near the rocks there was another 'crow', who knew them and spoke to them. They went among the rocks and entered a little grassy hollow. In the centre of the hollow there was a large patch of black peat-hag, trodden hard and flat.

There were about sixty men in the hollow, and they were standing two or three deep in an irregular ring around the patch of trodden ground. There was as wide an assortment of types as might be seen at any other sporting event. There were pale mill workers and muscular miners. There was a farmer or two, and some ruddy, horny-handed men who looked like outdoor labourers. There were butchers, bakers, and bookmakers. There were dressy men, and men in cloth caps with coloured kerchiefs tied round their necks.

Doug Savage, pot-landlord of the Prodigal Son Inn, was there. Laurie Lovett was there, and so was Clogger Roach. Three inveterate gamblers.

In the middle of the ring a fresh-faced young fellow was saying: "I'll head 'em for four," and there were four one-pound notes in the hands of the sturdy, red-faced man who stood beside him.

"Has he done it twice?" Bill Bragg inquired, and the reply was an envious "That's right, chum," from a shabby, gaunt, colourless man who looked as if he ought to be spending his cash-in-hand on a good meal. Evidently the challenger had started with a one-pound bet. He had won twice, leaving stakes and winnings in the ring.

"I'll have a nicker on," said Bill, making up his mind quickly, and feeling proudly resolute because he had done so. He handed a note to the red-faced man, who took it and nodded an acknowledgement. The colourless man, after a moment of obviously painful indecision, risked a pound himself. Then Lolly Jakes and Doug Savage stepped forward together, each offering two pounds to the stakeholder.

The stakeholder, whose remuneration largely depended upon tips from the day's winners, wanted to make no enemies. "Now then," he said with a dry grin. "Whose money shall I take?"

"I was first," said Doug.

"Nay, I'm damned if you were," Lolly retorted.

The two men eyed each other; measured each other. They were both burly men; the innkeeper clean and almost dapper in appearance, the other carelessly dressed. The onlookers watched them with interest.

Nearly all gamblers have ideas about the fickleness of luck. Any small incident might affect luck or point the way to the avoidance of misfortune. And one lucky bet might change the whole day's fortunes. Therefore it became important to both Doug and Lolly that they should make that particular bet. It seemed to each of them that the other was blocking his way to an important initial success.

"Split it. Have a quid apiece on," the stakeholder suggested.

"Fair enough," Lolly agreed.

"I was first," said Doug stubbornly.

"Spin a coin for it," somebody advised.

The disputants shook their heads. Such a course might put a hoodoo on the bet.

"Well, do summat!" the challenger snapped, because he was afraid that the delay might be allowing *his* luck to change.

"A quid apiece," said Lolly, and there was a general murmur of approval for this compromise.

Doug shook his head obstinately. He thought that he should make the bet. To split with Lolly Jakes, whom he despised, seemed as if it would be an unlucky thing to do.

But he could see that Lolly's reasonable offer had popular support, and the deadlock had to be broken. "I was first," he said sulkily. "But go on. Put your brass on seeing as you're so keen. We'll see what happens."

Grinning, Lolly handed his two pounds to the stake-holder. Then the challenger stepped out into the middle of the ring and held out his right hand palm upwards. The forefinger and the long finger were straight, held close together. The other two fingers were bent, and held by the thumb. The 'putter-on' carefully placed two halfpennies, 'heads' upwards, on the outstretched fingers. The challenger threw, and the two coins went almost exactly straight up into the air, spinning side by side, and to the naked eye spinning in perfect unison.

It was a bad throw. The coins showed one 'head' and one 'tail' when they landed on the ground. It was a void toss. The challenger threw again, and the coins showed two 'tails'. He had lost his four pounds. With evident satisfaction Bill Bragg, Lolly, and the colourless man stepped forward to collect their winnings.

As Lolly held out his hand for his money, Bill noticed that his fingers were stained green. Because they were dirty they did not seem to be quite the same colour as Gus Hawkins' but green they undoubtedly were. Bill wondered foggily about that, but in spite of his visit to Hallam and the green-handed thief he had seen there, his childlike mind did not perceive any suspicious connexion.

Doug Savage was furious, According to his way of think-ing, he had been robbed of two pounds. He took a folded five-pound note from the fob pocket of his trousers, and handed it to the stakeholder, who uncreased it reverently.

"I'll head 'em for a fiver," Doug rasped, and glared at Lolly. The challenge was obvious and, to those men standing around, it was rightfully given. Lolly had to accept it, or be considered a timorous man. He simply nodded, and gave five pounds to the stakeholder.

Doug was a skilful tosser. He threw, and 'headed 'em' at the first attempt.

"Leave it in the ring," he said to the stakeholder, and he looked at Jakes.

Lolly nodded again, and fumbled in his trousers pocket. He brought out a small handful of pound notes, and counted off ten for the stakeholder.

Doug threw again, and won. "Leave it," he said, grinning widely now. Everyone waited to see what Lolly would do. They did not have to wait long. He was counting off twenty pounds for the stakeholder.

Doug won again, and laughed in exultation. He was a good gambler who would ride with his luck, and he had a great contempt for men who grew cautious or timid when they were winning, only to plunge wildly to regain losses when the luck was against them.

"Leave it," he said confidently. There were forty pounds in the ring, only five of which had belonged to him. He looked round at the spectators,, because he did not think that Lolly would have a further forty pounds with which to gamble. But the men waited. They also thought that Lolly would be unable to 'cover' the bet, but they expected that he would partly cover it with what money he had.

Lolly did indeed give the impression that he was nearly at the end of his financial resources. He was fishing in his match pocket and bringing out folded fivers one at a time, and handing them, one at a time, to the stakeholder. The stakeholder unfolded each one, and solemnly counted.

"Seven . . . Eight," he said. "Eight fives is forty. Your bet's covered, Doug."

In the face of such determination Doug began to look serious. But neither his luck nor his skill were affected, because he tossed and won again.

"Eighty quid!" he cried exuberantly. "Oh boy, rags to riches!"

It was obvious that he intended to leave the money in the ring, but the spectators again waited to see what Lolly would do. Bill Bragg stared at him blankly, with his mouth open. That was a fairly normal expression for all occasions. He was greatly excited by the betting, but he was incapable of showing his excitement.

"Come on, come *arn*!" Doug urged the 'school'. "Put your

money on the drum. You come in rags and go away in Rolls-Royces."

Lolly Jakes showed no disappointment. His face was stolid, though his little eyes glinted. He began to fumble in his trousers pocket again, but someone who had appeared at his side put a hand on his arm to arrest the action of bringing out money. The newcomer was Laurie Lovett, who had been standing quietly in the crowd. Also from the crowd Clogger Roach appeared, and he looked at Jakes with hostility.

It occurred to Bragg, and to other men standing near, that Jakes had been gambling with money which did not belong to him. It was a reasonable conclusion. Jakes had been at various times a runner for any small-time bookmaker who would employ him. It looked as if he had found another employer, and that he was now wagering money which had been entrusted to him to pay out some people who had betted successfully on yesterday's racing. If it were his own money, there seemed to be no reason for Laurie Lovett to interfere.

Aware of listeners, Lovett said in a low, hard voice: "Don't be a fool, Lolly. You've lost enough. You're backing your bad luck. Play small till it changes."

"I'm not going to let this big swaggering devil get away with *my* money," was the dogged reply.

"You can't afford to cover him again," said Lovett. "I tell you, *you can't afford it!*"

"I can afford it one more time."

"All right," said Lovett. "But remember, it's your own neck."

To those who listened, that sounded like an entirely natural remark. If Jakes were gambling away the money of other gamblers, it *was* his own neck which he was putting in peril. He ran the risk of getting it cut with a razor as sharp as his own. Therefore they were not surprised when he in his turn began to look worried.

"You're right, Laurie," he replied with sudden meekness, because he was also aware of listeners. "I can't cover it again, I were only goin' ter try an' frighten him. I'll just put a fiver on till my luck changes."

Lolly placed his bet, and the stakeholder said: "All right

99

then. Who's bettin' agen' this eighty nicker? Make yer bets up inter fivers an' tenners, then I can remember who's who."

One man, a bookmaker, gave the stakeholder twenty pounds as an individual bet. The one-pound gamblers made themselves into small temporary syndicates and handed in £5 and £10 bets. Each man knew the members of his own syndicate, and there could be no cheating or confusion at the pay off. The sum of £80 was quickly made up.

"Right," said the stakeholder, and the putter-on stepped forward with the two halfpennies.

Doug threw, and once more he headed the coins at the first attempt. There was now £160 in the ring.

"Leave it," said Doug. "I'll skin the lot of you."

The bookmaker immediately increased his bet to £40, but money from the small gamblers came in more slowly this time. In the opinion of many, Doug was 'set' to head the coins eight or nine times. They noted his confidence. He was in luck. They preferred not to bet against him until he was nearing the end of his run.

The stakeholder raised only £95 to meet Doug's £160. "Only ninety-five," he said. "Yer all windy. One man is flayin' the lot on yer."

Bill Bragg, who had lost his original stake and another pound as well, withheld his bet this time. He was one of those who believed that Doug would make one or two more successful throws. He stood aside to make room for those who wanted to bet, and he heard Lolly Jakes mutter, as if to himself, that Doug would never succeed in heading the coins another time. He was also surprised to see that Lolly was pulling a really big wad of money from his pocket.

Other bystanders were no longer interested in Lolly. He had had his moment. Only Bragg saw the fistful of money. Bragg, and the two men who were watching Lolly—Laurie Lovett and Clogger. They closed in on him.

"Put it away, man!" Laurie whispered fiercely. "Have you gone wrong in your head?"

Lolly scowled at him, and in doing so he met the fanatical glare of Clogger: Clogger, the frenzied adherent of a cause, the cause being Clogger's welfare. That wild angry look daunted Lolly, not because he was afraid of the man but because he knew that the anger was justified.

"So help me," Clogger whispered. "I'll stop yer if I have to knife yer."

Lolly made no reply, but he thrust the half-extracted money back into his pocket and turned to watch the gambling with little hooded eyes.

Doug Savage threw, and lost. The stakeholder paid out the winners, and gave the innkeeper the £65 which remained.

Doug gave him a five-pound note. "Sixty quid isn't so bad," he said. "I think I'll call it a day. My luck turned on that last throw."

His obvious self-satisfaction enraged Jakes, who turned in fury upon Roach and Lovett.

"But for your interference I'd a-won me money back, an' that swanky devil would a-won nowt," he snarled in a whisper. "God rot yer!"

The other two did not reply. But they were united in disapproval of his conduct and they met his scowl coldly.

"Ah, go to hell!" said Lolly, and he turned his back on the ring and went off the way he had come. His accomplices watched him until he disappeared among the rocks.

With his open-mouthed, vacant stare Bill Bragg also watched Lolly. He had seen the whole incident and heard some of the conversation, and he thought that it would make a nice item of gossip.

It would be no use telling Gus, the boss, when he went to see him in hospital. Gus wouldn't be interested in small-timers. He had a habit of cutting off Bill's oral efforts in mid-sentence with a curt: "Stop blathering, Bill. It takes you half-an-hour to tell a two-minute tale."

But it would make a tale to tell at the club. And his workmate, Stan Lomax, would be interested. Stan would probably know something. At any rate he would figure out an explanation as to why Laurie Lovett and another fellow had stopped Jakes from making a bet with some money he had in his pocket. Happen Stan would know which street-corner bookie the money belonged to. Whoever the bookie was, he ought to have his head examined for trusting Jakes with so much money.

101

The man ought to have his head examined. That was what Bill thought. He had that sort of brain. The sight of a much larger amount of money than he had first seen did not cause him to abandon the idea he had at first formed. Bill's brain could not handle more than one idea at a time.

Moreover, having decided that he would remember to tell somebody about the idea he had, Bill stored it away in the dusty background of his mind and immediately forgot it. Nothing less obvious than a leading question was likely to bring it out again.

VI

That Sunday night, when Devery went to see his Silver, he gave her grandfather the news that Don Starling was now wanted for murder. To his surprise Furnisher again failed to show his usual lively appreciation of being 'in the know' before the newspapers appeared. Nor did he say "I told you so." He only shook his head, and his old eyes reflected a sober misgiving.

"He'll see the papers in the morning," he said. "Ther'll be his photo on every front page. He'll know it's all or nowt, now."

"It'll be nowt, I think. We'll soon get him. He won't be able to move without being spotted."

"He'll be desp'rate. It'll not be prison he's thinking about. It'll be the judge, putting the black cap on. He won't be saying 'Thank you, me Lord,' this time."

"No, I'm afraid he won't," Devery agreed. "It'll be the end of the road for him. He won't care what he does."

Furnisher looked at Silver before he spoke again. It was a good thing, he thought, that Devery was so busy. Because Devery was too busy to take her out, the girl stayed around the house. She was proper domesticated. Of course she had had no shopping to do since Saturday night. Tomorrow the shops would be open. If she went out, Furnisher would have to make an excuse to go with her, and he would take his old gun. It was more than half a century old, a service revolver of Boer War issue, but it would still stop a man; stop him immediately and permanently.

The old man's vigilance was not based on reasonable

expectations. Starling had no real motive for hurting Silver. He had made a bargain, and he would gain nothing by dishonouring it. And he would also be very busy saving his own skin. But Furnisher was taking no chances where Silver was concerned, and, in spite of the bold way he had spoken to Starling on the telephone, he had an instinctive fear of the man. It was easy for him to imagine what that dangerous criminal might do out of pique, injured vanity, fancied insult or mere senseless cruel whim. Until Starling was caught, Furnisher was determined to be always in a position to guard Silver. Whenever she went out of doors, there would he be also.

"Well, the sooner you catch him, the better for everybody," he told Devery. "But, by gum, watch yourself if you come up agen him."

"I will, don't worry," Devery replied with a smile. But he was thinking, as other young policemen were thinking at the same moment, that if he got a glimpse of Starling he would take almost any chance to make an arrest.

"Think on," said the other man, not entirely convinced. "Our Silver wouldn't like it if you got hurt."

Devery used that remark to open another topic. "Silver and I are thinking of getting married soon," he said.

Furnisher was startled. He looked quickly from the young man to the girl. Then he sighed. "Aye, I suppose it's only natural," he said. "A bit sooner nor I expected, though. What's all the rush?"

Devery grinned at him. "You were young once yourself, you know."

"Yes, and I were a proper buckstick, an' all. *I'll* not stop you. But there's no need for you to go off and set up for yoursel's. Silver'll none want to leave her old grandad on his own. This place is big enough for three—or maybe more."

"We thought you'd want us to stay," said Devery, and he could see that his use of the plural hurt a little. "We'll do that, temporarily at least. But Silver wants us to do the place up a bit. Some new furniture, and that. We'll want something of our own, so I'll buy it."

"No need, lad, no need. If there's one thing we aren't short on, it's furniture." He looked around the room.

"Silver's been bothering about new furniture for some time. Aay well, I suppose a young woman likes to see a change once in a while. We'll have decorators in, and if there's nothing in the shop what you want, you can see what's in the catalogues of the firms I deal with. Unless—" he looked hopeful "—you'd like to see if there's owt upstairs you want."

Devery looked at Silver, who was following the talk with interest. He made a brief soundless remark to her, and they smiled at each other.

"Nothing doing, old boy," he said. "We don't want to seem ungrateful, but we don't want any of your antiques."

The top floor of Furnisher's shop-home-warehouse was crammed with his 'antiques'. Most of them were pieces of Victorian furniture which were in appalling taste by any standard except that of their period. During his business lifetime he had acquired them for next-to-nothing because people would no longer have them in their houses. He believed that before he died, or shortly after his death, the circular trend of fashion would make them into valuable collector's items. He had so much old furniture on the top floor that he did not know what he had. Some of it he had not seen for years, because he did not go up there for an occasional gloat as he might have been expected to do. The furniture was covered with dust, mainly forgotten, and seldom visited. The top floor was a bothersome thing in Silver's tidy mind. She often threatened to go up there and sail into action with dusters and a vacuum cleaner.

Now, with her fingers, she repeated the threat.

Devery replied in a combination of sign and lip language. "You don't want a duster, sweetheart. Take an axe."

The old man took it all in good part. "You'll see," he said. "Thar's some good stuff upstairs. It'll be worth a mint o' money one of these days."

"I dare say you're right," said Devery tolerantly. "But we don't have to live with it, do we?"

VII

Martineau's wife may have been out at tea time—tea time on Sunday meant that she had taken a bus journey to

see her parents. Fair enough—but she was waiting, unshak-
ably decorous, when he arrived home at half-past ten.

"Hallo," he said as he entered the house. She looked at
him, but she did not reply. "Sorry about today. I was very
busy," he added, but still she did not speak.

He went into the kitchen. He was hungry. He had had
one sandwich since breakfast, and a few glasses of beer since
nine o'clock. Nowadays he always seemed to need a drink
after a long day's work; or perhaps it was not the work but
Julia, Julia waiting for him with a grievance. Dutch courage.

He looked in the oven. His dinner was there; cold, con-
gealed, unappetizing. Part of it was a cold rice pudding. He
removed the pudding—he did not want it—and switched on
the heat to warm up the remainder.

From his movements she guessed what he was doing. "Are
you going to waste that pudding?" she demanded.

"I'm not going to eat it, if that's what you mean," he
replied.

"It's sinful," she said. "I waited all afternoon with the
table set."

A slight exaggeration. He let it go.

"How would you like to spend a fine Sunday afternoon
sitting waiting to wash up after somebody?" she wanted to
know. "So busy. Such an important man. Couldn't spare one
minute in all the livelong day to phone his home."

He let that go, too. But: "Did you have tea at your
mother's?" he asked politely.

That checked her. In the same polite tone he followed
up: "How is the old hellion?"

She was coldly contemptuous. "Guttersnipe talk doesn't
become you," she said. "But perhaps you can't help it."

"No, I can't. And she is, isn't she? Look what she's done
to your stepfather. He started to disintegrate as soon as she
married him. One of these days he'll just fall to pieces, and
she'll be looking for her third."

She looked at him with narrowed eyes. He had never been
deliberately offensive about her mother before. He never
sought trouble as a rule. What was the matter with him?

In their most vehement squabbles she had never once
thought that their marriage might be broken up. They were

105

husband and wife, and if they quarrelled, well, he was in the wrong. It was—as she saw it—her duty as a wife to try and make him behave like the man she wanted him to be. She thought that she railed at him for his own good, to keep him up to the mark, to suppress his natural—but deplorable—masculine proclivity for low pubs, low companions, slack behaviour and general vulgarity. She would have been shocked and humiliated if she had known that he had wearily ceased to care what happened to their marriage, and that once or twice he had actually wished that she would leave him.

Her belief in the permanency of their union was reasonable. She was a product of the police tradition of happy marriage. If a policeman was not happily married, he had to pretend to be. Even in so-called enlightened times, divorce or separation was frowned upon by police authorities. Policemen had to be respectable, and ambitious policemen had to be *very* respectable. A break between Martineau and his wife, with maintenance or alimony decided in court, would destroy all his prospects of promotion. His wife never suspected for one moment that he would consider parting from her and ruining his career.

So, now, she could see only one reason for his unusual aggressiveness. He was intoxicated. He concealed it very well, but he had had too much to drink.

"You're drunk," she said.

"I am *not* drunk," he replied.

"You ought to think about your position before you go and get too much to drink in a pub. You ought to think about your wife and your home. You've got responsibilities."

"Responsibility. Singular. If it were plural there'd be a different atmosphere in this house."

Not that again, she thought. Always on about children! It was getting worse! Of course, drunken men always got sentimental about little toddlers.

She did not answer him, but rose from her chair and began to set the table. She thought she had better get out his supper and carry it from the kitchen. She was afraid that—being drunk—he might stumble and spill gravy on the carpet.

"You needn't bother. I can do it," he said.

She brought the warm plate and put it on a cork mat. "Get your supper," she said.

He began to eat.

"How is it?" she asked.

The roast beef was tender. "Not bad at all," he said.

"It was lovely at dinner time."

He grunted something which might have been agreement, or sarcastic comment.

"It serves you right," she said.

"You sitting there with nowt to do but natter, that serves me right too," he replied.

To hell with her. She could clear out of it for all he cared, and damn the promotion.

Still Julia did not perceive what was in his mind. "It's always a mistake to argue with inebriated people," she said. "I'm going to bed."

After supper he played the piano until she knocked on the bedroom floor.

<h3 style="text-align:center">VIII</h3>

The next day, when people had read their morning papers, the telephone operators at Police Headquarters became very busy. There was a great increase in the number of citizens who thought they had seen Don Starling. The police knew that nearly all of them would be mistaken, but they patiently investigated each report. That was work for subordinates, and Martineau left it to them. He phoned Vanbrugh at the County Office.

"Anything new from the hinterland?" he wanted to know.

"A little," the County inspector replied. "We found a shepherd who saw a dark-blue car at about half-past ten on Saturday morning. It was standing in that little dead end which comes out at the Moorcock."

"Near the lane leading to the quarry?"

"Yes, quite near. He thinks it was a taxi, but he has no idea of the number or the make. He's not even sure if it had a Hackney Carriage plate."

"Not a very satisfactory witness, but his time is right, if he's sure of it. That was their second getaway car, my boy. But where do you suppose they went from there?"

"I've been working on that. The check points were set, both on the Lancashire and Yorkshire sides, before they could have got away from the quarry. If Don Starling was with them, as we surmise, they could never have got through a check point. But there's one way they could have missed all the checks, if one of them knew his way."

"That other little road from the Moorcock?"

"Yes. I told you it went through to the main Granchester-Huddersfield road, which was checked. Well, it turns out that it crosses a road which passes through a place called Scammonden. From there they could have sneaked right out of the checking area."

"And gone where?"

"Joined the traffic on the Wakefield and Doncaster road."

The races again, thought Martineau. Always the races. The heavy traffic going to the St. Leger.

"You think they went a-racing?" he asked.

"They could have done. They *would* have done, if they had any sense. Nobody would notice 'em in race traffic, once they got in the thick of it. There'd be hundreds if not thousands of cars and taxis filled with ugly mugs. And if they did happen to be caught with the money on the way back, well, they'd won it at the races."

"That seems to be a good assumption."

"Good enough to work on till it's disproved. We can try and find out if anybody saw Don Starling at Doncaster. And who he was with."

"The gang would separate, surely."

"They might, and they might not. They'd probably think they were safe once they got on the course. There was a terrific crowd there for the St. Leger."

"Yes, there always is," Martineau agreed. "Thanks a lot. I'll keep you up-to-date with what we get."

"I'm hoping you will," said Vanbrugh. "I'm hoping we catch the lot of 'em, with enough evidence to swing 'em."

After that, Martineau put out the word for all officers in contact with informers to find out if Don Starling had been seen at the St. Leger meeting, and in what company. Then he turned his attention to the call book.

"Anything good here?' he asked.

The clerk grinned. "Starling's been seen all over the place," he said. "And sometimes in two places at once. Take your pick, there's plenty to do."

Martineau's glance followed his finger down the pages. The name 'Mrs. Lusk' caught his eye. He read the item which concerned her. Some woman peeping through a window alleged that she had seen Don Starling walk to Mrs. Lusk's door and try it, and hurry away. Apparently he did not knock, he just tried the door. That was early on Saturday evening. Lucky Lusk would be working behind the bar at the Lacy Arms at that time.

'So what was the idea?' Martineau pondered. 'One would expect the door to be locked.'

No police officer had put his initials in the margin beside the item. Martineau wrote: *Attention H.M. D.Insp.* and said: "I'll have a word with the lady."

He looked at his watch. It was too early for Lucky to have gone to work, and he thought he might find her at home. Devery was out on an inquiry. All the men were busy. He decided to go alone.

He stopped the police car at Lucky's door. When he knocked, she appeared at a bedroom window. She was wearing a bright silk dressing-gown, and she had a comb in her hand.

She opened the window. "Hallo," she said. "Wait a minute, I'll come down."

She was still wearing the dressing-gown when she admitted him. "You've come too late," she said as he followed her into the house. "Ten minutes sooner, and you'd have caught me in the bath. Woohoo! What a thrill!"

He was admiring the rear view of her, and the way she walked. "A thrill? For whom?" he asked, for the sake of saying something.

"For me, sonny boy. And for you, if you're human. I'm worth seeing, let me tell you."

"Now you're making me sorry I was late."

They were in the living-room. She turned and faced him. "No!" she said, wide-eyed in mock wonderment. "I don't believe it! You *are* human!"

She was vitally attractive: full of life. The dressing-gown, which was rather long and full, suggested intimacy and vulnerable femininity. Martineau was stirred by a quite strong feeling of concupiscence. It was years since he had lusted after a woman other than Julia; and a long time since he had wanted Julia.

Well, there was nothing to be done about it. "I came to ask you a few questions," he said.

"Oh-h-h-h!" she exclaimed in disgust, and flopped into an armchair. He sat down facing her, and gave her a cigarette. The thought of her was still worrying him a little, and the way she was sitting did not help him to concentrate on his work.

"I came in a police car," he said. "We can't use those for errands of private amusement."

Her eyes twinkled mischievously. "Why not?" she queried. "That makes it official. If you come sneaking around with your hat over your eyes the neighbours'll *know* you're up to no good."

He grinned at her. Lucky was a good woman—so far as he knew—but her sporty brand of humour would get her into trouble some day. "Give over," he said. "You'd be frightened to death if I made a pass at you."

"Try it and see," she challenged, but she was still sprawling quite unguarded in the chair, smoking her cigarette.

He was tempted, but he laughed, thinking of her sudden alarm if he took her at her word.

"Business first," he said. "I thought Don Starling and all his friends were on your list of things which mustn't be mentioned at mealtimes."

She sat up. "Don Starling! What about him?"

"Have you seen him during the last few days?"

"No," she said.

He thought he had detected a slight hesitation before the answer. "Are you sure?" he persisted.

"I haven't set eyes on him," she replied deliberately.

He frowned, watching her keenly. "Can you think of any reason why he would want to see you?" he asked.

She appeared to meditate. "No," she said. "I can't. I'm not the sort of person he'd come to for money, or—or for anything else. We were barely on nodding terms when he was

110

sent to prison. I don't have anything to do with such as him."

"He might come to you for shelter."

"I shouldn't think so. Well, he hasn't asked for shelter, anyway. I haven't seen him."

Martineau was not satisfied. There was something missing. If she had had no contact of any sort with Starling, why hadn't she demanded, indignantly, the reason why she of all people should be questioned about him?

"You did know him quite well at one time, didn't you?" he probed.

"Yes. But that was years ago, before I met Chris, Chris Lusk. I thought he was a bit wild, but when I found out what he really was I dropped him like a hot cinder."

"Still, he might come to you for shelter. He was seen hanging around here. He tried your door."

"He—he tried my door?" She was obviously terrified. She put a hand to her face, as if to protect it. "When? When was that?"

"Early on Saturday night."

"Oh," she sighed, curiously relieved. Then she was assailed by a new fear. "Do you think he might come here again?" And before he could answer she said: "Oh no, he won't come again."

"What makes you think he won't dare?"

"Well, I—I don't think he'd dare."

"You don't? He's pretty daring, you know. Do you keep your doors locked all the time? When you're at home, I mean."

"No, of course I don't," she said, and then she was on her feet, staring at Martineau. Her face was chalk-white. "He might be in there now," was her panic-stricken whisper. "He might be listening to us. He might have crept in while I was upstairs."

"No, now, take it easy," said Martineau. "Of course he isn't here." But he could not prevent himself from taking a speculative look at the pantry door.

Luck came to him, as if for protection. She seized his arm. "I'm safe while you're here," she said. She shuddered at an intolerable thought. "Don't go till you make sure he isn't here. Lock the doors and search everywhere." She stooped quickly to the hearth. "Here, take the poker."

He looked at her curiously. "Has Starling been threatening you?" he wanted to know.

"Yes—no. Go on, make sure he isn't here."

Her terror was very real. He locked the doors and searched the house. Lucky, tensely holding the poker, was at his elbow wherever he went.

The house was small, and it was tidy. It did not take long to make sure that no man was hiding there.

"Now then," said Martineau. "Put that poker down, and tell me about Starling."

"I daren't tell you," she said.

"Because he threatened you?"

"He said he'd carve me up."

"Well, never mind. I'll see that he doesn't. Why did he threaten you?"

"If I told you, it wouldn't help you one little bit."

"Let me be the judge of that."

"I daren't," she said, and ran to him. Her distress was undoubtedly genuine. "You don't know what it is," she said, with her head against his shoulder, "to have no man of your own to protect you from people like Don Starling. You *have* to pretend to be bold and tough, just to keep your end up." And then, though she was weeping, she said with a kind of anger: "I *never* had a man who was any bloody good."

He raised her chin and smiled down at her. "Now Lucky," he chided gently. "Don't be such a softy. There's nothing to be afraid of. I won't let Starling get near you. Why don't you trust me, and tell me all about it?"

She told him about Saturday night's phone call from Starling.

"You were right," he said, when the little tale was ended. "It doesn't help much. But thanks all the same. Nobody will ever know you've told me."

"What will you do now?" she asked.

"I'll put some men out," he said. "Starling has no reason to hurt you, but they'll serve the double purpose of protecting you and picking up Starling if he shows his face around this district. You haven't a thing to worry about."

She was still close to him, and he was holding her gently, with one arm around her. Suddenly she hugged him hungrily, pressing close to him. That was too much for him. He put both arms around her, and became aware of her nearly-naked torso beneath the dressing-gown. She smelled sweet and clean.

She was on her toes. "Ooh, you!" she said, and put her arms around his neck. She pulled his head down and kissed him fiercely. "You!" she said again. He kissed her, quite literally sweeping her from her feet; and then over his shoulder she saw the time by the clock on the fireplace.

She broke away from him. "That'll do, for a start," she said. Her self-possession quickly restored his, but he may have looked disappointed. Smiling, she reached up and touched his face. "Call it a promise, darling," she said. "Just now there isn't time. I've got to go to work."

He left her then, with a reminder that he would post some men to lie in wait for Don Starling. He thought it quite possible that the hunted man, with no place to go, might call at Lucky's house again. By intimidation he had forced her to help him once, and he would expect to be able to do so a second time.

Then, deep in thought, Martineau drove slowly back to Headquarters. 'I'd better take Devery the next time I go to see Lucky,' he decided. It was obvious that she expected him to call again, and without Devery.

He pondered, with some inward excitement, about Lucky. Would he go to see her again, without Devery? It was a delicious temptation. She was certainly attractive. Quite lovely, really. And she was a good girl. Or at least, she wasn't a bad one. She had been unfortunate: she had never had a man who was any good. She had been a good wife to the wastrel who married her. Fortunately she hadn't had any children by him. What sort of a mother would she have made?

IX

At Headquarters, Martineau heard some interesting news. A man with green fingers had been brought in for interrogation. And the man was Doug Savage, unofficial landlord of the Prodigal Son Inn.

113

At that moment, Martineau was informed, Savage was being put to the question by Superintendent Clay. The interview was taking place in a bleak, windowless, nearly sound-proof room at the far end of the C.I.D. office. The room went by various names, the most common of which were the Torture Chamber, the Sweating Room, and the Bank Manager's Office. But any torture practised there was purely psychological. The aspect of the room itself was a help to detectives. Suspects had a feeling that they were shut off from the free world, in a place where anything could happen.

Martineau said: "Doug Savage with stained hands?" and frowned. He had talked briefly with Savage a few hours after the crime, and at that time his hands had been quite clean. Moreover, he had an alibi.

"I'd better go along there," he said, and as he went he reflected that some of the dusted money might have been passed to Savage over the bar in his pub, simply to pay for drinks.

He entered the interrogation room. It had a bare concrete floor, white-tiled walls and an off-white ceiling, because it was really an uncompleted washroom. The only articles of furniture were a table and four chairs in the centre of the floor, and a small desk and a chair for a shorthand writer in one corner. Clay and Doug Savage were seated facing each other across the table. A burly detective stood behind the equally burly innkeeper, another detective stood beside the door, and a clerk sat at the desk.

Clay looked up when Martineau entered. It was a surly, irritable glance. Evidently the interview was not going well. Savage looked surly too, and wary; but not yet nervous. He was no stranger to the interrogation room.

"Hallo, Inspector," said Clay, and he rose. "Come outside a minute."

Outside the room, Clay said: "I've got to see the Chief now, so I'll turn Savage over to you. All we've got on him are his green fingers, and he won't admit a thing. Won't say a word except 'Why have I been arrested?' "

"Have you drawn his attention to his green fingers?"

"No," said the superintendent. "I never mentioned his fingers. You please yourself. I'm off now. He's all yours."

Martineau returned to the room and sat in Clay's chair. For some time he sat in silence, considering Savage, looking him up and down. The innkeeper was a big young man. He was quite handsome in a swarthy, bull-necked way. But in spite of his dark skin he always looked very clean and well turned out. This morning he was dressy—elegant with an ineradicable touch of vulgarity—in a well-pressed gabardine suit, a nylon shirt and a bright silk tie, for he had been picked up while doing some shopping in Castle Street.

"Have a cigarette, Doug," said Martineau at last.

"Thanks," said Doug, taking a Players from the proffered packet. "So you're going to try the soft stuff?"

"Call it that if you like," Martineau rejoined. "I'm going to give you the chance to show you've got some sense." He was looking at the other man's hand as he lit the cigarette for him. The green dye on his fingers was in faint small blotches and streaks. Considering that in all probability there would now be much less of the dry powder on the stolen money, it looked as if Doug had handled more than one or two of the stolen notes, though he may not have handled a great many. It looked as if he had been in contact with someone who had had quite a lot of the money. Within the last thirty-six hours he had met and probably spoken to one of the murderers of Cicely Wainwright.

"All right, get cracking," Doug challenged. "I've been here too long already."

Martineau mentally reviewed Doug's record. It was a record of violence and dishonesty, but not a record in which those two criminal characteristics ever appeared together. Doug's offences were disorderly conduct, assault on police, obstruction of police and malicious wounding on the one side, and many cases of fraud on the other: fraud connected with black market, with racing and football, with the money and property of the various people who had been unwise enough to enter into trade with him. He was an incorrigible 'twister', as untrustworthy as a starving mongrel. It was fortunate for him that his mother's inn was a free house, so that he could not defraud any brewer who had the power to throw him out. And his mother knew him too well to let him take more than small amounts from her.

115

But he was not a thief in the exact meaning of the word: he did not commit larceny. And he was never violent in cold blood, for the sake of gain. As a criminal, Doug had little in common with a man like Don Starling. The two disliked each other.

Martineau thought: 'Doug is innocent, and he feels very virtuous and indignant. It makes a nice change'.

He said: "I saw you on Saturday, and you told me you'd seen nothing of the crime which happened right outside your pub. You said you knew nothing about it."

Doug nodded. "That's correct."

"But now we have some evidence which implicates you."

"So I'm told. You'd better show me this evidence."

"We're not going to show you. Not yet, anyway. But the evidence is there."

"Nay, Inspector! I thought you'd have more sense. You expect *me* to believe a tale like that?"

"For your own good you'll believe it."

"The well-known phrase! When the hell did a copper ever worry about what was good for anybody but himself?"

Martineau grinned. "Not often," he said. "And I'm not worrying now. You're the one who needs to worry."

"You once told me that an innocent man never needs to worry."

The remark made Martineau pause. "A shrewd thrust, Doug," he said. He wondered how on earth he was going to get information from this man, this intelligent man, who had been taught from boyhood that he must never tell the police *anything*. There was only one way: convince him if possible of the honesty of police intentions, and then put the fear of God into him.

"An innocent man doesn't need to worry," he said, "if he's prepared to maintain his innocence by giving a full account of his actions."

"Ah, you mean you want me to open my mouth and put my foot in it. Having no evidence against me, you want me to give you some."

"How can you, if you're as innocent as you say?"

"I don't know. I'm not taking any chances."

116

"Listen, Doug," said Martineau. "How long have you known me?"

"Too long."

"Have I ever tried to fix you for something you didn't do?"

"You've walloped me a time or two," replied Doug reminiscently, and with a certain amount of respect.

"I've walloped you when you were being a rough boy. I've never laid hands on you to make you admit anything."

"I dare say that's true," was the reluctant answer.

"I repeat, have I ever falsely accused you?"

"No, I can't say as you have."

"Have I at any time exaggerated the evidence against you?"

"No."

"Well, I'm not exaggerating it now. We have evidence. You have an alibi, but there is such a thing as accessory after the fact."

"If there's evidence, you planted it."

Martineau shook his head. "You know perfectly well I don't go in for planting. Besides, this is something the police couldn't have planted. But you're on the right track. Intentionally or otherwise, someone has implicated you. They've dragged you in. But if you're innocent you can soon get yourself out."

"By talking?"

"By answering my questions."

"Ask your questions, and we'll see whether I'll answer."

"All right. We'll summarize your first statement. All Saturday morning you were in the Prodigal Son, getting ready to open. Then you had a bath and a shave, and your dinner; then you helped in the bar until some friends called with a taxi, and you went to Doncaster with them. You have witnesses, and all that has been verified. By the way, what sort of a taxi was it?"

"A Silverline. Your man verified that, too."

"Do you usually have a Silverline when you go to the races?"

"No. We usually have Laurie Lovett, but he let us down. He said he was booked up."

Martineau nodded, and made a note of the name, though he attached no significance to it.

"When you got back from the St. Leger," he continued, "you had your tea and then worked in the bar until closing time. Then you had your supper, read the *Sports Final*, and went to bed."

"You never said a truer word."

"Right. Now I'll tell you something. While you were in the bar I dropped in to see you——"

"Just when I was busy."

"——and while I was talking to you I noticed that the evidence which implicates you wasn't there. Get that clear, Doug. It was between that interview, and this morning, that you were drawn into the job. So now we get down to cases."

Doug began to show interest, and some uneasiness. "Do you mean to say there's some evidence in the pub?" he demanded. "Did you plant it while you were there?"

"The pub is being searched at this moment," said Martineau, "but the evidence I am referring to is not there. And, wherever it is, I couldn't have planted it. I can prove it. I came into your place and touched nothing and nobody, and I didn't have a drink."

Doug was bewildered. "I wish you'd tell me what this damned evidence is," he protested.

Martineau would have liked to say that it was the Mark of Cain, but he refrained. "I can't tell you yet," he said. "But the sooner I get my men, the sooner you'll know what the evidence is and who shopped you, if you were shopped. Let's move on to Sunday. Sunday morning?"

"Cleaning up. Putting a couple of barrels on. I never went out."

"Any visitors before opening time?"

"Only the cleaning woman."

"Were you in the pub for the full opening hours yesterday?"

"Yes. The whole time."

"Sunday is your long afternoon off, isn't it? You went out between two o'clock and seven, I suppose?"

Doug hesitated, and Martineau smiled. He saw the pattern clearly. The races, the tossing school. It was at the tossing school that the innkeeper had handled marked money. He could not have taken enough of it over his bar.

Martineau's pressure was very gentle. "If you went to a gaming school," he said, "it's no great concern of mine. I don't even want to know where the school was. It'd be in the County area, anyway."

"All right," said Doug. "I don't see as there's any harm in admitting I was at the tossing school. But it's a good job you don't want to know where it was, because I wouldn't tell you."

"We won't quarrel about that," said the inspector, "so long as you tell me the names of the men who were there."

"I'm not giving you any names at all."

Martineau did not immediately pursue the issue. "The place you went to was an alternative site to the one near the Moorcock?" he suggested.

"Yes, the Moorcock was off. But why are you asking me, if you know it all?"

"Confirmation, just confirmation. But I'm not interested in gambling, or a bit of illegal booking, or the extraction of loose cash from a mug. I'm talking about the brutal murder of a young girl who never did a bit of harm to anybody. You don't hold with that, do you?"

"Too right I don't."

"Well, it's the murderers I'm after. It was at the tossing school yesterday, or in your own pub, that somebody involved you in this murder. It was done quite unknown to yourself. You don't owe that person any protection, as I see it."

"You're damn right I don't. If you're telling the truth."

"I'm telling the truth. You were a winner at the school, weren't you? Or a winner for a time, at any rate?"

"Yes. How the devil do you know that?"

"Just a guess. I don't want to know how much you won, I just want the names of the men who were there."

"And I'm not telling you."

"Did you notice anybody who was abnormally flush with money?"

It was an old and very common police question. Doug shook his head. "I didn't notice anything."

Martineau was patient. "As I keep telling you, this is a murder job, not a gambling case. And in a murder job, personal considerations are not allowed to obstruct the investigation. If you won't help me, I shall set about the job in another way. I shall start at the Prodigal Son. Every customer will be questioned."

"It's blackmail."

"It is not. It's something that's got to be done."

"You'll get me a bad name. You'll frighten all my trade away."

"That's your worry. What's up with you, man? You know what I'm after. Murderers! Look, if you happen to give me the right names, it'll do you a bit of good with the Chief. He might be inclined to overlook the next licensing offence, if ever there is one."

"I'm glad you said the last bit. I run my pub right."

"I don't care how you run it. How did you get out to the gaming school?"

"I went in a car, with Les Norrish."

Even the name of Les Norrish was a starting point from which to work. Martineau was pleased. He said: "Les Norrish from the Black Bull? Right. Who else was in the car?"

"Nobody else."

"Who did you see at the school?"

Doug began to mention names. Martineau reflected that he would probably withhold a few, but that did not matter. By questioning the men whose names he had given, the police would get all the others.

"That's about all I can remember," he said, after some final pondering.

Martineau nodded. "Now give me the names of the people who were in the Prodigal Son on Saturday night and Sunday," he said.

Doug exploded. "I knew it was a damned trick!" he bawled, red with indignation.

Martineau stared him down. "It wasn't a trick at all," he said. "I shan't come near your place. But I must have some names to round off the inquiry. If it's necessary to interview 'em, we won't do it in your pub, and they won't know who's given their names."

Somewhat reassured, Doug began to give more names. Soon he became interested in the number of people he could remember. He gave over fifty names. "And that's not to mention the casuals I never saw before," he concluded with pride.

Martineau went to the head of the gaming school list again. "This Sam Jackson, where does he live?" he asked.

"Out Boyton way, somewhere."

"What's his job, if any?"

"I have no idea."

Martineau nodded, and asked for a general description, not forgetting physical oddities or abnormalities. He went on down the list, underlining the names of men he knew, and men of whom he had heard. They were the ones he would seek out first.

At the end, he had eighteen names underlined. Among them were Laurie Lovett, Lolly Jakes, and Clogger Roach. Roach was more or less a stranger in town, but he had spent his time in the area where the telephone numbers were indexed CENtral, and Martineau had heard his name.

X

Laurie Lovett's taxi garage was a wooden structure in a cindered yard behind a lemonade brewery. Outside, there was a small petrol pump. Inside, there was room for five or six cars, and a tiny office with a telephone. The doors were wide open, and a car was standing half-in, half-out of the doorway.

The car was a middle-aged blue Austin with a taximeter in the usual place near the edge of the windscreen. The bonnet was raised, and Laurie Lovett, in shirt sleeves, was stooping over the engine. When the police car stopped behind him he turned his hard, thin face to see who had arrived. Then he went on with his work.

Martineau and Devery got out of the police car and went over to him. Without speaking, they watched him work for a little while. His hands and his muscular forearms were quite covered with black grease.

Lovett was the first to speak. He stood erect and began

121

to wipe his hands with cotton waste. "What's up now?" he asked in an unfriendly tone.

"One or two things," said Martineau. "I'm looking for Don Starling, and I'm also looking for his mates in last Saturday's little job."

"I know what you mean. The murder. Why come to me?"

"You're a taxi man. You get around."

"Plenty of other taxi drivers too. They get around an' all."

"That is so. But your name gets mentioned."

"Ah. Who mentions it?"

"Your friends. One friend in particular. You've done business with him. You should know who I mean."

"How the hell *do* I know?" Lovett demanded. He had been busy with his hands, seemingly intent on wiping off the thick oil, but now he looked up, and his eyes met Martineau's bleak grey glance. The inspector did not like him; did not like the look of him at all. Why had he selected this man to be one of the first on Doug Savage's list? He remembered now. Lovett had been unable to take Savage's party to the races at Doncaster. He had had another engagement. With whom?

Before the question could be asked, another taxi came into the yard. It was driven by a young man of twenty or twenty-one. Martineau recognized him as the young driver who had been in the Moorcock Inn at noontime on Sunday.

The young man's glance shifted quickly from Martineau's, and he called out: "Owt come in, Laurie?"

"No," said Laurie. "Off you go down to the rank."

"Right," said the youth, but Martineau called sharply: "Just a minute! I want you."

"Who're you?" was the truculent demand.

"You know well enough who I am. Come here!"

For a moment it seemed that the youth would disobey, and Devery made a move towards the police Jaguar. That settled the matter. The newcomer got out of his taxi.

He lit a cigarette as he walked across to the group of men, and both the policemen looked hard at his opened right hand as he threw the match away. The hand was dirty; the grime on the balls of the fingers *might* have had a faint greenish tinge, but there could be no certainty about it.

It was Devery who spoke first.

"Passing Clouds," he said in a slightly mocking tone.

The remark drew everyone's eyes to the cigarette. It had a distinctive oval shape. The young driver flushed and glanced at Laurie Lovett. Then he said to Devery: "What about it? What's it got to do with you what I smoke?"

No further reference was made to the cigarette. But the thought was in Martineau's mind: 'A young fellow who might be expected to smoke Woodbines at two-and-eight for twenty was smoking Passing Clouds at a price somewhere in the vicinity of four shillings. Increased earnings would be unlikely to make a young taxi driver go for that type of cigarette, but sudden unaccustomed money might.

"Is this your young brother?" he asked of Lovett. "He looks a bit like you."

"He's my brother."

"What's his name?"

"Gordon."

Acting on an impulse, Martineau addressed the youth. "All right, Gordon. I want you to come to the police station with me. Im going to ask you one or two questions."

"About what?" Laurie snapped.

"About what he was doing on Saturday, for a start."

Gordon's face was red. "I've done nowt," he cried. "You can't pull me in when I've done nowt."

"Suspicion, Gordon, suspicion. We can arrest without warrant on reasonable suspicion that a felony has been committed. Just weigh that up."

Gordon did not pause to weigh it up. "What felony?" he demanded in a high voice.

"Murder."

"Bloody rubbish!" Laurie interjected. "You can't accuse that lad of murder. And you don't take him in without me."

"All right," said Martineau agreeably. "You come along as well. We'll wait till you've washed your hands."

Laurie glared at him, then he strode into the garage. Devery followed him casually; hands in pockets, staring around.

"You got a search warrant for this place?" the taxi proprietor demanded curtly, as he cleansed his hands.

123

Devery grinned. "Not yet," he said.

"Then get out!" Laurie snarled. "This is private property."

"All right," said Devery. He drifted a few paces towards the door, still keeping Laurie in view.

" 'Get out', I said!"

"Sure." Devery moved one pace.

Glowering, Laurie dried his hands. Perhaps he also did some hard thinking. He strode past Devery and said to Martineau: "I've changed my mind. I'm not coming with you. I'm too busy. I'll have to take on my brother's jobs."

"And I've changed mine," said the inspector. "You're the one I'm taking in." For Devery had taken his hands from his pockets. He was holding them up, and tapping the fingers of one hand with the forefinger of the other.

"You're taking *me* in!" Laurie exclaimed. Then he asked: "You're letting the kid go?"

"No. I'm taking him too. He can keep you company."

Laurie looked as if he were going to fly at Martineau. But the inspector had a reputation. Men who flew at him usually regretted the action. The taxi man had to content himself with a bitter protest. "It's a lousy deal," he said. "You coppers don't seem to realize that a man has his living to make. Who's going to repay me and the kid for our lost time?"

"Write to your Member of Parliament about it," said Martineau. "Come on, get into this car!"

"Just a minute. I'll have to lock up the garage."

"I'll send some men to lock it up," the inspector replied.

"Yes. They'll have a search warrant too," Devery added. He did not like being rudely told to get out of places.

XI

At Headquarters Martineau left the two brothers in separate rooms, under guard. As they were parted, Laurie said: "Tell 'em nothing, kid," and Gordon nodded, but he looked so nervously preoccupied that the message did not seem to register in his brain. His wild absent look told the experienced C.I.D. men that his thoughts were scurrying around in his head like rats in a cage. And rats are not conspicuously bothered by fellow feeling. They seek a way out for one, leaving others to follow if they can.

There was a message for Martineau. Inspector Vanbrugh had been trying to reach him on the phone. He remembered how helpful Vanbrugh had been, and he called him up at once.

The County man sounded impatient. "What's going on?" he demanded. "I hear you've made an arrest."

"We've picked up two brothers called Lovett," said Martineau cautiously, "but there's no charge yet."

"Do they keep a pub? I thought it was somebody who kept a pub."

"Oh, him!" said Martineau. He told Vanbrugh about the list of names he had obtained from Doug Savage. "The whole thing started with the theft of a bookmaker's money," he concluded. "The horse-racing angle has been there all the time, and gaming school types are usually interested in racing."

The explanation was unnecessary. Vanbrugh had been fully aware of the sporting aspects of the case. Nevertheless, he listened without comment. He seemed to be very thoughtful when he rang off, and he did not ask for any of the names which Savage had given.

Martineau sent a search crew, with a warrant, to the house where Gordon Lovett lived with Mr. and Mrs. Laurie Lovett. Himself and Devery, with another warrant, returned to the taxi garage. They searched the place thoroughly, and the last thing they examined was a dusty, battered old spare taxi which looked as if it were waiting to be dragged away by a wrecker.

They found nothing in the body of the car, but Devery was not satisfied to leave it. He had been puzzling over the significance of four pistons which he had fished out of a pail of dirty paraffin. He tried to start the car, and found that it had no battery. Then he tried turning over the engine with a starting handle.

"This thing's like a hurdy-gurdy," he said. "There isn't a ha'porth of compression. I think they've taken the pistons out."

125

Martineau looked at him thoughtfully. "We'd better have a look," he said.

The cylinder head block was not screwed down very tightly. They removed it, and found that the four cylinders were stuffed with wads of greaseproof paper. Each wad contained a thick roll of paper money: many one-pound notes and a number of fivers.

"The bees an' honey," said Devery coolly, concealing his elation.

"You're a good boy," replied Martineau, not to be outdone in imperturbability. "Handle it carefully. Fingerprints, you know. You've heard of fingerprints."

"Malachite green too," said the younger man. "There should still be traces of it. *And* we have the numbers of the dusted notes."

XII

Back at Headquarters, the rolls of money were placed on the table in the interrogation room. Then Martineau sent for the younger Lovett. He had been too long a policeman to be sentimental about the fraternal feelings of thieves and murderers, and he had no qualms about using the evidence of one brother to hang the other, if the other were guilty.

When Gordon was brought to the room, with a certain amount of grim ceremony, he looked as if the short period of waiting in custody had not been good for him. His face was pale and his eyes were dark. He was jumpy and apprehensive.

"Sit down," said Martineau, indicating the chair which faced him. "Nobody's going to hurt you—yet."

Gordon sat, and tried not to look at the money on the table.

"We found it," said Martineau. "Your hiding-place wasn't good enough."

"I don't know what you're talking about," the young man replied, now looking at the money in preference to looking at the inspector.

"I think you do. It's a quarter share of the money that was taken from a poor murdered girl. But before you tell me all about it, I must warn you that anything you say will be taken down in writing and may be given in evidence."

Gordon apparently took the caution to heart. He **said** nothing.

Martineau reflected, not for the first time, that the caution was needless hindrance to an investigating officer. "Search him," he said.

The search revealed nothing which seemed to be important. There was a wallet which contained a few posed photographs of girls, a driver's licence, and seven one-pound notes. Martineau extracted the notes and put them to one side, then he picked up a small diary. He glanced through it. There were many pencilled addresses, notes of calls which Gordon had made with his taxi. The writing was sprawling and childish, with much mis-spelling. The lad was practically illiterate.

"Your engagement book," said Martineau, then he frowned. There were a few ruled pages optimistically headed 'Bank Balance'. The pages contained one entry, with yesterday's—*Sunday's*—date against it. The entry was: '£10-0-0.'

"So you got your first payment yesterday," he commented. "You were to get yours ten pounds at a time, so that you wouldn't flash too much money all at once."

Gordon stared at the table. He seemed to be numb with despair.

Martineau snapped a question: "Who were the others, besides Laurie and Don Starling?"

"I don't know what you're talking about," Gordon mumbled.

The inspector did not seem to be disappointed. He looked at his watch. "All right," he said. "Take him back and let him think it over. I'm hungry, and I'm going to be home in time for my tea for once. There's no great hurry now." He turned to a waiting detective. "Ducklin, keep your eye on this stuff till I get back. Come on, Devery. You can run me home and then go and get a meal. We'll clear this job to-night."

XIII

After tea, when Martineau returned to Headquarters, he was told that Inspector Vanbrugh wanted to speak to him on the telephone.

"What again?" he said. "All right, get him for me."

Vanbrugh seemed to be remarkably cheery when he came on the line. "Hallo, Martineau!" he bawled. "Any more progress?"

"A little. With the Lovett brothers."

"Have you got 'em right?"

"It's just possible. Laurie Lovett has green fingers. Also, we recovered the best part of a thousand quid, hidden in his garage."

"Ha ha! You thought you'd shake me with that bit of news, did you? Well, I also have been trying to make a name for myself. I've been awful busy."

"Doing what?"

"I staged a raid. On a tossing school."

"On a Monday? I thought they only operated at week-ends."

"The big rings, yes. But on Monday afternoons there's a smaller one. The mugs have all gone back to work and this is for the *élite*: those who have had a big win on Sunday, and the ponces and layabouts and half-inch bookies who want to take their winnings off 'em. When you mentioned all those names you'd got, I thought I might as well interview some of 'em myself."

"Did you know the meeting place?"

"I found out. The taxis are the give-away. Our motor patrols had 'em spotted. The school was at a place called Chatty Clough, which is at the bottom of Chatty Hill. Not far from Stacksfield."

"I'm no wiser."

"Of course not. You city denizens ought to learn more about the land we live in."

"Get on with your tale. What did you do?"

"I got our Super on the job. He let me have all the men he could gather. Forty-two, with eight cars and two vans. We went out there and surrounded the place, and closed in."

"Was the raid successful?"

Vanbrugh chuckled. "I'll say it was. And the best bit of fun I've had in years. There was a crow on the top of the hill, and he had us spotted in no time. He went hareing down the hill, waving his arms and shouting—he fell twice—and when he got to the ring you'd ha' thought he was carrying a time bomb. What a scatter! Fellows fled in all directions. Fat 'uns, thin 'uns, bow-legged 'uns and pasty-footed 'uns. They did look funny; I couldn't run for laughing. One bloke tried to climb a precipice that Hillary and Tensing would have baulked at. Another sprinted straight into a bog, and we pulled him out as black as the ace of spades. Yes, it was a good raid."

"How many did you collar?"

"We got the lot, thirty-one in all. A very small school. We had a good look at 'em, and took their names and addresses, and let 'em go. All except one."

"Ah, you got something?"

"Yes sir. It was the guy who tried to make the alpine getaway. He had about two hundred pounds in his pockets—we're searching his house for the rest—and his hands were as green as lettuce. His name is Lawrence Jakes."

"Congratulations," said Martineau. "Lolly Jakes, eh? Can we have him?"

"Not without a written order from the bosses. We don't know yet if it's our murder or yours. But you can talk to him as much as you like. He won't sing for *me* yet."

"They'll all sing before we've done. Cheerio."

"Cheerio, old boy. You ought to try a little canter over the heather some time. The fresh air 'ud do you good."

"Oh, give over," said Martineau, putting down the telephone.

He went to the interrogation room, and asked for Laurie Lovett to be brought in. He waited leaning against the table, so that his body concealed the four wads of notes from anyone who was near the door.

When Laurie entered, his glinting eyes swept hungrily from corner to corner. "Where's my brother?" he rasped.

"Don't worry about him, he's all right," Martineau replied. "He's sitting down to think about what he's going to say next."

"You're daft. The kid can't tell you anything. He knows nowt—nor me neither."

"Well, if he knows nothing, he must have had a middling shrewd suspicion. We've already got Lolly Jakes."

Laurie's watchful eyes did not even flicker. "Who's Lolly Jakes, when he's at home?"

Martineau moved away from the table, and let Laurie see the wads of money which he had so recently regarded as his own. The prisoner looked at them for a moment, then returned his hard gaze to Martineau. Apart from that swift glance, not a muscle of his face moved.

"Sit down," said the inspector, himself taking a chair. And when Laurie faced him across the table he suddenly smiled, and offered a cigarette.

"Don't think I'm softening you," he said, when they were both smoking. "I don't think I need your statement. Statements by accused persons are sometimes a nuisance at a trial, and I believe I've got you right, without any words from you. I'll tell you now, I'm going to prove that you were the driver of that Buick car; the murder car."

Laurie blew smoke at him.

Martineau reached across the table and deftly took the cigarette from Laurie's fingers, and threw it into a corner of the room. Then he went on calmly: "You made a good job of wiping off the Buick when you dumped it in the quarry, but you forgot one thing." He paused to take a pull at his own cigarette, and said: "The driving mirror, you know. A very common omission. When you pinched the car you adjusted the mirror to your own height, and then forgot about it. You left a lovely thumb print on it. At least, I'm betting it's your print, when we come to make a comparison. Yours, or your brother's."

Laurie remained silent.

"We've got that, and this money which you hid so artfully, and your green fingers. . . ."

Laurie did not look at his fingers.

". . . I expect you've been wondering what that green stuff is. It's a dye. You got it from the stolen money, and from nowhere else. It's on your fingers, and Lolly Jakes', and Don Starling's, and it's on the fingers of that poor murdered girl. Green evidence. I'm hoping we shall find some of it on Gordon's hands when he washes the dirt off, but he hasn't handled as much of the money as you have. He's only had his ten-pound allowance."

"You've got nothing against the kid. Nothing."

"He seems to think we have. He's in a blue funk. And it all fits so nicely. There were four men in the Buick. You want four men, we've got em. Starling, Jakes, you and your brother."

"Nothing of the kind. I'm admitting nothing, but I can tell you this: you'll make a fool of yourself over our Gordon. He's innocent. Absolutely innocent."

"Then who was the fourth man?"

"How—how do I know?"

"You mean, how can you tell me without implicitly admitting that you were there? We *know* you were there, man. And if there was another man instead of your brother, I want to be knowing him too, before he hears of these arrests and clears off."

"You'll get nothing from me," said Laurie.

Martineau rose from his chair and paced about. He made an almost imperceptible signal to the clerk at the little desk, then he turned to Lovett.

"Listen," he stormed, throwing down his cigarette, "I want four men and I'm going to have 'em. If I don't get a fourth man, I'll have Gordon. And don't think I won't get him. It's my guess that all he did was to pick you up near the Moorcock and bring you back to town, after you'd driven your taxi out there and left it. But it's a guess I can easily forget. Gordon has guilty knowledge, he's in possession of some of the stolen money, and he's your brother. And you're in it up to the neck. He'll do for him."

For the first time, Laurie's face showed a faint trace of humour. "You can't kid me, Inspector," he said. "I've heard of you. If that's all you think my brother did, you'll not blacken the evidence against him. You're just trying to make me think you will."

Martineau stopped pacing. He glared. "Now who's softening who?" he wanted to know. He put a cigarette in his mouth and threw one to the prisoner, and sat down again. For a while he did not speak.

Then he said quietly: "I'm offering no inducements. But with a good counsel Gordon might get off scot-free. It all depends on how much grilling he gets while he's in our midst. All he did was to pick up his brother at the Moorcock. What is the name of the fourth man?"

"Clogger Roach."

"Thanks. And the finger?"

"Peter Purchas."

"That's the lot?"

"Yes."

"Now, would you like to make a statement?"

"No. You've got all you're going to get from me. And I'm admitting nothing."

"Fair enough," said Martineau. "Now you can go and sit down quietly while you try to remember the name of a good lawyer. You're certainly going to need one."

XIV

Strangely enough, of the five men arrested, the only one to retain some honour among thieves was young Gordon Lovett. Somehow, while he waited in the charge of a silent detective, he gathered enough resolution to face Martineau and remain defiantly unhelpful.

"I'm saying nowt," he said, "because I know nowt."

"You haven't any sort of alibi," Martineau reminded him. "You won't tell me what you were doing on Saturday morning."

"I can't tell you. I don't remember."

"You keep a record of journeys, don't you?"

"Aye, but I'm a bit behindhand. I haven't made out Saturday's sheet yet."

"Are you going to make it out?"

"I don't know, now. I'd have had to make something up, anyway, 'cause I've forgot what jobs I did."

"I'll refresh your memory, Gordon. You went out to the Moorcock and picked up your brother somewhere around there, and brought him to town."

"No I didn't. I never went near the Moorcock."

"Then where did you go?"

"I've forgot, but I never went near the Moorcock."

Martineau was not deeply concerned about that denial. Having laid hands on four out of five older men, he could afford to let this boy escape him. But he persisted a little while longer. He had to make a show of interrogating Gordon: a few pages of questions and answers for the eyes of Higher Authority.

"Laurie employs you," he said. "What wages does he pay you?"

"That's none o' your business."

"He gave you ten pounds yesterday. That was wages; the wages of sin."

"No it wasn't. Laurie didn't give me that money. I *had* ten pounds yesterday, what I'd saved up."

Martineau reflected that Gordon was fortunate. The money from his wallet had been examined, and the numbers of the notes did not correspond with any of the numbers received from the Hallam police. He had not received even one dusted note, and his hands were not stained.

"You say you'd saved ten pounds, but this morning you had less than eight. That's not saving, is it? Did you spend two pounds on a Sunday night?"

"No, I spent a pound. I—I lent a pound to a girl."

"Who was the girl?"

"I'm not saying. She has a husband. He wouldn't like it."

"I guess he wouldn't," said Martineau. "I suppose she repaid you, not in money but in kindness. You're young to be starting on that game, Gordon."

Gordon had the grace to look ashamed. He avoided the inspector's glance.

He wouldn't stand comparison with a sound, honest lad, Martineau thought, but he wasn't really a bad kid. But, good or bad, there was evidence against him. And if he remained consistent in his denials, there would be none. The police had failed to find a witness who had seen either him or Laurie travelling between Granchester and the Moorcock on Saturday morning. The statement of Purchas was only hearsay in its references to Gordon's activities.

So Laurie's betrayal had been in vain. He had sacrificed his only principle—and two accomplices—to save a brother who did not need saving. There was something about that: not poetic justice perhaps, not any sort of justice, but something. Irony.

Martineau had made a tacit bargain not to push Gordon

too hard, and he had no case against him. So he sent him home. Gordon was only small fry, anyway. Martineau had bigger fish on his hooks.

He went to have a look at Clogger Roach, who had been arrested at a railway station as he bought a single ticket to Liverpool. He was being given the waiting treatment. He sat in a small room under the eye of a bored detective who would not make conversation with him. Martineau looked him up and down, and liked him no more than he had liked Laurie Lovett. The bitter, discontented face was of a type he knew well. This man was a demander of rights; a fanatic in a purely selfish cause; always passionately aware of what he considered to be his due. He was badly frightened now, but when he saw Martineau his dominant characteristic asserted itself.

"You can't keep me here without telling me summat," he shouted. "I have a right to know what I'm charged with."

Martineau went away without speaking to him. The waiting treatment would do for Roach.

Peter Purchas was an entirely different subject. He was a despicable coward, ready to tell all; to say or do anything in the hope of lenient treatment. He had already made a statement, and signed it.

"Will I be charged with murder?" he wanted to know, with all his fear in his eyes.

"Accessory to murder," said Martineau shortly.

"Does that mean they can hang me?"

"Better ask your lawyer that," said the inspector, and left him.

After instructing Devery to relieve the man who was sitting with Roach, Martineau found himself with a little time to spare. He looked at the C.I.D. clock. Eight-five. He went out, and strolled into Lacy Street. There was an awning of grey cloud over the city, and it shut out the little daylight that was left. The many brilliantly lighted shop windows made a welcome glow along the pavements. It was a slack time of the evening, and there were not many people about.

Martineau reflected: 'Monday. Wash day. Women are doing the ironing. Husbands are figuring how much they've spent over the week-end, and deciding that they'd better stay in tonight.'

He entered the Lacy Arms and stood at the end of the bar. The place was quiet. Lucky Lusk was there, behind the bar, but a male customer was engaging her in conversation and she did not immediately see Martineau. Another barmaid served him with a half-pint of beer. Then Lucky saw him, and she ended her gossip with a brief remark and a smile, and came to him.

"Hallo, darling," she said, and her smile was intimate.

He said "Hallo" and asked her to have a drink. She hesitated and said: "Could I have gin and tonic?"

"Have what you like," he said, putting money on the bar.

She sipped her drink and talked with him, occasionally leaving him to serve a customer. He had started his second half-pint before she said: "When are you coming to see me again?"

He looked at her hair, almost the colour of mahogany, and thought about her. The thoughts were exciting. "I don't know," he said. "I *won't* know, till this job's cleared."

"Come tonight," she said with a certain urgency. "Any time you like after eleven o'clock."

He shook his head. "When I leave here I'm going to be awful busy," he said. "It might be three in the morning before I get away."

"Then come tomorrow afternoon, half-past three."

"Hold on, Lucky," was his smiling protest. "What are we starting?"

She raised well-groomed eyebrows. "Don't you know what we're starting?"

"And if we find we can't go on with it?"

She shrugged. "Nobody knows what's going to go on, and what isn't," she said. "Are you thinking of your position?"

"No. I'm thinking of yours."

Her smile was gay. "I'll take a chance," she said. "The other woman's chance. Is it a date?"

A woman who wanted him. A lovely, eager woman. At home there was a reluctant one.

"But I can't make dates," he said. "I haven't the faintest

135

idea what I shall be doing at half-past three tomorrow."
Then as her eyes clouded: "I'll tell you what, Lucky. If I can
make it, I'll phone you, here."

Her smile returned. "No, don't do that," she said,
promptly and shrewdly. "Phone me if you *can't* come."

XV

At Headquarters, Martineau found that Lolly Jakes had
been surrendered by the County Police. Because the assault
which ended in the death of Cicely Wainwright had started
in Higgitt's Passage, it had been decided by Higher Authority
that the murder was a City job.

Jakes was being put to the question by Superintendent
Clay, and, apparently, he was beginning to talk. Martineau
did not join in that inquisition, but told Devery to bring
Clogger Roach to his office.

The waiting treatment had taken Roach through and
beyond the period of fearful imagining, and now he was
bored and bad-tempered, and hungry for a cigarette. When
he saw Martineau he bawled: "What's the game? Keeping
a feller sitting around like this! What's the charge? If there
is one."

"The charge is murder," Martineau said. "You've been
kept waiting because we've been busy with your friends."

"What friends? I've got no friends."

"Maybe friends isn't the right word. We've got two
statements already. You want to watch your step."

"How, watch my step?" Roach demanded. Then his eyes
narrowed in suspicion. "Yers," he said thoughtfully, looking
at the floor. "Yers."

Then he looked up. "Who shopped me?"

"The same man who shopped Peter Purchas. And
Purchas has told us a thing or two as well. How he signalled
to you from Gus Hawkins' office. How you paid him off with
two hundred pounds."

Roach was not interested in Purchas. He was thinking
about the man who had betrayed him. "Jakes, for a quid,"
he said. "The dirty bastard. I coulda got away, and he
shopped me. What did he say about me?"

"I can't tell you what anybody said about you, but—watch your step."

"If he says I did it he's a liar!" cried Roach passionately. "I never laid a finger on that girl. Never even touched her! Jakes and that bloke Starling had her in the back seat. They're the ones who croaked her."

"And you were in the front seat with Laurie Lovett?"

"Ye—— I never said I was there, did I?"

"You were there, all right. There's no argument about that. They didn't give you nine hundred pounds for advice."

Roach did not reply.

"We've got the lot of you, except Starling," Martineau went on. "Where is he?"

"I don't know. None of us knows."

"He must have said *something.*"

"I'm telling you, I don't know where he is. He faded, and I wish I'd done the same."

"He can't stay in England. Didn't he talk of going abroad?"

"Not a word. For Chrissake gimme a cigarette, Inspector."

"Here you are. Did he say where he'd been since his escape?"

"No. He only said one thing. 'Keep moving.' That was his motto. 'Keep moving.' Gimme a light, Inspector."

"Sure, here. Now, about Saturday morning. . . ."

XVI

None of Don Starling's accomplices could help the police to find him. That was established by persistent questioning.

"He's the one who matters," said Martineau with savage regret, "and we can't get within a mile of him. He's moving around, and nobody ever sees him."

"He calls on friends, stays a few hours, and moves on," said Devery. "That way people don't get too fed up of him, and they don't get much chance to shop him."

"He can't have so many friends who'll harbour somebody as hot as he is. Still, he stays hidden."

"He can't hide for ever, sir."

"No. He's sticking around until he can lay hands on the plunder from the Underdown job. That's what I think. I'm

137

fairly sure he's the only one who knows where it is, because he's the one who hid it. When he gets that stuff, he'll clear out. What's worrying me is—he might have got it, and cleared out already."

Martineau took that worry home with him after the five prisoners had been charged and locked up. His wife had a good supper ready for him. He had been home to tea and he had come home to his supper, without, apparently, calling in a pub for a drink. He was a good boy. It appeared that he was about to regain his stripes.

He ate contentedly, with some absence of mind. If Julia wanted to be friendly for a change, he wasn't going to commit any breach of the peace. Then he found that he had to give her his attention. There was another reason for her benign, almost affectionate mood. She had been to the pictures. She had seen a film which she liked, and she wanted to talk about it.

It had been a musical film, and the male star had been a bull-necked tenor. The romantic story, the music, and the bellowing male had affected her. She had a faraway look: she visualized the picture as she talked about it.

"There was a man in the film—not Paolo Ascari, but another man—who was a bit like you," she said. "He was the wealthy business man who was in love with Gina when she was an unknown singer, before she became famous. He paid for her training, without telling her. He gave her father the money, you see. But she met Paolo and fell in love with him, and married him at the finish. So the man's part was a bit sad."

"He was the guy who loved and lost," Martineau commented, with his mouth full.

"It was a lovely picture," she said with a reminiscent sigh. "Absolutely lovely."

He so obviously failed to catch her enthusiasm that she thought he wanted to talk about his own affairs. "How did you go on today?" she asked.

He told her, briefly.

"Oh, that's good, isn't it?" she said. "You've done more than anybody. If only it's you who catches Don Starling. . . . They might make you a chief inspector."

"There's a chance," he agreed. "There'll be a vacancy when Ted Hollis retires."

Her thoughts dwelt luxuriously on a chief-inspectorship. More salary, more authority: more housekeeping money, more social prestige.

"You'll get promotion," she said, "if you get your man."

"Oh, I don't know," he replied, speaking his mind as he was used to speaking his mind on police matters to Julia, because it is one of the duties of police wives, to listen and allow their husbands to 'get things off their chests' with safety. "I'm up against stiff competition. There are some damn good men holding my rank. Picking up Starling would help, but it's not all that important. Not to make a bull-up of it, that's the thing."

She frowned slightly. "But you always said Starling would eventually kill somebody, and that you'd like to be the man who arrested him for the last time."

"True enough," he agreed. "He's trash, garbage, rubbish. He should be carted away and destroyed. But that's a *personal* feeling, wanting to arrest him. I want to be sure it's done right and proper, without bungling. No loopholes in the law for Mr. Starling. He wants seeing off. If you could have seen that poor kid we found on the moors. . . . Well, to tell the truth, Julia, I do have a feeling about Don. I think he'll walk into my hands. Wishful thinking, probably. He might be two hundred miles away from here."

He was silent, then he said: "That's the way it's always been with him and me. Always running into each other, usually head-on."

Julia was satisfied. Her husband would be the man who arrested Don Starling. He would handle it right. One thing about Harry, he was a big, strong, capable man. He did not make as much money as some women's husbands, but to compensate for that he was a complete man. He was neither bald, corpulent nor ailing. He did not wear spectacles and his teeth were his own. He was quite a husband, really—when he was at home. She was moved by a surge of possessive pride. There would be women who envied her such a husband. Yes indeed, she wouldn't be surprised if there were quite a few women who had an eye on Harry Martineau.

She rose from her chair and poured him a second cup of tea. He put it on a corner of the table, so that it was in easy reach when he moved to his armchair. He relaxed in the armchair, and lit a cigarette.

"I enjoyed that. Very good," he said politely. Then he yawned. It had been a long day.

She moved across the hearth and perched on the arm of his chair. She was a tall woman for a posture of that sort, but she managed it gracefully enough. Her left arm was on the back of the chair, behind his head. She looked down at his hair, and stroked it. Then she pressed his head against her breast; a firm breast, of satisfactory proportions.

He noticed that she had a clean pleasant smell about her. She always did have.

"It's a long time since you made love to me," she said.

He admitted that it was indeed a long time, and refrained from giving his opinion that it was her fault. It had been such a long time that he felt awkward and shy. Also, he had a guilty remembrance of Lucky Lusk. He had been strongly tempted to go to Lucky's house when he found himself off duty earlier than he expected.

"It's late. Let's go to bed," Julia suggested. "I'll come in with you for a little while, if you like."

"That's an idea," he said, "but—we don't have any of the doings."

She sat up quickly.

"Why?" she demanded.

"I keep forgetting to buy some."

"You never forgot before," she accused, though she did not seem to be angry. "You always made sure of having some."

"Times change," he said, for the sake of giving an answer. Then he went on: "It's time we did without those things, anyway. We're married, and we ought to behave as if we were married."

She relaxed to her former position. She stroked his hair pensively. For a moment he had a wild notion that she was going to say that she agreed with him. Then he thought: 'It's

140

a good mood she's in, but not as good as all that. No, not *so* good.'

He was right. She got up suddenly. "No," she said. "I think not. Not tonight, great lover. I'm going to bed; to my own bed. Cheerio."

"Good night," he replied, and as she was leaving the room he drank the last of his tea, and stood up.

"I suppose you're going to play your piano now," she said, without rancour. "One of these days I'll sell that thing and buy a television set."

"Buy what you like," he said, also in good humour, "but you'd better not sell my piano."

She went off to bed. He wandered into the front room and sat down at the piano. He played softly, because he did not want to disturb Julia. One thing was certain, if she could not sleep she would knock on the bedroom floor to make him stop.

XVII

In the flat over the furniture shop, the supper dishes had been cleared away, and Devery and his sweetheart were happily engaged with pencil and paper. They were making a list of wedding guests. Devery wrote: *My Uncle Ernest. He'll drink us out of house and home,"* and then rapidly at the bottom of the foolscap sheet: *This list is not for publication.* Silver opened her lovely lips in silent laughter, and from his armchair her grandfather smiled at her happiness.

When the list was finished, Devery began to write pleasing nonsense on the other side of the paper. Silver snatched the pencil from him, and with lips primly pursed though her eyes sparkled, she wrote: *The wedding is off. You are too silly to be married.*

He took the pencil and replied: *If you don't marry me I'll lock you up—and lock myself up with you.*

She wrote: *If I marry you, will you be good to me?*

He replied: *No. Ha ha, wait till I have you in me power.*

She got the pencil and scribbled over his writing, and then there was a tussle, and some laughter. Then he wrote: *What will you be doing tomorrow while I am working for your living?*

She put a finger to her lips, and wrote: *This also is not for publication. I am going to spring-clean the top floor. Grandad doesn't know.*

He answered: *You can't. It's too big. You'll be just about dead.*

The lifeless bride, she wrote. *You'll have to restore me.*

I'll bring you to life, baby, he replied.

She wrote: *You are a bad man,* and then the sheet was full. The two lovers sat and looked at each other. He was quite sure that he had never in his life seen anyone so radiantly alive and lovely.

XVIII

In the heart of the city Devery sat with his Silver and thought only of future happiness.

There, too, in the heart of the city lay four men whose liberty Devery had helped to restrain. Laurie Lovett, Lolly Jakes, Clogger Roach, and Peter Purchas could only look forward to an appearance before a magistrate in the morning, and probably an adjournment, and then another appearance where pleas would be made and evidence presented. Since miracles could not be expected, that trial would lead to a committal for trial at the Granchester Assizes. Before a red-robed judge, bewigged barristers, and a listening jury, there would be examination, cross-examination, and re-examination. Then the speeches of counsel. Then the judge's careful weighing of the evidence as he directed the jury. Then the agony of waiting for the verdict. Then the sentence. To what? Would the judge put on the black cap? Would there be the warden, and the chaplain, and finally the hangman on the grey execution morning? Would there be the final shivering stand on the scaffold, before the world dropped away from beneath the feet? And then what? Choking agony? It was said that it didn't hurt, that it was over in a split-second, but who could really tell. Oh God, said the men in the cells, who did not believe in God. Oh God preserve us from the death penalty.

Not far from where those men sat awake in the dark, Chloe Hawkins stood in a dark doorway in a side street. She was with a man, enjoying married life in her alley-cat way because her husband was in hospital. As she talked with the man she wondered if she dare take him home for the night. The man—who anticipated satisfaction there and then, having no intention of going anywhere with her—was wondering too, how long she was going to chatter, and what his wife would say when he went home so late: feeling guilty when he thought of his wife.

Not far away too, Lucky Lusk was drinking her nightcap (a cup of tea) and thinking about Harry Martineau. He had no children. All was fair when a man had no kids. If his wife couldn't hold him, that was her look out. If Martineau came tomorrow, would she go all the way with him? Could she do anything else? He would regard her invitation as a promise. Any man would. Well, she wanted him. She had wanted him for a long time. 'I won't be able to help myself,' she thought. 'I must have him. I'll keep him if I can. I never had a man who was worth a damn.'

Also in the heart of the city, where he had not ventured since Saturday morning, Don Starling was settling in his night's hiding-place. He was well content with the place, and with himself. Of the six men who were concerned in the murder of Cicely Wainwright, he was the only one who could escape from thoughts of the hangman. That was because he was still at liberty, and also because he was different from the others. They had remained, figuratively, immobile, hoping to avoid discovery. He had kept on the move to evade pursuers.

And in spite of pursuit he had done what he had set out to do. Beside him, within reach, was a small fortune in gems. He knew where to dispose of them—at a fraction of their value, unfortunately—and the money they raised would all be his. It was hard lines on the mob, but they shouldn't have gone and got themselves locked up. He could hardly be expected to share with them when they were in the hands of the police. And anyway, he needed the money himself. He had a long way to go.

There was just one thing. Martineau. He had promised to kill that clever, sarcastic devil. Killing Martineau couldn't make matters worse. In fact, it would make them better. Many people who despised him for killing a girl—the Lord knew he hadn't intended to kill her—would admire him for

143

rubbing out a police inspector whom he had previously warned. And those who didn't admire him would be scared silly of him. That would help, too.

But, simply for the double satisfaction of enhancing his reputation and making an end of a man he hated, the gesture of killing Martineau was too risky. Martineau, he remembered, was fly, very fly. Stalking him would be dangerous. It was no use taking a chance on losing everything just for the pleasure of closing an account with an old enemy.

No, no use at all. Starling was firm on that point. No use making changes now. It was all laid on. Wait here until eleven in the morning, then sneak out and go round to Sammy Toy's place. It was no use going before eleven, because Sammy couldn't be depended on to start work until then. He was a wizard mechanic, but slothful. He bought cars and overhauled them and sold them, making a good living that way. He always had a roadworthy vehicle of his own: a little car or a van. He did not know it yet, but he was going to transport his old friend Don Starling out of town. Not through the police road checks, but around them. The police hadn't enough men to block every back alley leading out of Granchester. Sammy would know how to get through. He was used to avoiding the police when he drove unlicensed purchases home.

Outside Granchester there would be checks on the main roads, but Sammy knew the byways. He would get through. His friend Don would give him a tenner to keep him sweet. A tenner to drive somebody a score of miles to Liverpool. Sammy wouldn't grumble. Sammy wouldn't dare grumble, because his friend Don would show him a gun.

In Liverpool dwelt the man who would buy hot sparklers. The same man would also know how to buy a new identity, the identity of an ordinary seaman or steward. At least, Starling had heard that this could be done. Some chief steward or bo'sun would be bribed, and he would get a place on a ship. Once safely out of Britain—that damned difficult place to get out of—he would land at a foreign port and assume yet another identity, that of an American. There were thousands of Americans abroad. If he met any real Americans, he would pretend that he was an American born and bred in England. It would work out all right. He, Don Starling, was capable of making it work out. Yes, it would be all right. It had better be.

It couldn't go wrong now. Look what he had done. Got out of Pontfield Prison as clean as a whistle, got a gun, organized a job and got nine hundred nicker (it was a pity that girl had to go and die) and this evening he had rounded it off by picking up the Underdown loot. That had been a good job well done. And all the time he had eluded the police. He'd given 'em the dummy proper. The police, the police, the bloody police, Martineau leading on. They hadn't had a smell of him. They never saw which way he went.

Starling lay in the darkness considering his uncomplicated plans, while around him the heart of the city pulsed more quietly as midnight approached. The sober crowds had dispersed to their homes, and only the denizens remained; the denizens, and the few who did not want to go home, and the very few who had no homes. He could hear the city's night sounds, and they were familiar to him: an occasional rushing car, the whirr of curtains being drawn across open windows, the click of a street-walker's cheap shoes, the hoarse bray of adolescent male laughter, the slurred voices of passing drunks in endless reiterative argument. He thought, with knowledge, of the adulterous embracing all around him; the whisky frisky, sherry merry, brandy randy, ginerous embraces. He grinned in the dark. That was life, as he liked it. That was the city, as he knew it.

Three miles away, in the suburbs of the city, Julia Martineau was knocking on the bedroom floor with her shoe, and swearing softly, her husband was moving away from the piano. The last knock was followed by the first whirr of the telephone bell.

"No, I'm not in bed," said Martineau. "Why? What's up?"

It was Detective Constable Ducklin on the phone.

"It's a queer affair at the Royal Lancaster Hotel," he said, with the unction of one who knows he is doing himself a bit of good. "On account of the connexion with Don Starling and the Underdown job, I thought I'd better tell you about it."

145

"You did right to tell me. Go on."

"Well, it seems they keep a cellarman on duty till eleven o'clock. He signs off at the same time as the wine waiters. At half-past ten a guest who was throwing a little party asked for some particular sort of wine; some sort of champagne. The waiter phoned the cellar, and got no reply. He thought the cellarman had dodged off home before his time, so he went looking for the wine himself. He found the cellarman trussed up. He'd been hit on the head. He doesn't know who hit him, or what with. We can't tell yet if there's anything missing. The manager has sent for the head cellarman, the old Frenchman, whatsisname, François."

"Very good," said Martineau. "I'll be with you as soon as I can. I want a car. At once."

"I took the liberty of sending a car, sir," said Ducklin, obviously taking great pleasure in his own forethought. "It should be there any minute."

"Right," said Martineau, and rang off. He was waiting at the gate when the car arrived.

When he walked into the Royal Lancaster Hotel he found Ducklin making much of what he called 'the mystery'. The detective's mystification was supported by François and the manager, a Swiss called Weiss, both of whom raised their hands, shoulders and eyebrows in complete lack of understanding.

"If it was Starling, looking for *something,* nobody knows how he got in, sir," said Ducklin.

"He could walk into the lounge or the bar, couldn't he?" Martineau queried. "There are several ways."

"Without being seen, sir? He once worked here. The doormen and the porters know him. And so do the waiters and the barmen, and the pages and the reception staff. The storekeepers and kitchen hands know him even better. It's reasonable to suppose he didn't come in at any door, and all the cellar windows are still secure."

"In a place like this there are bound to be ways of getting in. Anyway, we mustn't assume it was Starling. It could have been somebody else. Where is the man who was attacked?"

"I had a few words with him and sent him off to hospital.

He got a pretty bad crack on the head. The person who hit him wasn't worried about breaking his skull."

"That sounds like our Don. It's getting to be a habit with him. Didn't the man see or hear *anything*?"

"Nothing, sir. He says he was working at a little desk they have down there. He must have been attacked from behind."

"Obviously," said Martineau. He rubbed his chin thoughtfully.

"I had the hotel surrounded, sir," said Ducklin helpfully. "There's just a chance he might still be with us."

"You've done very well," the inspector conceded. He turned to the head cellarman: "Shall we take another look downstairs?"

"Certainly," François replied. He led the way. Martineau, Ducklin and Weiss followed.

"We turned this place upside down two years ago," the inspector commented as he looked around the wine cellar.

François smiled. "I remember thinking that you would impair the foundations," he said.

"We found nothing, anyway. Are you sure there's nothing missing now?"

"Without taking stock I cannot tell," the old Frenchman admitted. "But I cannot *see* anything missing."

They went on, into a portion of the cellar where there was no wine. He looked into a disused, ill-lit chamber which contained a few broken cases, some old dusty bottles, some empty kegs and three huge casks which loomed shadowy in the background.

"I've looked in there, sir," said Ducklin.

"Of course," said Martineau absently, staring around.

His gaze lingered on the casks. He remembered them from the previous search. They were immense, taller than a tall man, and of tremendous girth. Even when empty they were much too heavy for one man to handle. François had declared that they were two hundred years old: storage casks for rum or brandy. Nowadays, who ever had that much liquor to store?

Two of the casks were equal in size; the third one was slightly smaller. Its outline seemed to be proportionately narrower, too. Martineau stepped forward and peered, at the same time feeling in his pocket for his flashlight.

"What's the matter with that end cask?" he asked.

"The smaller one?" Ducklin asked quickly. "There are a couple of staves missing."

"What?" cried François, fairly leaping forward. "The old casks? Who has done that?"

All four men made their ways around kegs and cases to the big casks. Ducklin did a balancing act and nearly fell when he put his foot on an empty bottle, but he was there first. He hesitated only when he was quite close to the broken cask, and he made the final approach as if he expected Don Starling to be lurking inside. Reassured, he stood at the long opening and looked right into the cask.

"There's nothing——" he began, and then an object glittering in reflected light made him draw back so quickly that he collided with François.

"There's a one-eyed rat in there!" he exclaimed, and the tone of his voice indicated that he definitely did not like rats.

Martineau was there with his torch. "Let's look," he said. He stooped cautiously, exploring the cask with his light, for he also did not like rats.

There was no small rodent, but still the red eye glittered from the floor of the cask. Martineau squatted on his heels, and reached, and picked up a small ruby.

"So now we know," he said, turning the stone in his fingers. "He's got the stuff, and he's on his way."

"Weren't these casks examined just after the Underdown job, sir?" Ducklin wanted to know.

"We looked on top," the inspector said, "then we tilted 'em up and looked underneath. It's obvious we didn't tilt 'em enough, else we'd have heard the stuff sliding about." He smiled wryly. "These casks are a bit too big to pick up and shake, you know."

He reached up and tried to pull out the bung. It was firm. "Starling hammered it in after he dropped the stuff piece by piece through the bung-hole," he said. "He didn't even disturb the dust on top of the cask. Very crafty. Very crafty indeed."

Ducklin picked up a stave and looked at it closely. "He

used a jemmy, inch-and-a-quarter," he announced. "Would he find it down here?"

François led the way back to the cellarman's desk. In the desk there was an inch-and-a-quarter case-opener. But, he insisted, there should have been two.

Martineau nodded. "All right, we can assume that Starling now has a case-opener."

They went upstairs to the kitchen level. There, on the little landing, was the door giving access to the cellar steps, the big swing doors leading to the kitchen, the service stairs, and a service lift.

Martineau looked from the narrow service stairs to the cellar door. "Four strides," he said. "And the cellar door wasn't locked. It's a piece of cake."

He stepped to the foot of the stairs and looked up. "They used much?" he asked.

"In emergencies," the manager replied. "When the lift is out of order."

"How far do they go?"

"Past every floor, right to the roof."

"Evening sir, evening all," said a newcomer. It was Devery. "I was passing. Saw the place surrounded. Thought I'd see if I could be of help."

Martineau looked at his watch. "Have you been courting till this time? Well well, you'll get no sleep now. You've stuck your nose into a job."

Devery grinned. "I said I could do it, sir."

Martineau's own grin was slightly mischievous. "So you did," he said. "You and Ducklin had better tackle those stairs, as far as the roof. Mr. Weiss and I will go up in the lift."

The lift stopped at the top floor. From there the police inspector and the hotelier took the stairs to the roof.

"This door should be barred on the inside," said Weiss with some asperity, as they stepped out into starlight.

"Somebody has unbarred it," said Martineau calmly. "I suppose one could get off this roof without going back into the hotel?"

"There are four fire escapes."

"Show me," said the policeman.

Devery and Ducklin arrived, a little leg-weary. They followed the other two men around the roof.

Two of the fire escapes gave access to the hotel yard. The third was in a side street, and near to the front of the hotel. The fourth was near the back, and it zigzagged down into the narrow alley between Little Sefton Street and Lacy Street.

"I guess he made his departure by this route," said Martineau, leaning over the parapet and looking down. "He could have used any of them, but this is the likeliest."

Far below, there was a very faint, brief glow of fire. Some uniformed policeman, detailed to watch that way of escape, was holding a forbidden cigarette in his cupped hand. A fugitive on the roof would have seen it. It was very bad police work; a man having a smoke in the wrong place, at the wrong time.

Martineau was not stirred by the facile indignation of the superior officer. He was not even slightly annoyed. His mood was one of extraordinary calm.

"I wish we had some used light bulbs, good big ones. We'd frighten the life out of that fellow," he said, and the others laughed.

He stood up straight, and looked out over the starlit city. He was above it looking down, because Granchester, after the fashion of English provincial cities, did not have many buildings taller than eight storeys. The light of street lamps reflected on darkened windows sent faint illumination skyward, so that there was a glow even where lights could not be seen. Distantly, steam from some huge condensers shone eerily white, while in another direction the red glare of a steelworks could be seen. Even at this late hour fumes from many, many chimneys drifted upward, and the stars had smoke in their eyes.

Away down below there was the sudden hoarse bray of an adolescent male excited to mirth. It sounded like the veritable voice of ignorance. A creature of the abyss?

Martineau quoted: " 'Hell is a city much like London—A populous and a smoky city.' Much like Granchester too, if you ask me. Who wrote that?"

There was no immediate answer, then Weiss said: "Do you really want to know?"

"No, Mr. Weiss, not really. I'm just trying to impress these two dumb coppers. Shelley, wasn't it?"

"It was," said Weiss, in a tone which suggested that any puns or limericks about Shelley would not be appreciated.

Martineau looked over the parapet again. From that height the alley seemed to be very narrow. It almost looked as if a fugitive could jump, across and downward, from the fire escape to the roof of the four-storey building across the alley. Yes, he decided, an active man could do it, but there was no point in it.

"It looks as if our man got clean away," he said. "Up the fire escape, through the first window he could open, down the service stairs and into the cellar: then, because he couldn't find the window again, up to the roof *via* the service lift, down the fire escape, and away. Perfectly simple. He's quite a boy, is our Don. Quite a boy."

His words were a true reflection of his mood. Four times in a few days he had crossed the trail of Starling, without ever getting near him, and he was beginning to be philosophical about it. His intuitive feeling, that he would have a chance to arrest the man, might be nothing more than a strong wish. Every policeman in the city might feel the same. It was a large city, and a very big world. He could not count upon being the man among thousands who would find another. It was better to be easy about it. 'If I set eyes on him, he's mine,' was the attitude. 'If I don't, well, good luck to the man who gets him.'

It was to be expected, now, that Starling would try to get away from Granchester. If he did the obvious thing—which could also be the double bluff—he would head for Liverpool and the docks. The Liverpool police were expecting him. They were looking out for him.

But if he stayed in Granchester even a day longer. . . . The police were methodically blocking the rat holes. They would find him. Well, probably they would.

Martineau casually shone his torch on the lower roofs, then turned away. "We can't be sure he's gone," he said to Weiss. "In the morning there'll have to be a thorough search of the hotel. I'm afraid we can't do it tonight, with all your guests asleep in bed."

"I should say not!" said **Weiss.**

"Tonight, though, we'll search as far as we can without disturbing anybody. All unoccupied rooms and service rooms.

The Swiss nodded. He did not like having the police in his place, but he was a reasonable man. The police had their duty to do, unfortunately.

xx

Sustained by coffee made by the night porter, the C.I.D. men stayed on duty at the Royal Lancaster throughout the night. When the hotel had been searched except for the bedrooms, Martineau arranged with the obliging manager to spread a network of plain-clothes men and hotel employees in the morning. The men would be stationed at strategic points looking along corridors, so that Starling could not move about if he were still in the hotel. And as the suites and bedrooms became unoccupied at the breakfast hour, they would be searched by floor valets and police. So long as there was a slight possibility that Starling might be in the hotel, the search had to be made, though Martineau himself summed up the general opinion by saying that it was like looking for a needle in the wrong haystack.

At Police Headquarters, Superintendent Clay was also up and doing, directing a wider search than Martineau's. Within the city boundaries there were check points, foot patrols, motor patrols, and roving detectives following information and hunches. Outside the city, in borough and county areas, a second, wider cordon was in operation. In places further distant, country policemen and city detectives had Starling's likeness and description stuck in their pocket books and imprinted on their memories.

It was an army searching for one man, in a land where the habits and ideals of the people make the prolonged survival of a hunted criminal almost an impossibility, and where geographical obstacles preventing his escape are enormous. He might evade capture for a few days, or even a few weeks, but eventually. . . .

Superintendent Clay was soberly confident that Don Starling would be captured.

PART FOUR

STARLING AND MARTINEAU

I

At ten o'clock in the morning, with the breakfast dishes washed, the beds made, and the old man safely out of the way in the shop, Silver Steele blithely climbed the stairs to the top floor, to make a preliminary assault upon the dust and dirt which lay upon her grandfather's huge collection of Victorian 'antiques'.

She carried a vacuum cleaner and a cardboard case containing a flexible pipe and extension brushes because, first of all, she had to remove the thick dust which lay upon everything.

She put down her tools and looked around. Sunlight was streaming dustily through the windows 'of the big, square warehouse room. On two sides she could see blue sky and a vista of roofs, on the third side there was the back view of some big shops in Lacy Street, and on the fourth side, across the alley, were the third floor windows of the Royal Lancaster Hotel. She blushed warmly as she imagined what the people in the hotel rooms would think about the dusty windows of her grandfather's top floor.

She worked for a few minutes, moving along with the humming cleaner, then she stopped. She had a feeling that someone was watching her. Her glance went to the hotel windows opposite. She thought that one of the chambermaids might be wanting to wave to her.

Then her sensitive nose made her aware of a stale tobacco smell. Cigarette tobacco. Near her, she knew, was someone who had been smoking quite recently. She stopped, just in time to avoid getting within reach of a man who crouched, waiting for her, around the end of a big wardrobe. She was suddenly afraid, and she turned to go. But now she was too late. As she hurried along an alley between wardrobes arranged in rows, she could not hear the man who ran upon the other side. He stopped and faced her when he was between her and the stairs.

Don Starling! Terrified, she stood open-mouthed. Her very soul was screaming, but she could make no sound.

When he observed that silent scream, Starling relaxed. He remembered that the girl was dumb. She was no danger to him, so long as she did not get away down the stairs. He would soon be going down the stairs himself, and he hoped to sneak out of the shop without being seen. He could tie up the girl with the flex from the vacuum cleaner, and leave her to be found.

He smiled. "Steady," he said. "I'm not going to hurt you."

She backed away. Her eyes were wild with fear.

"Take it easy," he coaxed, as he advanced. "There's nothing to be afraid of."

She fled from him. With an exasperated growl he followed. But at the end of an alley of sideboards she slipped through an opening, and he had to turn and race back, to keep between her and the stairs.

He pursued again, but she was not easy to catch. She wore flat-heeled crêpe-soled shoes, and she was fleet and agile. She was slim enough to pass through openings between heavy pieces of furniture which were too narrow for him. And he was always hampered by the vital necessity of keeping her away from the stairs.

He tried new tactics. He began to push furniture around, closing ways of escape as he advanced. It became obvious that she would eventually be cornered. She stared around in desperation, looking for some way out. Then she picked up a heavy black marble clock, the pride of some nineteenth-century mantelpiece. She managed to raise the clock in both hands and hurl it through the window. There was a great crash of glass, and a second crash as the clock landed like a bomb in the street below.

"You hellcat!" cried Starling, in astonishment and alarm. He abandoned his earth-stopping measures and went after her in headlong pursuit.

As she ran from him she caught up, with one hand, a bronze statuette of a muscular man with two rearing horses, and slung it through another window. Then, when she had barely eluded his clutching fingers by squeezing between two huge mahogany sideboards, she picked up a vase. It was a big, wide vase which had at one time held a prized aspidistra. It made a great noise as it went through a third window and burst on the concrete of the street.

Starling reacted according to type. He brought out his pistol. "Stop it!" he shouted. "Stop it, or I'll shoot!"

The pressure of swift and alarming events made him forget that the girl could not hear him. It seemed that she just wasn't heeding him. She was defying him. He saw her lift a small but ornate lacquered chair, and run at a window with it.

At that moment he had only one thought and one intention; to stop the infernal din. "I'll shoot!" he threatened.

She knew that she was temporarily out of his reach. She never looked at him. A second chair followed the first.

He fired one shot. She heard neither the report of the pistol nor the smack of the bullet as it struck the wall behind her. She reached for a bronze ornament. He fired again. He was not an expert with a pistol. It was the third shot which struck her and sent her reeling against the broken glass in the window frame.

II

Devery persuaded Martineau to turn up his nose at an hotel breakfast. "Come round the corner with me and see my girl," he urged. "She'll be delighted to meet you." He smacked his lips. "There'll be ham and eggs, I wouldn't be surprised. Plenty on your plate."

"But it's after ten o'clock," Martineau demurred.

"That makes no difference," he was assured. "She'll have 'em ready in a jiffy. She's as good as gold."

They left the hotel, and they were walking along Lacy Street when they heard the first crash. They stopped and stared around. Traffic was running smoothly: there was no commotion. "Somebody smashed a window somewhere," Devery commented as they walked on.

They did not hear the second and third crashes, because those were in Little Sefton Street, but when they turned the corner into the alley they saw a uniformed policeman run past the other end.

"Something up," said Martineau.

Then they saw two chairs, one after the other, sail through a top floor window of Furnisher Steele's and fall and break their limbs on the cobbles of the alley.

Devery said "Silver!" and sprinted along the alley. The inspector did not immediately follow. He stood there, looking up. He heard a shot, then two more. A bronze statuette dropped to the ground. Then a bright golden head rocked for a moment in a frame of broken glass, and disappeared. He waited, and saw the face of Don Starling peering down. He smiled grimly, and waved. So they were to meet, after all! Starling seemed to say something, and his dark eyes suddenly glowed with devilish intent. His hand holding a pistol appeared, but Martineau had leaped towards Steele's building, and he was running along close to the wall.

When the inspector reached Little Sefton Street he met a hurrying sergeant. "Get your men around Steele's place," he said, pointing. "Somebody's been shot. Starling's in there, and he's armed."

The sergeant said "Yessir," and turned away. Martineau entered the furniture shop and ran up the stairs. He ascended the four flights without meeting anybody. But on the top floor he met Devery, carrying Silver's limp body. By his side Furnisher Steele hovered anxiously. A uniformed constable was there also. He was staring up at an open skylight.

Silver's eyes were closed. Her face was pale and her head lolled. She had lost her dust cap and her lovely hair hung down.

Martineau looked a question.

"In the back," said Devery tightly. "It looks bad to me. I'll put her in the ambulance and come back here. Starling's on the roof."

They went down the stairs. Martineau turned to the P.C.

"Did anybody see him?" he asked.

"Me and the old man, sir," the constable replied. "We arrived up here together. Starling's legs were just disappearing through the skylight."

He pointed. Martineau had already noticed the light cane table which had been placed on a bigger table beneath the skylight.

The constable held up a big service revolver which he had been holding at his side. "The old boy took a shot at him with this," he said. "He missed by a mile. I took it off him before he hurt hisself."

Martineau held out his hand for the revolver. "Did Starling return the fire?" he asked.

"No sir. He took a look at us—that's when I saw his face —and pointed his pistol. Then he seemed to change his mind. He scarpered without shooting at us."

"Saving his ammunition," said Martineau. "It sounds as if he hasn't a spare clip." He 'broke' the revolver carefully, so that the six shells were ejected into the palm of his hand. There were five unused. He reloaded with them, and put the gun in his pocket.

"If we aren't careful," he said, "some good man is going to lose his life on this job. Go and get on the phone to Superintendent Clay. Tell him what's happened. Tell him it's my urgent request that the men surrounding this building be issued with firearms. The sooner the better."

"Very good, sir," said the constable. He turned away, and almost bumped into Ducklin, who was taking the last flight of stairs at speed.

"What's happened, sir?" asked Ducklin breathlessly.

"Starling's on this roof," said the inspector shortly. "You go back to the Royal Lancs, and take the lift and get on the roof. I'll be near that skylight. You'll be able to look down and tell me what's going on. Away you go, at the double."

"Yessir," said Ducklin. He went pattering down the stairs.

Left alone, Martineau took the revolver from his pocket. "Now then, Don boy," he said as he went towards the skylight, "We'll see what we can do for you."

He climbed on to the two tables and stooped beneath the open window. It was propped open to an angle of forty-five degrees by an iron bracket. He put out his head for a fraction of a second, looking in one direction only. Then he looked around the tilted window. The section of sloping roof was deserted, He climbed out on to the slates.

This was no roof with a strong parapet like that of the hotel across the alley. If a man slipped on the slates, there was only a narrow iron rain trough to stop him from falling into the street below. But beyond this outer slope there was another bay of the roof, where two sections of slates sloped down to a gutter. That was half of the roof. Another inner bay and an outer slope made up the other half.

Martineau approached the crest of the outer slope. Before he showed his head against the sky he looked up at the roof of the Royal Lancaster, but Ducklin was not yet in position. He decided that he could not afford to wait for Ducklin. He reached up and put his fingers over a ridge tile, then he pulled himself up and took two quick looks. The first inner bay was empty. He scrambled over with relief. Now, at least, he could not roll off the roof.

He looked up again, and saw Ducklin staring down. The man's red face was redder than ever with excitement, and his prominent blue eyes were popping. The inspector could see the colour of them even at that distance.

"In the next bay," the detective bellowed. "Behind the chimney stack."

There was the sharp crack of Starling's pistol, and stone dust flew from the parapet. Ducklin discreetly bobbed down out of sight.

"That's four," Martineau muttered. "He should have six left."

He did not relish the idea of looking over into the next bay and being sniped from behind the chimney stack. What was Starling doing there anyway? Was he going to fight it out from there? Or was he looking for a way down?

He crawled up the slates and raised his head just high enough for him to see the top of the chimney stack. It was at the end of the bay, over-looking a two-storey drop on to the sloping roof of an adjoining brush factory.

He walked along the gutter to the end of the bay, then he got on his hands and knees to look over. Starling was doing the same thing. Martineau pulled back out of sight as Starling fired.

"Hard cheddar, Don," the inspector called mockingly. "You need some practice with that thing."

Starling's reply was a mouthful of lurid invective, and Martineau grinned. He had seen what he wanted to see.

There were no fall pipes on that side of the building, but the chimney stack itself jutted like a buttress into the adjoining property, and it was roughly masoned. A descent could perhaps be made by means of fingers and toes, but it would be a hazardous task even for a good climber.

"If you try to climb down that stack, I've got you," he called. "You can't get away."

"I'll get away, you swaggering monkey," Starling shouted, evidently beside himself with rage.

Martineau pondered. Why not make the man fight? It was an even chance. It might mean promotion, or it might mean a vacant inspectorship in the Granchester City Police. It was sometimes an advantage for a man to have no children, after all. He could take chances with an easy conscience.

"I've sent for some more men," he shouted. "If you want to have a bash you'll have to do it now. There's only you and me on this roof."

Apparently he was not believed. The shouted reply more than suggested that he was a liar, a very special and unprintable sort of a liar.

"Come on, Don," he urged, not caring a great deal what happened. "I'm waiting for you."

If Starling accepted the challenge, and proved himself the better man with a gun, who would be sorry? Julia, for a few weeks, until she saw somebody who might make her a second husband. Lucky Lusk? For a day or two. His mates in the force? There would be an even balance of open regret about his death and secret pleasure in a sensation. Life must go on, and men soon forget. Every sergeant in the C.I.D. would contribute towards a wreath, and hope to be promoted into the vacancy made by the death of an inspector. Ducklin up there would express his sorrow in a very ostensible sort of way, and hope to be promoted into the place of the sergeant who was made inspector.

Martineau turned his head and looked up. Ducklin was kneeling behind the parapet. Only part of the red face could be seen. The blue eyes were gazing intently in the direction of the chimney stack.

The inspector wondered why Starling was sitting still. That was not his way at all. If there was a move to be made,

159

he would make it. One thing seemed obvious. He hesitated to start making the difficult climb down the chimney stack while there was a policeman on the roof with him. Did he think that the police were murderers? Did he think that a policeman would shoot him or dislodge him while he was making the climb?

"I didn't know you were windy," Martineau taunted. "You must be getting old. Scared of a fight with one copper!"

"I'm not scared of you, you bastard," came the reply.

"Of course you are. You know I can always lick you. It's all right making threats when you know I can't touch you. What about it now, when there's just the two of us?"

Starling did not reply, but Ducklin up above appeared to go suddenly crazy with excitement. "Look out, look out!" he screeched. "He's coming!"

Martineau took Furnisher's old revolver from his pocket, and thumbed the safety catch. He grinned, because he felt curiously irresponsible. This was it, the last encounter. Don Starling was coming, because he had remembered that Harry Martineau was never a liar. And possibly, he expected to meet an unarmed man.

Looking up, Martineau saw fingers appear on the apex of the roof. They were followed by the head and shoulders, hands and arms of Starling.

Both men fired. Martineau felt a hard blow on his chest, and he was knocked backward against the slope of the bay. He saw the pistol fly out of Starling's hand and go spinning in the air above and behind him: a mediocre shot but an extremely lucky one.

Starling disappeared in pursuit of the pistol. Martineau sat up. There was a feeling of numbness in his chest: no pain but a trickling uneasiness. He had no time to think about it. He scrambled up the slates and looked over the apex in time to see Starling stooping in the gutter in the next bay. He was picking up the pistol with his left hand. His right hand hung useless, and it was red with blood.

Martineau fired and missed. Starling vainly squeezed an immovable trigger. Martineau could not steady his gun again, because he was seized by a sudden irrepressible need

160

to rid his lungs of something by coughing. He clung to the ridge tile and coughed, and never took his eyes from Starling. The latter failed to free the damaged mechanism of the pistol and in anger he threw it at his enemy—a poor throw with the left hand—and fled. He ran along the bottom of the bay hopping from side to side of the narrow gutter.

The coughing bout ended. Martineau spat bloody fluid on to the slates. Then he put his revolver in his pocket and went after his man.

With an injured hand it was impossible for Starling to climb down the chimney stack. The only thing he could do was to go over the edge at the end of the gutter, with the desperate intention of hanging for a moment by his one good hand and then dropping two storeys to the roof of the brush factory. He swung his legs over, but he was holding the coping with his head and shoulders above it when Martineau tackled him.

The inspector flung himself full length. He appeared to reach for Starling's throat, but his big hands did not seek the windpipe. He grasped great handfuls of the coat at the lapels, and held them stiff-armed. Starling could go neither forward nor back.

The brown eyes blazed into the slightly glazed, calm, relentless grey ones. The fugitive struck once, and once only, with his wounded right hand. Then he let go of the coping and punched with his left. Hampered by the coping, he could not put much weight behind the blows, but they stung Martineau. Still keeping his arms rigid, the inspector wriggled and pushed his way forward. There was a second of dreadful strain when, with all his captive's weight suspended, the edge of the coping seemed about to break the ulna bones of his forearms, and then his own head and shoulders were over the edge. Lying flat in the gutter, he had Starling hanging straight down below him, suspended by the lapels of his coat. Starling's left hand could no longer reach the face which looked down at him.

Hanging there, Starling tried to pry loose the inspector's grip with his left hand. But it was an iron grip: the fingers were locked around the strong worsted-and-buckram of the lapels. The captive could have swung up his feet and pushed

161

against the wall of the building, to break the grip with the strength of his legs, but even Don Starling did not have the nerve to push himself away like that, and fall head first for two storeys.

"Let me go, blast you!" he stormed, tugging and jerking desperately.

Martineau had another coughing fit, but it did not affect the rigidity of his arms and hands. He spat blood, turning his head slightly and carefully avoiding the man who hung below him.

"You've had it," Starling panted. "I got you in the lungs. You'll go before I do. You'll be the Chief of Police in Hell by the time I get there."

Martineau was silent, saving his breath. He could not even grin.

"You're dying," came the breathless insinuation. "You'll have to let me go. You can't hold on much longer."

Martineau spat more blood.

"You're killing yourself, man. The effort is killing you. Let me go and save your own life."

But Martineau did not let go.

"Oh, God damn and blast you," the captive snarled, out of patience. "Die and rot. Die and be bloody burned. I'll laugh at your funeral notice, you stupid swine. You always were a smug, clever, stupid swine. But you've had it, chum, you've had it. Don Starling's got you, like he said he would. Remember that when your throat's rattling, will you? I said I'd get you, and I did."

They were in the same position when help arrived: Starling arguing, jeering, and struggling; Martineau just holding on. Two strong young constables lay down on either side of the inspector, and the three of them hauled Starling up on to the roof. As soon as he was on his feet he tried to kick Martineau, but the constables yanked him away. He fought them. He succeeded in giving one of them a swollen eye. They restrained him and overpowered him, but they did not strike him. It would have been a shame to hit him. One does not hit a man who has not long to live.

PART FIVE

THE HANGMAN'S MERCY

I

THE condemned man did not eat a hearty breakfast. He pushed the food aside and asked for more coffee. He also demanded his daily allowance of ten cigarettes.

They offered him one cigarette and told him that this did not count as a day. Nine o'clock in the morning was his time, when the day had only just begun. At nine o'clock he would be leaving them, and according to the rules. . . .

He said to hell with the rules. It was a day all right for him, and he was entitled to a condemned man's ten cigarettes. He became excited and slightly hysterical.

For the sake of a quiet death they gave him the cigarettes. They knew that hysteria could be highly infectious on execution mornings, with a thousand uneasy fate-ridden men still locked in their cells. The prisoners knew why they were still locked up, and they were disturbed by a vague fellow-feeling for the man who was about to die. All night they had been restless, and now one yell could create a cursing, bawling, rattling, banging pandemonium.

Starling, the condemned man, smoked incessantly as he waited for death. He had little to say, and his warders were relieved that it should be so. Better a man preoccupied and surly than one who moaned and pleaded. Let him be quiet, that was all they wanted. Let there be no uproar.

When the chaplain came Starling scarcely listened to him, but the chaplain—a young man—was insistent. He begged the prisoner to listen, to join him in prayer, to trust in God's mercy.

Starling looked at the young man with many years to live, and laughed in his face.

"God's mercy, yes," he said. "Maybe, but I doubt it. There's no evidence. The hangman is the visible hand of God and the Sheriff, and I'll get no mercy from the hangman."

Pleased with his own words, he lit another cigarette and blew smoke at the chaplain. It was the only way to deal with

163

this thing, he believed. Be tough, treat it as nothing, refuse to think deeply about it. Don't think at all, in fact. It was nothing but a short walk, a few seconds of numb waiting, a brief agony perhaps, and then oblivion.

There, he *was* thinking about it. All through this inter-fering priest.

"The worst thing about this job is having to listen to a bloody parson," he said. "Am I to be hanged or bored to death?"

The chaplain was too sorry to be offended. And Starling, a fool but not a blind fool, knew why. The chaplain did not want a man to die unrepentant, with awful sins burdening his soul. Starling could have talked to him about the crime, explaining how he had not really intended to kill that girl or any girl, and it would have been repentance of a sort. But he had already explained to a jury—or at least, his counsel had—and the explanation had not been accepted. So what was the use of talking to a parson? Besides, to die excusing himself was not Starling's idea of stoic behaviour.

He snarled at the chaplain. His voice again warned of unwanted hysteria, and the chaplain regretfully withdrew.

Starling knew how he was going to die. Like a man. Why seek mercy where mercy was not? He would get no mercy from the hangman.

He knew how he would meet the hangman. Cool and sardonic, he would say: "I always wanted to make your acquaintance, mister, but not as a client of yours." That would be remembered. It would get outside. People would know that he had not cringed at the final test.

II

There was a stir outside the door of the condemned cell. The hangman had arrived. Starling lit the last cigarette he would ever smoke, but in spite of his determination to be cool his hands trembled and his heart thumped. The Chief Prison Officer and a subordinate entered the cell. They were his escort to the scaffold, and they were followed by the hangman and his assistant.

Starling had imagined that the hangman would not be able to meet his glance, but his imagination had misled him.

It was he who looked away first. And, somehow, he could not utter his brave remark. He could not summon the mood, the ease of manner. The hangman's level glance would make the words seem silly. He was a burly man, clean and fresh-faced; a type who might be seen on any street in any English town. He offered Starling his hand according to custom, and his grip was casually powerful. His assistant was a younger, fresher-faced edition of himself.

Then Starling saw the strap, and his courage ebbed. A new rope for every murderer, but not a new strap. The thing of brass and leather was like a symbol. The hangman's assistant moved behind him with the strap, and at a signal pinioned his shaking hands with one adroit jerk. The remaining length of leather was put over his shoulder, and the extra buckle dangled close to his chest.

More of Starling's resolve deserted him. He had convinced himself that he could meet death calmly, but that was yesterday and the day before. *Now* was the time. *Now* he was going to die. And he found that he was afraid of the ordeal of dying.

He heard himself whisper: "Will it hurt?"

The hangman shook his head. "Not a bit. You'll be all right."

They were ready. The Walk began: a prison officer on each side of Starling, the chaplain behind, the executioners last.

They went out of the cell, and through a doorway which led to the execution shed. They passed an opening, beyond which some evergreens grew. Among the trees were small birds which twittered heedlessly.

Starling never heard the birds, never saw the trees. He did not take a last look at the soft grey sky. An instinct, the most powerful of instincts, had sent its most desperate appeal to his brain. It was Self Preservation, the parent of avarice, cowardice, discretion and last-resort fighting fury. 'You must not die!' the instinct clamoured. 'You are not ready to die!'

The instinct totally displaced the reason which told him that it was useless to struggle or plead. But it did not entirely vanquish pride. Some vestige of self-respect kept Starling walking, in silence. He would not ask for mercy.

165

In the execution shed there waited the fortunate people who were privileged to witness an execution, and the less fortunate who were compelled to witness it. Outside the prison gates, a considerable crowd waited to see the posting of the notice which would say that justice had been done. In the rows of cells, convicts gnawed their knuckles and waited for the spark of hysteria, the single shout which could start a riot.

Starling's pride did not carry him up the steps of the scaffold. The executioners had to assist him. "Stick to it. You're doing all right," murmured the hangman, who understood.

The encouragement helped Starling. In his extremity it made him the hangman's creature. He did as he was told. He managed to make his shaking legs support him when they stood him on the three-way trapdoor.

Now was the time for speed. The hangman slipped a white hood over Starling's head, then he adjusted the rope with quick professional care. The assistant took the remaining length of the strap and began to secure it around Starling's ankles. But his adroitness seemed to have left him. He fumbled.

Starling realized that the last moment was near. It was suffocating knowledge. His heart pounded and he could hardly breath. The moment would come when the assistant had fastened his ankles and moved away. It would be the last agony of waiting for the drop. Starling knew he could never bear it. He would lose all control. He would scream, hop from the trap, fall over.

"You're doing fine," came a reassuring whisper.

A half-second later the hangman extended his mercy to the condemned man. While his assistant still crouched fumbling on the trap, he pressed the release. The trap fell away and Starling dropped. And according to plan the assistant dropped too, on to the soft sand beneath the scaffold. Starling had been spared the last brief time of dreadful waiting. Before he could know that moment, he was beyond knowledge and beyond pain.

The prison clock began to boom the hour of nine. The condemned man had died with fortitude.

PART SIX

MARTINEAU

The day—the January day—of Don Starling's execution was the day before Harry Martineau was due to return to duty after a long disablement and convalescence. In the morning he arose at eight-thirty and prepared to breakfast at leisure, but he knew what day it was and his mood was sombre.

"Are we going to have another day like yesterday?" his wife wanted to know.

Yesterday had been a bad day too. He had been oppressed by the knowledge that it was Starling's last. In the evening he had gone out for a drink—the first in months—and it had led to many more. He had come home late, and Julia had been angry. She was still angry.

He picked up the morning paper, and the first item he read—his glance was drawn to it as if by a magnet—was a small announcement that Starling would be executed at Farways Prison that morning. He threw the paper down.

He looked at the clock. Five minutes to nine. Five minutes to go. He found that he had no appetite. Pushing away his plate, he reached for the coffee pot. Julia frowned.

At two minutes to nine he closed his eyes and prayed silently. It was a prayer for Don Starling, but Martineau did not mention any names even to God, because he did not know what to ask God to do about Starling. He simply repeated the Lord's Prayer in his mind until the minute hand of the clock was well past the hour. Julia watched him with an enigmatic gaze. No one could have told whether there was amusement, scorn, or sympathy for him in her expression.

Julia may have wondered why her husband allowed himself to be distressed by this matter of Don Starling. It was not the first time he had helped to send a man to the gallows, and never before had such an occurrence made him miss a meal or lose a wink of sleep. He had detested Starling, and Starling had deserved to be hanged, so what was all the fuss about? Certainly she could not see why there was any need for him to go out last night and get a lot of drink. She failed

167

to understand why a man could not be sorry in a decent way, without going out and hitting the bottle. She did not agree with that at all, and she was determined not to tolerate any more of it in silence.

Martineau did not notice her expression. He was thinking about Starling. Queer, he reflected, how a man could feel the loss of an old enemy almost as much as if he had been a friend. Starling had had a place in his life. Now there was an emptiness.

He guessed it was time he went back to work. There were plenty more thieves and fiddlers in the world. Enough to keep a man busy, leaving him no time to think about what had happened to a murderer.

The other three still had a chance of escaping the hangman. Roach, Jakes and Laurie Lovett had appealed, and it was possible that for them the death sentence would be commuted to life imprisonment. Starling had not appealed. If he could have escaped death for the murder of Cicely Wainwright he would have been hanged for the murder of Silver Steele.

A bad do, that, Martineau thought. A lovely young life snuffed out like a candle flame. And to no purpose. Starling had lost his head on that occasion. He had muffed it. His nerves must have been getting pretty worn.

Young Devery had taken it very badly, so it was said. Martineau remembered that the young fellow had never been to see him in hospital. Well, there could be a very good reason for that. Devery may have thought that it would look rather like lick-spittling for a P.C. to go sick visiting an inspector. Anyway, somebody would have been sure to say that it was lick-spittling.

Old Furnisher Steele seemed to have taken it badly too. He had shut up his shop and never opened it since. Those broken windows on the top floor had never been repaired. Poor old boy.

Julia interrupted the unhappy train of thought. "What are you doing this morning?" she asked.

"I think I'll go down to Headquarters and see what's stirring," he said. "I'll get ready for starting tomorrow."

She nodded her approval. Two weeks ago the Watch

Committee had promoted him. He was a Chief Inspector now. He would have a lot of administrative work to do. He would be able to do it, but it was a good idea to have a preliminary look at it.

"You'll be back for lunch?" she asked.

He thought about that. He did not expect to be at Headquarters for more than an hour or two.

"Sure," he said. "I'll be back."

"Think on, you're not later than one o'clock," she said, but not aggressively, because she was still pleased with the thought that he had been made a Chief Inspector.

He nodded. He was a good husband in one respect; his intentions were usually good.

He went to Headquarters. Julia went to the fishmonger for a piece of halibut, because Martineau liked halibut. She hoped he would be at home to eat it. If he were detained in town—she could see no reason why he should be—he could phone in time to save the halibut from the frying pan.

But if he started his old larks—if he didn't come home or phone—there would be trouble. She wasn't going to let him start pub-crawling again as soon as he went back to duty. He might be a big man in the police, but at home he was just another husband. An absent husband. Out all day and coming home last thing at night and playing that damned piano. No, Julia wasn't having any more of that. She was determined to make a firm stand against it right at the beginning of this new stage of his career.

II

At Headquarters Martineau talked with Superintendent Clay about his new duties. Then he gossiped for a while in the main C.I.D. office. Then he looked at his own new office and decided what small changes he would make when he had settled in. He began to feel more cheerful.

But when he was leaving the office just before noon he met Devery.

"Glad to see you back, sir," the young man said. He offered his hand hesitantly—there was now a vast difference in their ranks—and Martineau took it.

"How are things with you?" he asked.

169

"Oh, I just keep on keeping on."

"That's the spirit. You do a good job, Devery. I've watched you. There's no reason why you shouldn't get a bit of promotion one of these fine days."

"Thank you, sir," said Devery. But his superior thought that the sparkle had gone out of him. Tragedy had sobered him. He had grown up. Ah well, he would get over his trouble in time.

Martineau strolled to the bus terminus. The meeting with Devery had brought a return of his depressed mood. Both of them had avoided mentioning either Silver Steele or Starling. Too carefully they had kept away from the subject of dead people.

Dead. Starling's body would already have gone the way of all murderers' bodies: buried in quicklime in a nameless grave, according to the ancient and relentless custom of the law.

The chief inspector shrugged under his overcoat, trying to throw off the irk of returning melancholy. He started to cross Lacy Street. The wintry sun was shining, and there was a happy bustle of people and traffic.

Starling had said that Martineau would be Chief of Police in Hell by the time he—Starling—got there. That had been just one more mistake in a short but mistaken life. It was Starling who would now be showing his credentials to the Prince of Darkness. What saving graces had he? Courage, no doubt, and loyalty of a sort. And on the devil's side a host of sins, deadly and otherwise.

"Well, we're none of us so marvellous," said Martineau.

He stopped on the corner. He did not want to take his depression home just yet. He needed company, masculine company; football talk, gossip, jokes.

'I'll have a drink. Just one,' he decided.

He walked along to the Stag's Head and entered. For a while he did not find the company he sought. He stood alone at the bar and drank two half-pints of beer, and the laughing and droning groups of men around him made him feel set apart. He stared into his beer and argued against his own mood. 'What's the matter with you, man?' he asked himself.

170

'You've got your promotion, so what the deuce have you got to worry about?'

That was it. In a way he had profited by Starling's death. That was the thing which worried him.

Gus Hawkins entered the bar and saw him.

"Hallo, hallo," said the bookmaker, approaching and offering his hand. "You better?"

Martineau nodded as he took the hand. "And you?"

"I'm all right. A bit of a headache sometimes, that's all. It was a right good swing I stopped. What're you drinking?"

"Beer. I'll get 'em. What's yours?"

"Beer? Nonsense. I owe you a decent drink. You got my money back. Most of it, anyway. George, two double White Labels, please."

Martineau accepted the whisky. He raised his glass silently.

"Cheers," said Gus. "Absent friends. Your pal Starling. He'll be a long way from the land of the living now."

Martineau drank three-quarters of his whisky. "I'm afraid so," he said.

"Little you care, eh?"

"I don't give a damn."

"Me neither. He might have killed *me*. What a business! I wonder how old Purchas likes it at Dartmoor. Seven years in that place! Serves him right. You take pity on a man and give him a job, and he stabs you in the back."

"He did well to get off with seven," said Martineau.

"He sure did. Have another?"

"Yes. I'll get 'em."

"Oh no you won't," said Gus vigorously. "Two more of the same, George."

Martineau looked at his watch. "Excuse me, I'll be back," he said. He sought a telephone, and dialled his home number.

"I won't be in to lunch," he said. "I'm staying in town."

"Oh, I've just put the halibut on!" cried Julia. "Can't you come home?"

"Sorry, no," he said. "I'll have the halibut for my tea."

"Where are you lunching?"

"Nowhere. I'm not hungry."

"You'll be ill again! You're drinking, I suppose. Who with?"

"I'm with Gus Hawkins. We have a lot of things to talk about."

"A lot of things to talk about with a bookmaker? Harry Martineau, you come home at once!"

"No. Not yet," he said. "Good-bye."

He put down the receiver and returned to the bar. More trouble. But he was not going home to sit staring at the fire all afternoon. He had done too much of that lately.

He returned to Gus, but two minutes later a voice paged him on the hotel intercom. There was a loudspeaker above the bar.

"Mr. Martineau," said the voice. "Mr. Martineau, wanted on the telephone."

That was Julia, he knew. She had guessed where he was. Anyone else but Julia would have asked for Chief Inspector Martineau, but she would not want to have his rank shouted up and down an hotel. That was sensible, he had to admit.

"Aren't you going to the phone?" asked Gus in surprise.

"No," said Martineau.

"That sounds like domestic evasion," said Gus. "Dearie me, these wives!" Then he grinned. "I got rid of mine, you know."

The manner of the announcement made Martineau raise his eyebrows, but Gus was not abashed. He laughed.

"Gentlemen don't talk about their wives, eh?" he said. "But they talk disrespectfully about bags and trollops, don't they? My wife is one of those. I found that out. There was the late Mr. Starling and a few more. Oh, I was upset, but I got over it. I give her something to live on. More than she's worth. Someday she'll start living with some fellow, and then I'll get *completely* rid of her. A queer woman is like a queer horse. You can't cure 'em. The only thing to do is to get shut of 'em."

"Did you have trouble?" Martineau asked, in spite of a desire to seem uninterested.

"A little," said Gus, with a slight growl in his voice. "She had about as much pride as a spaniel dog. She wept and begged. I knew too much. I couldn't live with it. So she went."

"And are you happy?"

"As the day is long," said Gus, looking at his whisky before he swallowed it.

III

At half-past one Gus went into the grill for a meal. Martineau declined the offer to go with him, and remained at the bar. Gloom drank with him. That, and the shade of the man who had been executed that day. He was not superstitious, but he wryly reflected that if hatred could bring an elemental soul back to the physical world to haunt a man, then the spectre of Don Starling was due to arrive at any moment.

At three o'clock Martineau decided to return to Headquarters. To go home smelling of whisky immediately after closing time was bad tactics. It would be better to spend an hour at the office, and then go home to tea like a worker.

He went into the C.I.D. and picked up the new file of the *Police Gazette* and took it to his office. Whatever work he would be doing, administrative or otherwise, it was as well for him to know what was going on in the criminal world. The office was pleasantly warm. It would be a comfortable workplace, he decided. He browsed through the file for half an hour. Nobody disturbed him. He began to feel sleepy.

He thought it would be a good thing for him to have a brief slumber. If he went home and fell asleep in front of the fire, Julia would say he had been drinking heavily, and he would have to admit that she was right. He could sleep here in the office. Half an hour would do. He would not sleep longer than that.

Sitting at the desk he laid his head on his arms.

His slumber had an uneasy, distorted background. He dreamed. He was a boy late for school, and all kinds of obstacles prevented him from getting there. At the same time, somehow, he was a youth transporting money for the bank, and he could not get the money to its destination. Also, apparently, he was a young constable on a beat, and he was unable to be at the right places at the right times.

When he awoke, the room was quite dark. He sat up and shivered, though the place was still quite warm. He sneezed, and came fully awake. Yawning, he found the switches and turned on the lights. He looked at his watch.

"That's torn it," he said. The time was five minutes to eight.

He rubbed sleep from his eyes with a handkerchief. He straightened his tie, and smoothed his hair with his hand. "The drink," he said ruefully. He sneezed again. He had no headache, but his mouth was as dry as the inside of an ashcan.

The drink had got him into trouble again. Himself, the responsible, successful police officer, had behaved like a wilful, will-less sot. Julia would be furious, and, to be honest, she would be justified in her anger. He had behaved like a fool. This was truly Don Starling's day.

"I feel shocking," he said, and wet his lips. He could think of only one cure for his condition. A hair of the dog. A hair of the tail of the dog that bit you. A double whisky, then a glass of beer to slake that dry tongue. It was no use going home: not until closing time. He would stay on the booze and forget Julia; and, maybe, forget what day it was.

There was a mirror on the desk, used by his predecessor to see who entered the room without turning in his chair. He examined his reflection. "Chief Inspector Martineau, Your Worship. . . ." he said. "Gad, what a bright sample you are!"

He got his hat and coat, picked up the *Gazette* file, and turned off the lights. There was only one plain-clothes man in the main C.I.D. office, and he stared open-mouthed when Martineau emerged from a room which had apparently been unoccupied. Martineau grunted "Here you are," and gave him the file, and walked out of the office.

For two hours he wandered from bar to bar, pouring liquor into his depression. The liquor only dulled the edge of his uneasiness. He argued with himself, and occasionally his lips moved, and people who noticed looked at him curiously.

At ten o'clock he knew that he was not, and would not be, visibly drunk. He was in the soberly reckless state which is beyond ordinary intoxication. He could still converse fluently and, in everyday matters, sensibly. He was unhappy, and he did not care what happened, and yet a part of his mind kept him aware that closing time would be a good thing for him.

It was about ten o'clock, in a tavern called the Maid of Athens, that two men approached him glass in hand. The leader of the two spoke politely but breezily—a strong breeze from far Kentish hopfields—but his companion was a picture of quiet alcoholic misery.

"Excuse me speakin' to yer, Inspector," said the confident one. "My friend here could do with a bit of advice. He's havin' trouble at home."

Martineau sighed, and glanced around the bar at the examples of married manhood. "Aren't we all?" he said.

The man laughed immoderately, though his glum friend only stared. Martineau waited stolidly for details of the complaint. The breezy one too quickly stopped laughing, and said: "Ar, but this is serious. My mate here, he can't trust his wife. She's proper fly. He don't know where she is half the time. He seen her once, gettin' inter a taxi with another feller, an' she denied it was her. Point blank denied it! Tha's right, i'n't it Lionel?"

Lionel nodded gloomily. "Tha's right, Willie," he said.

"What can yer do with a woman like that, Inspector?" Willie wanted to know.

Martineau cast around in his mind for a suitable non-committal reply. He remembered that Julia would be very, very angry. 'To hell with her,' he thought.

"I've told him what ter do," said Willie. "Let her know she's wed to a proper man. Let her know what it is to be married. Give her a kid or two ter look after, before somebody else does it for him. That's the only way to keep *her* quiet."

Martineau grinned. "I've heard worse advice than that," he said.

"Yers, lots worse," said Willie in wholehearted agreement. "I don't have no trouble, I can tell yer. I've got three sons at home. They're three little imps o' Satan, but I wouldn't sell 'em for three million quid." He paused and thought about that, then improved on it. "I wouldn't sell 'em for three million, but I wouldn't give yer thruppence for three more of the same sort."

Lionel shook his head doubtfully, and Willie looked at him in exasperation. "Well, Mr. Martineau's told yer, hasn't he?" he demanded. He thanked the policeman for the advice he had not given, and led his mournful friend away.

Martineau watched them go. "When in doubt, let 'em know what it is to be married," he murmured, and ordered another drink.

IV

It was a fine, cold night, and as the crowds moved along under the lights of Lacy Street their breath showed like horses' breath in the frosty air. When he had quitted the Maid of Athens, Martineau sauntered among them, with no destination in mind. His gait was quite steady, and he was able to respond with every appearance of sober urbanity to the respectful greetings of the policemen he met.

He wandered on. He did not know what he wanted, but he knew what he did *not* want. He did not want to go home.

A girl spoke to him. She was standing in shadow at a corner. "Where you off to, love?" she asked.

He stopped, astonished. Most of the street women knew him by sight, and those who did not were quick to guess at his occupation. They usually managed to keep out of his way. This one, perhaps, was a newcomer.

She looked up into his face. "My word," she said shrewdly. "You've had a drop tonight."

"True," he agreed. "Too true."

"Finish your evening in style," she said. "Come with me."

"Where to?"

"A place I know. It's not far. We don't need a taxi. We can walk it in three minutes."

"I haven't any money," he said.

"That's what they all say. What about three pounds? That won't bankrupt you."

He considered the girl. She was dark and pretty, and quite young. She was smartly dressed and she looked respectable. How hard or how far was the step from respectability to the oldest profession in the world? Neither hard nor far, he suspected. Most of the girls were in that game because they liked it, or at least because they had liked it in the beginning. What about this girl? Curiosity was the only feeling he had about her.

"All right," he said, somewhat to his own surprise.

She took his arm. Immediate affection. "This way, love," she said. They walked along the side street.

"What's your name, love?" she asked. "Or what shall I call you?"

"Lionel," he said. And to himself he said: "This is a proper mug's game."

"Lionel. That's quite nice," she said. "My name is Anne Marie."

"Did your parents call you that?"

"Well no," she admitted. "It's a sort of professional name. You can't get anywhere with Annie."

She laughed and looked up into his face. They were passing the lighted window of a snack bar. She looked again, and her mouth formed a startled O. "Ow! You're Martineau!" she said in a fright, and she released his arm and ran away.

He gazed after her stolidly. He was not amused, but neither was he disappointed. 'The social handicaps of being a prominent copper,' he mused as he returned to Lacy Street. 'The leper of the law.'

There was still time for one drink. Thirty yards away was the Lacy Arms. He had kept away from that place since he came out of hospital. 'I have an appointment,' he remembered. 'Must keep my appointment. I'm only about four months late.'

Though she was busy, Lucky Lusk saw him as soon as he entered the bar. She came straight towards him, and stood opposite him. Around him, customers were clamouring for rounds of drinks before closing time. He grinned at her. "One large whisky," he said.

"Why didn't you come before this?" she asked.

"I've been a wounded hero, didn't you know?" he said. "I'm better now. I start work tomorrow."

She could not carry on the conversation. There were too many calls upon her attention. She gave him the whisky. "I'll talk to you in a minute," she said.

177

When the manager had firmly shouted: "Time, ladies and gentlemen please," she returned to Martineau. "Will you wait for me?" she asked. "I have to tidy up here."

He nodded, and pushed his empty glass towards her. "Never mind," she said. "You can have a drink at my place."

As she collected glasses she stole glances at him. To her, he looked as if he were in a reckless mood. 'This is it,' she thought, but she was afraid of keeping him waiting too long. She held a brief conference with another barmaid. The other girl looked curiously at Martineau, and nodded. She would wash the glasses for Lucky.

"I'm ready now, love," said Lucky to Martineau. "I'll just get my coat."

Soon they were walking towards Lucky's home. His hands were in the pockets of his overcoat—a posture not usual with him—and she hugged his arm and kept very close to him, matching his strolling step. Martineau thought that this was a very cosy way of getting along. They walked in harmony. When he walked with Julia they were always going somewhere, full of purpose: he strode and she stepped briskly beside him, with her hand scarcely resting in the crook of his arm.

This was better, just sauntering along. Martineau began to feel very affectionate towards Lucky. He could drift along nicely with her.

Lucky was thinking of what might happen. She had to be prepared. She was quite sure that Martineau would not be. He wasn't the type.

They were strolling towards a corner where the windows of an all-night chemist's shop poured a flood of light on to the pavement.

"How would you like it if we eventually got married?" he said rashly.

"I'd like it all right," she said.

"So would I. We could have a youngster or two."

She was silent for a while. Some part of her thoughts made her squeeze his arm. Then she said: "No. The marrying part is all right, but I don't want any kids. I'm not the sort of woman to have kids."

"Don't you *ever* want any children?" he asked. "Not even when you're married?"

"No. They're not my cup of tea at all." She squeezed his arm again. "I just want you."

They came to the corner where the chemist's shop was open. "Wait here," she said. "I won't be a minute."

He stood at the kerb and lit a cigarette. He blew out smoke pensively. So Lucky was another one who would not have children on any consideration. 'You do find 'em, Martineau,' he reflected.

It was a busy corner where he stood. Crossing lights winked, and traffic stopped and started. People were hurrying home after their evening's entertainment: the anonymous thousands, going back to the places where they scratched and toiled in innumerable ways to make a living. They did not really belong to Granchester. *This* was Granchester, this less-than-a-square-mile in the centre of things. There was no hotel district, no theatre district, no financial district, no administrative district. There was just the middle of Granchester, which, for Martineau, had everything. *He* belonged here, and so did Lucky Lusk. Julia did not. She was a suburbanite to the core.

He thought of Julia's Granchester; and of other districts, within the city boundary, which were not the real Granchester. Not half-a-mile from where he stood there was a section which housed many coloured people. It had no name, but some called it Dixieland. There were Jewish and Irish sections. There were sections, recently respectable, which had been made into slums by new inhabitants. There were the residential areas. But they were not recognizably Granchester, because they could have belonged to any city. Here, around here, where the buildings—and very often the people in them—had definite and perceivable characters, was the real Granchester.

Don Starling had belonged here. Martineau still did. Lucky did. Sinners. Sinners, rats, and people who unwillingly fed the rats.

'I wouldn't like to be anywhere else,' Martineau decided.

A taxi passed near, with a young coloured man at the wheel. Coloured taxi drivers and coloured bus conductors.

That was something Martineau had never seen in London, the Big Smoke. Well, well. What Granchester does today, London does tomorrow.

Another taxi approached. The driver checked, and swerved hopefully to the kerb. Martineau put up his hand.

He got into the taxi and gave his address. Then he said: "She doesn't want any kids. She never had a man who was any good."

The taxi driver took no notice. People said all sorts of daft things to him, especially at this time of night.

Martineau did not speak again until he had alighted at his front gate. He paid the driver and gave him his tip. "Good night," he said solemnly. "When in doubt, give somebody a kid or two to look after."

v

"This is it," said Martineau as he walked round to the back door. "Home, the place to go when every other place is closed."

The door was unlocked. One thing about Julia, she wasn't afraid of things. She had courage and good nerves. "Well, I must have married her for *something* besides her looks," he murmured.

She was waiting for him. She looked at him searchingly. "You've excelled yourself today," she said with surprising calmness.

"Yes indeed," he agreed. "Very sorry. I fell asleep in my new office."

He threw his hat in the general direction of a chair, and never looked to see where it fell. Then he slipped off his overcoat and absently reached out with it, to where there used to be a hook behind the living room door. Julia had removed the hook about the time he was made Chief Inspector. He never noticed when the overcoat dropped to the floor.

She watched him impassively.

He rubbed his hands together. "Any supper?" he asked, suddenly realizing that he was hungry.

"In the oven since tea time," she said. "As usual." Then, quite coolly: "I don't know how long you think I'll stand this state of affairs."

"Me neither," he said, walking towards the kitchen. "I don't know how I stand it myself."

"Stupid brute," she said, suddenly and clearly. "I'm going to bed."

"Good night," he answered, turning the oven switches.

Julia went to bed. Martineau lit a cigarette, and decided that his life was in a mess. It occurred to him that some soft piano music couldn't make Julia more angry, and he went into the front room. He turned on the light and then stood in complete amazement. The piano was missing. In its place, grandly alone on the fitted carpet, was a console television set.

"What the devil—?" he began. Then he noticed a sheet of paper lying on the top of the otherwise shiny and immaculate console. He went forward and picked up the paper. It had a printed billhead, thus:

HINDLE CLEGG and SON

79   Castle Street   79

Radio   TV   *Piano*

MUSIC   MUSIC   MUSIC

and underneath:

To one Viselux Console	£103 19	0
To aerial, plug etc.	6 10	0
	110 9	0
Allowance Stein piano	50 0	0
Balance to pay	£60 9	0

His own name and address followed. Naturally. "Send the bill to my husband. Chief Inspector Martineau, you know." It was cool, very cool. Julia had nerve, all right. To flog a man's piano and expect him to pay the balance on a blasted television set! To imagine that this thing was worth more than his piano!

He crumpled the bill in his hand, and threw it into the fireplace. He went to the foot of the stairs and bawled: "I'm going to change your mind for you. You'll bring my piano back tomorrow, and I'll let you know when we can afford television."

She did not answer, so he continued to shout: "You never wanted television. It's just a dirty trick. But it won't work, see? You get my piano back tomorrow. Not me, you!"

She appeared at the head of the stairs in a handsome dark blue dressing gown. There was no doubt of it, she was regally beautiful.

"Is it necessary to inform the neighbours of our affairs?" she demanded in a low, clear voice. "They'll all know you're drunk."

"I'm not drunk!" he thundered, aware that he was certainly not sober. "And the neighbours can go and take a running kick at themselves for all I care."

"You *are* drunk, and you'll care enough if somebody sends an anonymous letter to the Chief and tells him so."

"He won't believe it. I am not drunk. I'm just a frustrated husband. I'm a frustrated *man*."

"You're a drunken man," she said with utter contempt.

"And you're cold sober, always sober," he retorted in a quieter voice as he glared up at her. "But what good are you? You're neither a wife nor a mother."

"Hallo, we're off again," she said. "I'd look nice, having children to you. Then I could sit here *all* the time and wait for you to come home."

"You wouldn't have to. If we had some kids I'd be home a lot of the time. I'd come home to lunch as well."

"That's what you say. I know different."

"It'd stop your gallivanting off to your bridge clubs and tea fights, an' all. You don't know what it is to be married."

"If I don't, nobody does."

"I tell you, you don't know what it is to be married. You don't even know if you're married to a proper man. You don't know anything. A man can demand his rights as a husband. Every man has a right to have children if his wife can bear 'em."

"Well, you won't get me bearing yours."

"Oh, won't I? You wait till I've had my supper."

"Ridiculous! You're not only drunk, you're insane."

182

"You mean I'm just coming to my senses. Come to think of it, our marriage has never really been consummated."

"It won't be tonight, either."

"Oh yes it will."

"You're crazy. I'll lock the bedroom door."

"That won't make any difference. You can't keep me out of my own bedroom."

"I won't let you come near me."

"Oh no? You wait."

For the first time since she had known Harry Martineau, Julia was afraid of him. Would he do such a thing to her? Her knowledge of his *domestic* character—the man when he was at home—informed her that he would not be so brutal. But there was another aspect of him which, recently, she had allowed herself to forget. He was a very determined man. She remembered some of the startling, audacious and ruthless deeds which had earned him his reputation and his promotion. Oh, dear!

He was strong-willed. Even this business of lingering in pubs was not weakness. He liked strong liquor, but normally he drank only a moderate amount of beer. He stayed out in spite of her upbraidings because he wanted to stay out. No amount of pressure from her had ever succeeded in bringing him home before he was ready to come.

He was a man who did what he wanted. And he had always wanted a child or children. That was a very real desire, she knew quite well. And now he was in this mood! Julia was afraid.

"You can't," she said. "It's wrong. You could be arrested. I could have you arrested.

"You couldn't," he said. "We are man and wife, and we are not judicially separated."

"I shall scream," she said desperately.

"Scream all you like. I don't care."

She stared down at him. For once in her life she had nothing to say. It seemed to her that he was absolutely determined. He had always wanted children.

"Supper first," he said. "I won't be long. I'll soon be right there with you."

"You wouldn't be such a beast," she said. For the first time there was a pleading note in her voice.

"Ah, but I would!" he said.

He turned away and got his supper from the kitchen. He took it into the living-room and closed the door.

As he ate, his temper cooled. He realized that he had done an unpardonable thing. He was still indignant when he thought of his piano . . . but really, he shouldn't have talked like that to Julia. Threatening her. After all, she was his wife. A man didn't threaten his own wife.

He supposed she would leave him now. There and then, that very night. It would be like Julia to make up her mind and do it straight away. He guessed that she would be packing a bag, quickly and neatly as usual.

Well, maybe he shouldn't have talked to her like that, but he wasn't going to crawl and ask her to stay. She could go. It wouldn't be much of a life for her, he thought, living with her mother and her stepfather. He felt rather sorry for her. She was losing a good husband: himself, Harry Martineau. Well, a fairly good husband. He had his faults, he supposed. Julia had plenty of faults, too. Everybody had faults. If only they'd had a youngster or two, maybe there wouldn't have been so many quarrels. They would have had to learn to tolerate each other's shortcomings. Quarrelling parents were bad for kids.

She seemed to be taking a long while to pack one bag. He had eaten his supper. She would only take one bag, he figured. She would come back for the rest of her stuff when he was out. She could take her damned television set too.

He got up and made some tea, and lit a cigarette. After this, he reflected, there would be a separation, and ultimately a divorce. He would have to pay maintenance, and later, alimony. The Chief wouldn't like it: there would be no more promotion. Well, a chief inspector's pay wasn't so bad. The pension was all right too. Eventually he might meet some young woman who would want to marry him and have a baby or two, a proper home, a proper going on.

He threw away his cigarette. Julia would be ringing for a taxi anytime now, he thought. 'Good-byeee. I get along without you very well. Don't smoke in bed.'

He waited, but there was no sound made by movements overhead. Julia had gone to bed. She would leave in the morning, probably. There was nothing for him to do but go upstairs and get into his own bed.

He turned off the light and went upstairs. There was a light in the bedroom, and the door was open. Julia was in bed; in his bed. She opened her eyes as he entered the room, and said drowsily: "You've been a long time."

"I made some tea," he said, covering his surprise.

He was nonplussed. Had she believed that he would really carry out his threat? And instead of resisting, she was going to use the wiles of her sex? 'Come to bed, husband, but—no babies.' If that was the idea, it wasn't going to work. He would have no more of it.

He brushed his teeth in the bathroom, then he undressed and put on his pyjamas. He got into bed beside Julia. Lying flat on his back, he pushed his feet right to the bottom of the bed. Julia put an arm across his chest, and squirmed her lovely elegant body closer to him. The confiding movement stirred him. In spite of his suspicions, excitement mounted in him.

"We'll talk a bit," she said. "Till you get warm."

"Sure," he grunted, relaxing. He was asking himself: 'Whats the move? Does she think I'll drop off to sleep?'

He had never felt less like sleep.

"I've been thinking," she murmured in his ear. "I think I shall like it, starting a baby."

He made some sort of reply. He could scarcely believe that this was happening.

"I've been thinking," she repeated. "I'll have to pull you round somehow. Things had gone too far. We needed a fresh start. I thought selling your piano would pull you together and make you realize. . . . But it didn't work in quite the way I expected."

His astonishment was complete. She had never for a moment thought that there might be a parting! In all their quarrels she had never once thought of leaving him, or of him leaving her!

"It came to me suddenly, after you got so wild and

185

threatened me," she said. "I think you're right; a baby *is* the only answer. It'll make you feel more responsible: bring you home oftener, and sooner I hope. And now—well, I rather like the idea."

She moved against him, and gently bit the lobe of his ear. "I hope it's a girl," she whispered, "then I can make lovely dresses for her."

"Any daughter of yours will be the smartest girl in town," he said, and he meant it.

That pleased her, and the idea of a girl-child opened up a whole new range of interests.

"I'll have everything beautiful," she breathed. "I'll have her as pretty as a picture."

He thought of Julia with a little girl of four or five; a straight-limbed, tall child, dark-haired like her, or fair like himself.

An effort of will was needed. He made it.

"Yes, but not tonight," he said. "We've got to think about the child."

"Not tonight?"

"Not tonight," he repeated, aware that he was risking a change of mind in her. "I've had quite a lot of whisky. That wouldn't be very good for our little girl. Tomorrow night, when I've got some of the alcohol out of my system."

She thought about that. She realized that such a decision, against his own strong desires, was a true acceptance of family responsibility. It made her deeply happy. He was already pulling himself together. He had the right idea. He would be a good father, and the sort of dependable, humdrum husband she wanted. Through the child, she would be able to 'make him behave'.

"Tomorrow night then," she agreed contentedly, and closed her eyes to go to sleep.

'By God,' he thought. 'We'll make a go of it, after all. I guess I shall have to mend my ways a bit.'

He remembered that he had not thought of Don Starling for a long time. That was over. Justice had been done. A life for a life. . . .

THE END

>>> If you've enjoyed this book and would like to discover more great vintage crime and thriller titles, as well as the most exciting crime and thriller authors writing today, visit: >>>

The Murder Room
Where Criminal Minds Meet

themurderroom.com

www.ingramcontent.com/pod-product-compliance
Ingram Content Group UK Ltd.
Pitfield, Milton Keynes, MK11 3LW, UK
UKHW040435280225
455666UK00003B/96